Then There Was You

A TWIST OF FATE NOVEL

A.J. DANIELS

To Katie
xoxo
♡ Andrea Key

Then There Was You is a work of fiction. Names, characters, businesses, places, events, and incidents are either the product of the author's imagination or used in a fictitious manner. Any resemblance to actual persons, living or dead, or actual events is purely coincidental.

Copyright © 2019 by A.J. Daniels

Cover Design: ©Just Write. Creations
Edited by Joanne Thompson
ISBN: 978-1-9992413-0-8

Dedication

To Caleb, you're forever missed. R.I.P cousin

CRWR 471 class of 2019 – I owe a lot of this book to you. Thank you for your feedback and encouragement through the workshops over the last year.

Author's Note

There are several trigger warnings for this book. If you think this subject matter might affect you, please don't continue further.

Trigger warnings: physical and sexual domestic abuse, suicide, rape.

*Spelling in this book is in British English because the majority takes place in South Africa.

Blurb

Annika Holt believed that Jackson Carter was the sole love of her life. Then fate took him away from her when Jack is killed while on deployment with his SEAL team. Angry, she finds herself falling deeper into depression, Annika decides to move back to Cape Town, South Africa. The city where she spent the first part of her childhood and where her family has recently returned. Thinking it will help her grieve her late husband. What she didn't count on is Nathaniel Walker. The tall carpenter and primary school teacher. He awakens something in her she thought had been buried with her husband. Is it possible to have two epic loves? She never thought so.

Just when she has finally given herself permission to love again, fate throws her another curveball when someone from her past returns.

What happens when our past and our present collide?

Trigger warnings: physical and sexual domestic abuse, suicide, rape.

South African Slang

Bokkie –Term of endearment. Sweetheart, Honey, etc.

Boot – Trunk of a car

Braai – BBQ but it's done over an open woodfire.

Bukkie – Pick-up truck

Cooldrink – Soda or pop

Fok – Fuck

Howzit – How are you? / How's it going?

Ja - Yes

Ja-nee – Yes-no.

Jislaaik – positive or negative surprised expression.

Koeksister – Sweet pastry that's been fried and dipped in a honey syrup. Often rolled in coconut flakes afterward.

Lekker – Cool, nice.

Moffie – gay male (used in a derogatory fashion)

Ne? – Do you know what I mean/Do you agree?

Pavement - Sidewalk

Potjie – cast iron pot

Potjiekos – Meat and vegetable dish that is specialty cooked in a potkjie. Traditionally slowed cooked for hours. Served during a Braai.

Reno – Short for Renault. Type of car.

Robot – Traffic light

Slap chips – French fries but better. Usually served with vinegar and salt sprinkled over.

Snoek – Type of fish found in South Africa. Also known as Barracouta, not to be confused with Barracuda.

Spar – Name of a grocery store chain in Cape Town.

**Not slang but Clifton Beach in Cape Town is broken up into four beaches; Clifton 1st, Clifton 2nd, Clifton 3rd, and Clifton 4th

Prologue

WE'RE SORRY.

Two words. Two words that have the power to change everything. Two words that can end life as you know it. Those two words rush over me like a tsunami until I'm drowning. I didn't know I was quite literally falling until one of the men in his dress blues reaches forward and catches me before I hit the floor, scooping me up in his arms. I can hear the other curse under his breath while making his way into the apartment.

The cold leather of the sofa greets my skin as I'm laid across it. A glass of water appears on the coffee table in front of the sofa, but I don't want it.

"Is there anyone we can call for you, Mrs. Carter?" The water-fetcher asks, his hands wringing the white hat.

I shake my head, staring up at the hideous popcorn ceiling. There is no one. My parents moved back to Cape Town last year and Londyn, my best friend, is still on the other side of the country, in Florida. And the one person I had here has just… I swallow back the burn of the tears threatening to spill.

A throat clears, pulling my gaze away from the little bumps of white paint. "Do you need us to stay?"

I shake my head again. "N-No. That's okay," I say in a hoarse whisper, managing to find my voice again. I have no idea who these two men are other than they are officers in the Navy and sent here to deliver the bad news. They aren't even his teammates. Hot white anger surges through my veins when I hear the click of the front door closing behind them. His teammates couldn't even come to tell me the news themselves. I would much rather hear it from them than the two strangers who were just in our apartment.

My apartment now, I guess. Fuck.

I turn on my side, and curl into fetal position on the cold leather. Jackson is gone. The man I fell in love with at fifteen and married straight out of high school, is gone. Killed in action they said.

Right there on the sofa, I pray that God takes me too because there is no way He could possibly subject me to the living hell that is life without the love of my life. The other half of my soul.

Chapter 1

"HONEY, WHY DON'T YOU come to Cape Town? I heard that P.N.P.S. is looking for a new teacher, you could go work at your old school."

The sentence every adult dreads hearing from their parents. She might as well come right out and say, "Your dad and I think you're unable to function by yourself anymore. Come home so we can keep an eye on you." I can't fault her for caring though. It's been eighteen months since my husband died, and somewhere during those months I forgot to give a damn… about my life, about everyone else. I've been stuck in this never-ending cycle of sleep, Netflix, and trying to remember to eat. Hell, I even left my job at the school a year ago. I've been doing website design to keep me afloat whenever I muster up enough energy to drag out my laptop.

So, yeah. I guess my mother has a point. Plus, I know she's right. My old principal is still the principal of the primary school I attended from Sub A to the end of grade six before we immigrated to America. I've seen her post on the school's Facebook page. I'm sure if I went to talk to her, she could help get me a teaching job there. It would be so cool to teach at the school I used to attend. And I'm a still a dual citizen so there'd be no added stress of trying to acquire a work visa. I do have a lot of my support system in Cape Town, but Xander and Londyn wouldn't be there.

It's been eighteen months since I had last seen Xander, my husband's older brother, the morning after Jack's funeral. I woke up the next morning with a bitching hangover and discovered that Xander was already gone. The note he left said he had an early morning flight, but I had to wonder if he left so early because he couldn't stand to be in his brother's house without him. And Londyn… God, she's been such a rock for me these last eighteen months. She couldn't get the time off work to fly out here for the funeral, but she helped me organize as much of it as she could from where she was. She even helped set up online payments for some of the bills so that I wouldn't have to think about them for a while. And her daily texts in the morning help make the day a little easier. They aren't anything extraordinary, just a few motivational quotes interspersed with some funny memes. And when the pain gets to be too much, she just listens while I cry over the phone or FaceTime. It doesn't matter if she is still at work or has an early morning meeting. She's there, and I know I can count on her.

I mean, I guess that part won't change much. We can still FaceTime and if I get an international SMS package for my phone, I can still text her. The time difference will be the major hurdle. Cape Town is six hours ahead of Miami. Right now, there's only a three-hour time difference for us.

"Annika?" my mom's voice sounds worried as it comes through the phone and I realize that I haven't heard a word she's been saying.

"I'm still here. I'll think about it, Mom."

I can tell she's disappointed in my answer when she sighs a little on the other side and then stays quiet for a couple of beats. "I just worry about you, honey. You don't have anybody there…"

I wince at the stab of pain her words cause. I know she doesn't mean to do it but she's right. I don't really have anyone in San Diego anymore except for Caleb and a couple of the other guys from Jack's team, but I hate calling Caleb. I feel like I'm a burden to him. Like a problem he just can't seem to get rid of.

"I… I'll think about it, okay?"

"Okay, Honey. Your dad and I just worry about you," she says again.

"I know," I say, crawling back under the sheets of the unmade bed. "I'll call you guys later. Love you."

"We love you too, Annika."

After hanging up with Mom, I sink further into the big bed and pull the covers over my head, blocking out the mid-afternoon sun shining through the blinds. Could I give up this last piece of Jack?

Before tucking the phone under a pillow, I shoot a text off to Xander, needing to know what he thinks of me possibly moving back to Cape Town.

Me: My mom just tried convincing me to move back again.

X: Are you?

Me: I don't know. I don't have anyone here, X.

X: You have me.

Me: You're not in SD

X: Then move back to Florida.

I don't reply to his last message. Mostly because I don't know how. I've thought about moving back to Florida and being closer to him and Londyn. At least I wouldn't be totally alone in Florida like I am in San Diego, and Miami is big enough that I wouldn't have to run into my in-laws if I chose not to. But there's something about the thought of moving back to Cape Town, moving back to the city that holds so much of my childhood before Jack. It would be like starting over, nobody there knows me except my parents and most of my extended family probably don't remember me outside of the thirteen-year-old girl I was when we left. With my mind somewhat made up, I fall into a restless sleep.

3 weeks later

"I'm so glad you're here," my mom says, gathering me in her arms as soon as I clear security and baggage pick up.

"We both are," my dad chimes in, wrapping an arm around my shoulders the second my mother releases me.

"It feels weird being back here," I say, hitching my carry-on higher up my shoulder.

"Well you haven't been back here since we left when you were thirteen, honey," Mom says like I've forgotten that fact. The flight here was enough to remind me that I haven't had to travel like that in fourteen years.

Chapter 2

THE FIRST THING I notice when I turn the car onto the street that held my childhood home is that everything still looks exactly the way it did when we left so many years ago.

The second thing I notice is that the tree in the front yard of our house is missing and the in-between owners had ripped up the brick driveway, paving it instead. I shake my head, pulling up to the carport door and putting the car in park. It looks horrible.

I wonder if my dad had a fit when he saw it earlier. This house was his baby. He built the carport and added the door when he and my mom first bought the house in the 80's. They also planted the tree that used to be in the front yard. The same tree we took my first day of school pictures under every year until we had immigrated to America in 2001.

I briefly wonder if the other owners had taken down the six-foot tall, rusting metal clothesline in the backyard too. The same clothesline I would try to climb every spring and summer but instead would just get rust stains on my palms. I hope they just replaced the poles instead of removing the line altogether. I guess I'll be finding out soon enough, though.

Shutting the driver's side door of the Opal, I fish the key out of the front pocket of my shorts and start towards the door. Grinning at the memory of sneaking out of the house while my mom was taking a nap after cleaning all day, I had accidentally locked the door behind me while I ran across the street to play with one of the neighbourhood kids.

Oh man, were my parents pissed at me that day. I couldn't sit comfortably for a couple of days after that, but I learnt to always make sure the door wasn't set to lock behind me after that incident. Probably not the lesson my parents had wanted to teach me, but whatever.

Pushing open the front door, the stark reality that this hasn't been my home in about fourteen years comes crashing to the surface. Gone are the carpet floors in the living room I used to fall asleep on during the hot summer months because it was a cool reprieve from the blazing sun, and no one in Cape Town had air conditioning at that time. Air conditioning still is a luxury in Cape Town. At least outside of stores and malls.

In its place are white tiles. I tip my head to the side, taking in the bright floors. I get why they would want tile floors instead of carpet. Cape Town summers get ridiculously hot and tiles do tend to stay cooler, but I can't wrap my head around tile floors in anything other than the kitchen and bathroom. I make a mental note to have my cousin over and see how much it would cost me to rip up the bright flooring and put the original tan carpeting in. On second thought, maybe I should look into wooden floors as well.

I make my way down the narrow hallway to the left. The house is a rancher style with no basement – no one in Cape Town has basements in their houses. I poke my head into the first bedroom on the left and what used to be my younger brother's room. Or I guess, *was supposed to be*, would be the right description.

I swallow back the lump that forms in my throat. We don't talk about Kody. Twenty-five years later and it's still too painful to even think about. Mom had a healthy pregnancy. Her doctor didn't find anything wrong during the multiple check-ups and ultrasounds over those eight months, but right before Mom was about to give birth to him, the baby had stopped breathing. The doctor had gone in for an emergency C-section, but the cord had been wrapped too tightly around his neck and he had turned blue from lack of oxygen. Dad said they tried everything they could to get him breathing again, but nothing had worked.

While my parents were going through all of this, I was happily playing at my grandparents' house, excited to meet the new baby. I was finally getting a baby brother. Then the news came by phone call at close to midnight. At first I couldn't figure out why Granny and Grandpa were crying and so sad. They should be crying tears of happiness. We had a new baby. And then Granny sat me down at the kitchen table and told me that my brother hadn't made it.

People don't think young kids understand what's going on in the world around them, and for the most part, maybe that's true. I would beg to differ though. I think kids understand more than what we give them credit for. At three years old I knew what had happened before my granny said the words. I knew after they had hung up the phone with my dad and Granny's cries turned to small screams as Grandpa tried to comfort her in his arms. They wouldn't have had that reaction if my brother were alive. I'm not sure how I knew it was Kody who didn't make it and not Mom, but somehow I knew.

I move on to my parents' bedroom after that. The large wall-to-wall, dark wood armoire my parents had built still takes up the far wall. The matching vanity nowhere in sight. My heart soars as I step up to one of the doors of the armoire and pull it open, seeing the tie hooks still on the inside of the door. I remember pulling open this very same door as a kid and seeing all of my dad's ties hanging neatly from the hooks, before stepping into the closet and closing it behind me. It was my favourite hiding spot when Dad and I played hide-and-seek.

"No running in the house," my mom would yell as I raced past her in the kitchen from the backyard door as fast I could to get to my hiding spot before Dad stopped counting.

I giggle at the memory of hearing my dad search the whole house, loudly closing doors as he went. I had no doubt that he knew where I was hidden but he always pretended that he never did. When he found me, he would pick me up under my arms and twirl me around in the air before the tickle monster would come out.

I sigh, closing the armoire door. My dad and I had the best relationship while I was growing up. After exiting my parents' bedroom, I head towards the door at the very end of the hallway and inhale deeply before turning the knob and pushing it open. My room.

It's funny how everything we thought looked so big as kids, looks a shit-ton smaller when we're adults. As a kid, I thought my room was huge and it was usually the location for one of my many imaginary games. Like, teacher. We had a plastic kids table set I would eat meals at because I was too small to eat at the normal table. You know, back before booster chairs and all that stuff. Anyway, I would grab the two plastic chairs from the set and drag them to my room, setting them up against the wall. Then I would sit my teddy bears up in the chairs and pretend to teach them from the other side of the room with a ruler in my hand.

I'm happy to note that the white built-in wardrobe is still there even though most of the red handles are now missing. I'll have to take a closer look at all the shelves on the inside and see if it will need replacing. The built-in vanity and oval mirror are still here too. It's rare for a house in Cape Town to have what Americans would call closets. So, we make do and build our own. Sometimes it's great because it means you can customize it to match your individual taste and the style of the house. Other times, it's not so great. Especially if you're on a budget and don't already know a carpenter.

I step up to the only accessible window in the room and peak out between the net curtains. My eyes bug out at the sight of the same concrete fence my dad had installed when I was a kid.

No, it can't be.

When I first turned onto the street it looked like a lot of the houses had undergone an exterior makeover, including tearing down some of the fences to build newer, higher ones. So, it's a shock to see the original concrete fencing still in place around this house.

I turn on my heel and rush out of the bedroom, down the hall, and out the door in the kitchen, heading to the far side of the fence. I stare in disbelief at the chip my dad and our neighbour caused when they dropped the concrete slab the day they installed the fence. I reach out and tentatively run my fingers over the chip just as the side door to the carport opens and closes.

"I thought you would be back here," my mom says coming to stand beside me. "Wow," she whispers. "I can't believe it's still standing."

I nod. "Well, it was definitely built to last a long time."

"It is concrete," my mom jokes, nudging my arm.

I laugh. "Touché." I turn, and loop my arm around her waist, laying my head on her shoulder. "What are you doing here?"

"Your dad wanted to see if you had found the place okay."

"Where is Dad?" I ask, looking over her shoulder to see if I can spot him in the backyard or through the window into the kitchen.

"He's checking out the house. He wants to make note of any repairs that need to be done and make sure all the bars are secure on the windows so it's safe for you to stay here by yourself. This neighbourhood isn't what it used to be."

"It feels weird being back here," I comment as we turn and make our way back through the kitchen door.

"It's been what? fourteen years since we sold the house and immigrated to Florida?"

"About that, yeah."

"Well, the burglary bars will need replacing. The armoire in the master bedroom still looks good, but we can get someone in here to renovate it if you'd like, Peanut. The built-in located in your room will need replacing," my dad says, walking out of the far room and down the hallway to meet us in the dining room.

I let out a hard exhale. "Does Uncle Dave still know the carpenter who built the original ones?" I ask my dad, leaning into him when he wraps his arms around me for a sideways hug.

"No, he passed away years ago. But the man who took over for him is just as good. I'll get in touch with Dave and get his number again. He works as a carpenter during the weekend and school holidays. He's a primary school teacher during the week."

I pull away from him and tilt my head up. "Is Uncle Dave sure about this guy, Dad?"

"You know your uncle; he wouldn't have recommended him if he didn't think he was good."

"Well," I say, stepping out of my dad's embrace and sticking my hands in the back pockets of my jeans. "If Uncle Dave recommends him then it wouldn't hurt to try him out."

"Good," my dad says, pulling out his cellphone. "I'll give Dave a call now."

"Did he happen to say what the carpenter's name was?" I ask, as his thumb moves across the screen, dialing my uncle's number.

"Nathaniel Walker," my dad replies before lifting the phone to his ear and retreating back down the hall to the bedrooms, his voice carrying down to us as my uncle picks up on the other side.

I look around the space one more time as I hear my mom rummaging around in the kitchen and a sense of coming home settles in my belly. I spent so much of my childhood in this house, building memories, reaching milestones. It's weird being back here with the knowledge that I'll be here for the foreseeable future. Who knows, maybe I'll even get to watch my own kids grow up in this house. But does it still count as *moving back home* if this hasn't been my home for more than half my life?

Chapter 3

"**HOW DOES IT FEEL** to be back there?" Londyn asks, taking a sip of her morning coffee.

This was the only time that fit in both of our schedules where we could FaceTime each other. Miami is six hours behind Cape Town. So, while it's inching on to four o'clock in the afternoon here, it's only just before ten in the morning there.

"It's weird," I reply, sipping from the red wine I poured just before we connected the call. "I remember so much of it, but there's still so much that I've forgotten."

"You're back in your childhood home, right?"

"Yeah." I prop up a foot on the chair I'm sitting on and rest my chin on my knee while I talk to my best friend. "You should see this place, Londyn. The in-between owners changed so much of the interior. They ripped up the carpet and put down tile everywhere." I shake my head.

"Isn't that the norm there though? Because it gets so hot during the summer?" she asks, leaning down until all I can see is the top of her head in the camera. I assume she is trying to get her new puppy, Kingston, to cuddle on her lap.

I sigh. "It is. I mean, my uncle's house has tile throughout except in the bedrooms. I think it was more just a shock at first. I was so used to seeing carpet in the common areas. Plus, I think he got tired of my cousins leaving wet footprints on the carpet every time they came inside from the pool."

Londyn sits back in her chair again, a ball of spotted white and brown fur wiggling in her arms.

"Oh my gosh, Londyn! He's so cute!"

She laughs, scratching behind the puppy's ears. "Kingston meet Annika. Annika meet Kingston."

"He's so fluffy!" I gush, suddenly sounding like the little girl from *Despicable Me*. God, I love that movie.

Londyn giggles when the puppy reaches up, putting his paws on her shoulder and licks up her face. His tail wagging playfully.

I laugh. "Seriously, Londyn, he's so cute."

She manoeuvres the puppy, so he's playing on her lap while she gently pets him. "He wasn't so cute this morning. Little shit chewed up my favourite pair of underwear."

"Maybe this will teach you to actually pick up your clothes. Your bedroom floor is not a closet." I grin.

Londyn rolls her eyes. It's a conversation we've had multiple times growing up together. It doesn't matter if it's clean or dirty, all of her clothes end up on the floor of her bedroom until she needs to do laundry. She calls it an 'organized' mess, claiming she knows which articles of clothing are clean and which are dirty. I call it chaos.

"When is the carpenter supposed to get there?"

I glance down at the gold watch on my left wrist. "In about an hour. He wasn't supposed to get out here till next week, but he'd called Dad and said he'd had a last-minute opening."

Londyn grins. "Your dad's taking over the renos isn't he?"

"Ding ding ding." I raise an eyebrow. "Did you really expect anything less from my dad? This house was his baby before we immigrated."

"I honestly thought he would've had it all done before you got there."

"He probably would have," I agree. "But I didn't get the keys until after a couple days of being here. He had no way of getting in before then."

The puppy lets out a little growl around the rope Londyn's using to play tug of war. "Have you at least researched this guy, Nika?"

"Not yet. I kinda completely forgot about it until my dad called this morning to say the guy had some time today after all." I look around the table for my phone, figuring now was as good a time as any to look this guy up. "One sec," I tell my best friend, remembering I left my phone on the charger in the bedroom.

"What's his name again?" Londyn asks, the puppy now chasing a ball around the room behind her. Every once in a while he gets one of his long floppy ears under a paw while running causing him to tumble, but he shakes it off and goes right back to playing with his ball.

"Nathaniel Walker," I answer at the same time I type his name into the search engine and hit enter.

Londyn lets out a low whistle just as the search results are loading. This is one thing I miss about North America. The fast Wi-Fi.

"Damn, Nika."

"Fuck, it's taking forever to load. The video stream is slowing down the connection."

Londyn laughs, holding up her phone to the webcam so that I can see the picture she has pulled up on her phone. The guy in the picture looks tall, sculptured abs lead down to a narrow waist and that V muscle that makes most women dumb. The picture cuts off just below the blue waistband of his swim shorts. My eyes trace up his bare chest again, to broad shoulders, and a square jaw. I can't get a good look at the rest of his face because the glare from the setting sun hides it, but it's obvious that whoever had snapped the picture had taken it right after Nathaniel had gotten out of the water. The scenery behind him looks like one of the local beaches. I can't tell which one exactly because Cape Town is home to many and the glare makes it even harder to distinguish.

"So, how long exactly is the flight to Cape Town?" Londyn's question interrupts my wandering thoughts and I swallow hard.

"About thirty hours travel time," I manage to say past my dry throat. "You wouldn't make it in time." I laugh as she sticks out her bottom lip in a pout.

"Dammit. Take pictures!"

"What? No! I am not taking pictures like some creep."

She groans. "Come on, Nika! I'd totally do it for you!"

She totally would. Between the two of us Londyn is the pro at taking stealthy pictures. I'm not sure whether to be creeped out at that trait or a little envious.

"Fine! But if I make a complete fool outta myself and he decides to not come back, that's on you. You'll have to explain to Dad why he has to get me a new carpenter."

A wide smile splits her face. "Deal."

"I hate you," I groan before taking a longer drink of my wine.

"Nah, you love me." Londyn takes a drink of her coffee. Her nose wrinkles when she places the mug back down. "It's not fair that I have to watch you drink wine while I'm stuck with coffee."

I laugh. "It's after four in the afternoon here!" And just because I can, I make a show of lifting the wine glass to my lips and taking a drink. "Hmmm, so good."

"Asshole," she mumbles.

"You love me," I repeat her words back to her.

We talk a little more and discuss her plans for maybe coming here for a month over Christmas. After we graduated high school, Londyn's parents decided that they wanted to spend the winters skiing in Aspen from then on. From what Londyn told me, they'd made it perfectly clear that she was not invited to join them. She seems to be okay with it at first, but I can tell it slowly started to weigh on her. And anyway, I would love nothing more than to have my best friend here while I celebrate my first Christmas back in Cape Town after so many years.

I miss the green Christmases here. Miss going to the beach on Christmas Eve and spending Boxing Day in my uncle's pool. I glance outside to my backyard wondering just how hard of a hit my savings account will take if I were put a pool in. It's something I remember my parents talking about a lot while I was growing up, but we never had the time nor the money. Now with the savings I have put aside and Jack's life insurance, I have more than enough to put the pool in and live comfortably.

"Londyn, no," I say looking down at the too tight, too short dress she made me put on.

"Stop fussing, Nika. You look fucking hot and Jack's going to eat his heart out."

She picks up her phone from its charging place on my bedside table, a smile lighting up her whole face.

"That was Kyle. He wants to know where we are."

"I don't understand why you guys aren't together. You'd make the perfect couple," I argue while grabbing a tube of lipstick from my makeup desk and sliding it in between my boobs and bra. I didn't want to take a purse and Londyn absolutely refuses to let me change into a pair of tight jeans instead. So, everything is going into the boob holder tonight. Lipstick, emergency cash, and cell phone.

"Because I'm a free soul, Darlin'. I can't be tied down," she answers dramatically, pressing the palm of her hand over her heart.

I roll my eyes wanting to call utter bullshit. Londyn might look and act like a wild child, but under the surface she's really just an old soul. She enjoys lounging around in pajamas and working on her latest arts and crafts project most nights. Whether that's knitting, crocheting, sewing a new outfit, or painting a new piece.

I believe that's what drew us together that first English class at the beginning of freshman year. She strode into the class, sat down next to me, and declared that we would be best friends. She could just tell, was her reasoning. And hell, she was right. We slowly built a friendship in that class that leaked out into our lunch hour and eventually outside of school.

That's also how I know that when she loves, she'll love hard. I just wish she would either forget about Kyle or stop waiting for him to make the first move. They've been circling each other since sophomore year with neither one of them acting on it. The odd time Kyle dated, Londyn would get upset and he'd break up with the girl and vice versa. Except Kyle didn't get upset. No, instead he tried to intimidate the guy Londyn was with. In short, he would turn into a grade-A asshole until she broke up with the guy.

Their non-relationship makes my head spin and makes me glad I found Jack when I did.

Jack.

My heart soars at seeing him in just a few short minutes until I remember what happened in the parking lot of the school, and then I just feel sick. What the hell am I supposed to say to him tonight?

'Gee, I'm sorry for freaking out. I guess this is the end for us then, huh? Good luck in the Navy.'

My stomach rolls at the possibility of saying goodbye to Jack tonight. I hate that it's even an option. But what other choice do I have? Just wait here for him to finish training and hope he doesn't get deployed right away?

I wouldn't even be a military spouse and I'm not a family member. Would I even get access to him while he's deployed? And how long would he be deployed for? I have no idea. I had plans to research all of this when Londyn and I got to my house, but she started in on my hair and makeup right away, plus I don't know

19

where my laptop currently is. Probably still in my backpack from yesterday but I wouldn't look for it now. I plan on researching all of it tomorrow.

"Let's go, hot stuff." Londyn slaps my ass on her way out of my bedroom, continuing down the hall to the front door.

"God help me," I mutter, picking up my phone and following my best friend.

Jack's house is already packed with high school seniors and some juniors by the time Londyn and I make it down the street from my house to his.

The bass of the music is turned up so loud I feel it reverberating through my chest as soon as we step through the front door. It's an odd feeling and one I could never get use to despite the parties we all attended together throughout our high school education.

"Looks like we have some party crashers tonight," Londyn nods towards a group of people standing in a corner of the living room.

I sigh, not really feeling like dealing with idiots tonight. "Hopefully they don't get out of hand like the last group who crashed a party."

"Amen to that," Londyn announces, taking the lead as she pushes her way through the crowd and into the kitchen where the guys are standing around the island.

"Budgie!" Kyle hollers, his words slurring already.

"I'm not a damn bird, Kyle Montgomery," Londyn admonishes him.

"No, but you are cute." He grins, throwing an arm around the back of her neck and offering her a sip from his drink, which she declines before proceeding to make her own gin and tonic.

"I'll have one of those."

Londyn nods at my request, grabbing another red plastic cup from the upside-down stack.

"Can we talk?" Jack asks, his strong hand splayed on the counter in front of me as he leans a hip against the marble.

"Now you want to talk? Wouldn't the time for talking have been before you decided to enlist?"

Jack lets out a small breath. I stiffen a little when his hand lands against the small of my back. I know the movement is meant to be reassuring and I guess it still is in a way, but I am pissed.

"I didn't even know if I would make it past the initial tests. I signed up for BUD/s in hopes of eventually becoming a SEAL. I didn't want to make a big deal about it until I knew for sure, babe."

"That's the thing, though, Jackson," I say, taking my cup from Londyn and making sure to not make eye contact with anyone because if I do, if I look up and see genuine remorse in Jack's eyes then I know I wouldn't be able to say goodbye to him tonight. "Just deciding to try and enlist is a big deal. We had plans, Jack. Plans that involve both of us and you just…" I wave a hand in front of me not sure how to describe how hurt I am by his actions. "Shat on it."

"I'm sorry, baby," he whispers into my neck. His lips brush the sensitive skin there and I shiver. The scent of his cologne wafting up to embrace me in its comforting smell.

"Don't," I choke out, grab my drink, and head for the stairs to the second floor where it's a bit quieter.

I gingerly poke my head into Jack's room, half expecting a couple having sex but praying there's no one. When I push open the door and see no one naked, I breathe a relieved sigh and close the door behind me, momentarily debating on whether to lock it or not.

"If this is the last time for the two of you to be together then you should be making the most of it." *My best friend's words echo through my head, so I leave it unlocked.*

I place my drink on Jack's nightstand before taking a seat on his bed. Swinging my legs up on the bed, I lay back and stare up at the darkened ceiling, but something pokes me in the back of the head from under the pillow.

Curious, I sit up again and reach under it, my hand pats back and forth until it comes into contact with something hard. I pull it out and turn on the bedside lamp. My hand freezes midway back from under the lampshade when I get my first good look at the object that poked me.

It couldn't be.

"*I was planning on giving that to you this weekend.*" *Jackson's voice startles me so much, I jump and drop the box on the floor, watching as it rolls to a stop by his feet.*

"*Wh-what is it?*" *I ask, as Jack bends down to retrieve the small box from the floor.*

"*I guess since you've seen it, there's no point in trying to make it more romantic.*"

He runs a hand through his shaggy hair. Suddenly, he looks around the room, holding a finger up to tell me to wait a second while he plugs in the white Christmas lights we strung around his room several years ago and never took down, then switches off the bedside lamp.

A soft glow is cast over Jack's bedroom. He clears his throat, taking both my hands in his and turns me until I'm fully seated on the edge of the bed. Jack then proceeds to get down on one knee in front of me, never letting go of my left hand.

"*I'll never be able to tell you how sorry I am for keeping my enlistment from you. I never want you to feel like you don't have a say in our future because you do. I meant it when I said I would always be the only one who you lay down next to at night and wake up beside in the morning. I want you on this journey with me, baby.*"

Jack fingers the box open revealing a beautiful but simple square cut diamond in a white gold band.

"*Annika Michelle Holt, will you marry me?*"

My eyes bounce between Jack and the ring and back again. My brain unable to compute what's happening.

"*But what will people think? We're only eighteen, Jack.*"

He grins. "When has that ever stopped us?"

He has a point. We've practically been together since we were fourteen, but only officially since we were fifteen. Everyone in our lives has told us our relationship could never work past high school. We have an opportunity to prove them wrong. Jack is my one, my only. I can't imagine feeling towards another what I feel towards him.

"Okay," I whisper, still in shock.

"Is that a yes?" Jack asks, trying to hide the smile threatening to split his face.

"Yes."

He whoops, swinging me up in his arms and twirling me around his room.

"I love you so much, Annika."

"And I you, Jackson."

The thought of my late husband sends a jolt through my heart. Londyn must notice the tiny flinch I try to cover up because her eyes turn worried.

"You okay, Sweetie?"

"Yeah," I croak out, massaging the area just above my heart. "Just some heartburn is all." I paste on a smile and hope that she doesn't call my bullshit this time.

Just as I'm about to respond there's a knock at the front door. *Saved by the door.* Londyn's eyes light up at the sound and I wonder how sensitive my microphone is for her to have heard it.

"That's him, isn't it?" She bounces in her chair.

I roll my eyes. "I have no idea until I answer it."

"Well, go answer it." She shoos me. "And don't end the call just yet," she manages to get out before I hit the end button.

I raise my eyebrow and would've said more but there's a second knock. Londyn motions me to go again. I reluctantly leave the connection open but pull up a different window so that he won't see Londyn on the webcam when he comes in, and hurry to the door before he can knock a third time.

I flip the lock and pull the door open. My eyes land on a pair of tan work boots before travelling up the long expanse of denim covered legs, a t-shirt that's tucked into a narrow waist and seems to pull across a wide chest that'll make a football player envious, then up further to a square jaw I saw a hint of in the picture Londyn showed me on Instagram earlier. I bite my lip, my gaze travelling higher to full lips that pull into a lopsided grin and higher into a pair of whisky eyes.

"Howzit, are you Annika Carter?"

Here's the thing about the South African accent, to anyone who hasn't heard it before, it may sound like a weird mix of the British, New Zealand and Australian accents. People most often confuse those from South Africa with being from Australia, New Zealand or England and I admit, to those who grew up here and around the accent, it's not the most... sexiest sound. I have to disagree with them. It might be because I haven't lived here in several years, and no longer have the accent myself, but as soon as he opened his mouth and I heard him say that first word, I think I may have sighed dreamily a little.

"Uh, yeah. Come on in," I say, taking a step back and opening the door wider so he can step through.

"You must be Nathaniel."

"Please call me Nathan." He offers a gentle smile as he steps inside and takes a quick glance around the living room.

"The built-ins are in the back bedroom." I motion for him to walk ahead of me mostly so that Londyn can get a good look at him as he walks by my computer sitting on the dining room table. Also, because I can't help but look to see how his ass fills out those jeans.

As Nathan and I pass by the dining room table, I shoot a warning look at my open computer. I can't see my best friend, but I know she can see us. The last thing I need is for Nathan to hear her giggle or the puppy to bark. I inwardly cringe and wonder why I let her talk me into keeping the video connection open while he's here.

I follow Nathan into the back bedroom where he doesn't hesitate to begin checking out the already existing built-in wardrobe. He opens one of the doors, examines the inside and the hinges before he closes it and moves on to the next. I try not to remember the time when I was eight and found a snake curled up in the corner. A cold shiver runs over my skin at the memory of running to the kitchen telling my mom, who didn't believe me, and then to my parents' bedroom where my dad was on the phone. I practically had to drag him because he didn't believe me either. But sure enough, when I opened the door to the built-in, the snake was still curled up in the corner.

"It's not in too rough shape considering how long ago it was built. The handles and some of the hinges could use replacing, but if you want to completely gut it, I could make you something new. Something more updated?" He asks, closing the last door on the far side and turning back to me.

"That would be great actually. I was thinking of turning this into more of an office, so maybe something smaller that doesn't take up that whole far wall?"

Nathan nods along as I explain what I want for the room, his gaze roaming over the existing wood again as if he's already picturing what he'll build. We move on to the master bedroom after that, but I have a hard time giving the go-ahead to replace the built-in armoire in here since it holds so many memories. We agree that for now it will stay the way it is but Nathan will polish it up a bit and bring it back to its former glory.

"Is it possible for you to build a headboard that would match it?" I ask.

He steps up to the carved wood and runs his fingers over the intricate designs. For a moment, I wonder how those fingers would feel tracing lines over my body. I shiver and push the thought away.

"Shouldn't be a problem."

The last bedroom we enter is the hardest. A part of me wants to keep the door closed permanently, but I know that isn't fair to Kody or to his memory even if he hadn't ever seen the inside of it. I swallow hard, straighten my shoulders, and lead Nathan into the center of the room.

"As you can see there's not much going on in here so it's pretty much a blank slate. I would like to make it into a guest room, though."

He doesn't say anything as he strolls around the room. "If you hardly plan on using this space then you probably don't want something as built-in as the ones in the other bedrooms?"

I nod my agreement.

"I can build a tall dresser or something a bit smaller if you prefer that. Maybe a couple of matching side tables?"

I beam up at him. It's like he can see exactly what I have planned in my head. "Sounds great."

I leave Nathan to do his thing and take measurements of the three rooms, reminding myself to ask him about building a new dining room table and maybe a bench that opens up against the wall for maximizing space.

When I sit back down in front of my laptop and pull up the window again, Londyn's grinning at me. I roll my eyes and begin typing out a message, not sure how good Nathan's hearing is but not wanting him to accidentally overhear our conversation either. Londyn gives me a weird look through the webcam and opens her mouth to say something but shuts it again when I send the message I was typing.

Me: *Let's switch to chat only. Don't want him to accidentally hear anything.*

I see her smirk and then the three dots appear indicating she's typing but then stops. I watch as she shakes her head, another grin pulling up a corner of her lips.

L: *I could make a dirty joke right now but I'm choosing not to. Fine, chat only it is.*

My face flames as I read her message. Londyn has always had the dirtiest mind between the two of us but sometimes I think she makes apples out of oranges. I click out of the video chat just as another message comes through.

L: *He's so fine! Tell me you're going to hit that.*

Me: *I just met the man! Plus, he kinda works for me.*

L: **eye roll* When are you going to learn to let loose and have a little fun? This seems like the perfect opportunity to me. The two of you fool around while he's working there then call a quits once he's done.*

Me: *Absolutely not.*

L: *Fine. Can I have him? I bet those arms of his could do some damage!*

Me: *He's not a toy, Londyn!*

"Okay, I think I have everything I need. I'll draw up some designs and come by tomorrow and see what you think? Maybe get started on some of the bigger pieces."

Nathan's deep voice startles me so much I jump and automatically reach out to snap the lid of the laptop shut.

"Oh, er… sounds good."

I swallow hard then glance up, hoping my face doesn't look as red as it feels. That in itself is a mistake because as soon as I lift my gaze, my eyes land on his arms.

I bet those arms of his could do some damage!

I'm going to kill my best friend. Not that she's wrong. Far from it actually. But because I now have images of my legs wrapped around Nathan's waist as he slams my back into the wall. His one hand pinning both of my wrists above my head as he trails the other up the inside of my thighs…

"Is there anything else you'd like me to take a look at?"

"Um…" I clear my throat and drop my gaze from his arms. "Yeah. I was wondering if you'd be able to build another dining table and bench to replace this one." I wave my hand indicating the table I was currently still sitting at. "I was thinking of maybe a bench where the top opens up and doubles as a storage area."

Nathan eyes up the set then nods, pulling out a small notebook from his back pocket. "I'll see what I can do. The built-in shelving will be my first priority though, but it shouldn't be a problem."

"Sounds good," I say, walking him to the door.

"I'll be back tomorrow morning," he says and then jogs down the driveway to his car.

Chapter 4

JACK PARKS THE CAR *at the pier. The light from the moon casts a glow over the ocean, making it sparkle. Some people love the ocean in the morning when the sun is just rising over the horizon, some love it in the evening when the sun is setting and casting beautiful shades of pinks and purples, while some just love it when the beach isn't packed full of people. Me... I love it just like this. When the water matches the colour of the dark sky while the moon casts its glow from above.*

It's a bit menacing, but it's peaceful the way you can see the gentle ripples of the water in the moonlight, hear the sound of the waves rushing the shore.

I still miss Cape Town, my birth city, something fierce, but Florida makes up for it with things like this. I think it made the move a little easier knowing I didn't have to give up everything. I still have the ocean and the comfort it provides me.

As soon as I round the front of the car, Jack takes my hand in his and begins walking down the sandy path to the shore. The sound of the crashing waves gets louder and louder as we near the water's edge.

When I'm close, I slip out of my ballet flats and walk farther until my toes touch the water as it slowly rolls in. I sigh in contentment, my hands in the pockets of my shorts, and tip my head back to look up at the stars.

"You really do love the ocean at night," he comments, sliding his arms around me from behind, his feet planted firmly on each side

of my own. I notice he too has kicked his shoes off and slid off his socks.

"You can't tell me this isn't the most peaceful time to enjoy the sounds and smells of the ocean," I say, leaning my head against his solid chest.

"You're right," he murmurs, his lips brushing the skin of my temple. "I can't."

"You really think we can make it, Jack?" I ask after the silence has stretched on for a while.

"What do you mean?"

I blow out a fast breath, turning in his arms to lay my cheek against his chest. "Everyone thinks that when we graduate we'll both move on. I mean, you have your heart set on NYU and following your parents' dream of wanting you to become a doctor. And I have no idea if I'm staying here or going to UCLA. It really all depends on where I get accepted."

"We have two more years before we graduate high school, Nika," he says with a small smile.

"I know that, but they'll want us to apply to schools after next year which means we need to start really thinking about our futures soon."

"My little planner," he smirks, brushing a few loose strands of hair out of my face.

It's true. I am a planner, especially when it comes down to big decisions like my future. I already know what I want to study in university and what I'll be declaring as my major. Plus, what I want to eventually get my master's degree in. Oh, and also what career I have hopes of achieving after I complete my degree. It gives me anxiety and solicits attacks to not have a plan for something so big. Something that can determine how the rest of my life will turn out.

"They don't know what they're talking about, babe. They don't know us. I think we can make it." He runs his thumb along my jaw, stopping at my chin to tip my face up. "The question is, do you?"

"I do," I reply, already knowing that Jack is it for me. There'll never be another man who makes me feel what he does.

Jack grins, his eyes dancing in the moonlight and taking on a teasing quality. "I like the sound of that."

I roll my eyes and turn back to the water, taking in a deep breath of the salty ocean air. This was always my anchor, but now so is Jackson. I'm afraid without one or the other I'd drown.

"Do you want to walk some more? Or are you ready to head home?" He asks, bending down to retrieve the shoes we left in the sand.

The decision I made earlier flashes in my mind and I bite my lip, wondering if tonight is the night. There's only one way to find out.

"No," I say, my voice pitched low, taking on a breathy quality. "I'm not ready to go home yet."

Jack swallows hard, his Adam's apple bobbing just barely visible in the darkened light, and I wonder if he can see the desire in my eyes. "Up for a drive then?"

I nod and slip my palm in his when he reaches out his hand for me to take.

It's closer to midnight by the time he drops me off at home and I'm not sorry in the least that I'm an hour late for my curfew and am grounded for the next week.

Later as I lay on my back in bed, I replay everything that happened on my date with Jackson and can't help but smile.

No. I am not sorry at all.

The hard knocking at the front door jolts me out of my dream of Jack and my first official date when we were sixteen. It's been two years of the same recurring dreams. Our first date, our high school graduation and the night he asked me to marry him, our wedding day, me moving to San Diego halfway through his BUD/s training, and then the day I found out he had been killed while on a mission. I never know which dream it'll be until I close my eyes at night.

Grumbling curses under my breath, I stumble out of bed and wipe the sleep from my eyes while grabbing a zip-up sweater to throw on over the sheer tank top. I zip it up when there's another knock on the door.

"Yeah, yeah," I say, moving across the living room to pull open the door.

"This a bad time?"

I gape at the man standing in front of me in worn jeans and a t-shirt. The same uniform he was wearing yesterday.

"Um, no. No, this is fine," I say, managing to push the words out of my dry throat.

Nate just stares at me, his eyes darting down to the front of my sweater and back up again. He clears his throat and rocks back on his heels. I cock my head to the side and study him when his gaze darts back down but he's quick to look away again, running his hand over his head. Confused, I look down and gasp when I see what has him so uncomfortable. The sweater I absently grabbed in my haste to answer the door is white. Almost sheer white. Which means I just flashed him my nipples. Frigging awesome.

"I, um... I," I stumble over my words, quickly folding my arms over my chest to hide my boobs. "I'm going to go get dressed and make coffee. Lots of coffee, and then lunch. You can start on the guest room if you'd like." I leave the door open and back away farther into the living room.

Nathan hooks a thumb over his shoulder, still not making eye contact with me and says, "I'm just going to grab my things from the truck. Mind if I set up shop under the carport?"

"No, that sounds great. I'll be right out."

I turn and dart back as fast as I can without running to my bedroom. After pulling on a pair of jeans from yesterday and an old t-shirt over a bra, I open the door again and check to see if Nathan is in the guest room. He's not. But I hear a saw start up outside. When I enter the kitchen, I see him bent over a wooden workbench in a black wife-beater undershirt. His shoulder and back muscles are impressive, the way they contract and release with every movement.

I groan, turning away from the window and going about making us lunch. This is bad. I haven't been interested in a guy since Jack. Some might think eighteen months is a long time to go without having sex or being interested in anyone, but when your husband was your whole life, those months can seem like no time at all.

I wait for the saw to stop before I go out and place two plates filled with sandwiches and fruit on a nearby table I keep out here for days like today.

"I thought you might be hungry," I say, gesturing to the plates I brought out.

"Ja. Thanks." He wipes away the sweat from his forehead with the back of his arm. "You mind if I wash my hands really quick?"

I laugh. "No need to ask."

Nathan takes off for the bathroom halfway down the hall and I take that time to get us a couple drinks. Foregoing the coffee once I notice that it's after noon.

"Beer or cooldrink?" I ask when he comes back down towards the kitchen.

"Beer. Thanks." He takes the one I offer him and sits at the table in front of one of the plates.

"Howzit going out here?" I ask, picking up half my sandwich and tipping my head to indicate the workbench.

"I started cutting a couple of pieces for the empty room. But I'd like to break down the built-in in the other

33

room and clear it out so I can get an accurate measurement of the walls."

I nod, taking a couple bites of the ham, cheese, lettuce, and tomato between the triangle slices of bread. "Can I help?"

Nathan pauses with the beer bottle halfway to his lips then shrugs. "If you want. I have a couple of extra gloves and goggles in the truck."

I sit up straighter in my seat and can't fight the big-ass grin that spreads across my face. Nathan doesn't know but he's just given me a big gift. I use to love helping my dad repair cars in this very carport, and that love of repairing things bled into my life at school when I was finally able to take woodwork class. That love hasn't been fed in so long. Too long for me to remember when the last time was that I picked up a piece of wood.

Nathan and I finish our lunch, and I wash up the dishes while he runs out to his truck to grab the protective gear for me. When he comes back, I suit up and follow him into my old bedroom.

"Do you want to take a couple of swings or drag the pieces out to the carport?" he asks, but when I eye the sledgehammer excitedly, feeling the adrenaline already start to take hold, he laughs and hands it over to me. "Alright then. Just let me take the doors off, then you can go crazy."

Nathan and I spend the rest of the weekend removing the existing built-ins and replacing them with new ones. On a whim, I decide to paint the guest room. Before Nathan brings in the new wardrobe he built, he helps me prime the walls and paint it a light sky blue.

By the end of the weekend, the guest room is completely done. The double bed has a brand new, custom made headboard that matches the new wardrobe and side tables. A three-piece painted canvas of Clifton Beach sits on the far floor ready to be hung. The colour of the ocean waves matching seamlessly with the paint on the walls. We got my old room clear of all the wood pieces and Nathan's already mostly done cutting the pieces for some new floating shelves, a custom bookshelf, and a desk. The man's a machine and by Sunday night I'm disappointed to see him leave without asking for my number. The disappointment doesn't last long before it turns to guilt.

Jack's hand wraps my upper arm, stopping me in my tracks. When he spins me, I turn right into his chest. Hands splay out on his pecs to keep me from headbutting him. He curls a piece of hair behind my ear and his thumb tips up my chin until I'm forced to look him in the eye.

"You can look," he rasps, his voice deepening. "But I will always be the only one taking you home at night. The one you fall asleep next to and wake up beside. The only one who'll get to see this gorgeous body naked."

I shiver. Fingers curling into the material of his shirt.

"After graduation," I whisper.

"After graduation," Jack repeats with a soft kiss to my lips.

Chapter 5

"I'm so happy to have you start here as a teacher. It's not every day that alumni come back to teach," Pam Morton, the principal of Pinelands North Primary School says as she leads the way to the room that will become my home away from home, at least during the school year.

"I'm happy to be here. This place holds so many memories," I say, glancing around at the various pictures that still decorate the hallways of the school. Then my eyes land on the class pictures of previous years and search until I see a familiar group of faces. "Oh, my goodness, we were so tiny."

Pam laughs beside me. "You know Mrs. Casserley just retired last year."

"Really?"

Mrs. Casserley was my grade five teacher and probably one of my favourites, only beat out by Mr. Andersen and that's only because I may have had a little crush on him. Truth be told, I think all the girls had a crush on Mr. Andersen. He was cute, but he was also an easy teacher. He could be serious when the subject required it, but he was mostly trying to get you to laugh during class, and when the sun came out and the temperature rose again, he didn't make us spend the day inside. He would have us grab our notebooks and pencils and we'd have class outside in the courtyard or on the field if there wasn't already a gym class out there. We'd spend the class time in the sun and enjoy the fresh air. I remember a few geography and history classes where we spent the time outside. I think I remember more from those few classes than I did from the ones spent inside the classroom.

"This will be your class while you're here."

I follow Pam into the familiar class and look around. Not very much has changed about the room since the last time I was in here as a six-year-old. The carpet in the front of the chalkboard looks new though. The wooden floors towards the back of the classroom look like the originals. The round tables and chairs also look like they've seen an upgrade in the last several years. But the student cubbies against the outside walls look the same and the layout is definitely the same, with the teacher's desk in the front right corner.

"This feel all so surreal," I tell Pam, taking in the rest of the classroom and the books on the two mini-shelves. "I remember sitting here," I say walking to the middle of the carpet, "for reading time. We each had our own books we used to follow along while Mrs. Ansty played the tape."

"Believe it or not, I think we still have those around here somewhere. Gale might have them in the library." I look up at Pam, my eyes wide in surprise and she laughs. "Some of the kids, especially the younger ones, still love listening to them from time to time. And it helps those who aren't as quick to pick up reading the words."

I walk to the windows overlooking the courtyard and watch the kids play as they prepare to start the day. Their uniforms still clean with zero wrinkles. I always loved this classroom, even as a kid. It's one of the few that open up into its own little courtyard that leads to the bigger courtyard. There's a door the kids can enter through rather than having to walk all the way down the hallway to get to their class.

"I've left the gym and pool schedule on your desk so you can have a look at it and see which works for your class for PE. I think Mr. Walker is planning on having his kids play cricket on the field today so the pool would be open for your class," Pam says coming to stand beside me.

"The older grades still have PE after lunch?"

She nods. "Nothing much has changed in terms of schedule since you've left." She smiles over at me, a slight blush to her cheeks like she's embarrassed by that fact, but I don't care. If it works, it works.

We both turn back to watching the kids out the window and it's quiet for a few beats before she speaks again. "So, what do you think? Can you be happy here?"

I grin. I can't believe I have my own Sub-A class now. I guess it's called grade one now. Sub-A was used when I was still in school here and then it changed to grade one the year after. "It'll take some getting used to, but I think I will be, yes."

"Good, I'm glad." She turns and heads back towards the door that leads into the hallway. "If you have any questions, don't hesitate to come see me. Mr. Walker's class is on the same schedule as yours so I'm sure he'd be happy to help you with anything as well."

"Thank you so much, Pam."

She lifts her hand in a small wave then disappears through the door just as the bell rings to signal the kids to begin lining up.

"Well, this is a surprise," I hear a familiar voice say as soon as I've sent my class into their respective changing rooms to get into their PE uniforms.

I turn and gape at the man walking towards me in basketball shorts and a tight t-shirt, a whistle hanging around his neck, and clipboard in hand.

"Cat got your tongue?" he says, grinning playfully when he comes to stand beside me as we wait.

"What are you doing here? I thought you were a carpenter?"

He shrugs. "Primary school teacher by day, carpenter by night… and on the weekends. It's like my superpower."

Right. I vaguely remember one of my parents mentioning that. I snort. "Your superpower? And what's your superhero name? Captain Fix-it?"

He laughs and I can't help but stare. He's gorgeous. His black hair shines in the mid-morning sun. I can see a couple of freckles dotting his face around the bridge of his nose that I hadn't noticed over the weekend when he came to my house, and he towers over me by at least five inches. "Bob the Builder was taken."

"Bob the Builder isn't a superhero."

He gasps, clutching his hands to his chest over his heart. "You wound me."

I roll my eyes and try to fight the smile threatening to pull at the corners of my mouth.

Nathan laughs, bumping his shoulder playfully into mine. "You guys heading out to the field too?"

I nod. "Yeah, still seems a little cold to make them get into the pool."

"Want to make things interesting?"

Now he has my curiosity piqued. I turn to him with an eyebrow raised. "I'm listening."

"Class against class? You pick the sport; soccer, field hockey, netball, tennis…"

"And what's the wager?" I ask.

"No wager. Just the knowledge that my class kicks ass."

I laugh, "You really think your class has what it takes to beat mine?"

By this time, the majority of both classes have begun filtering back outside from the changing rooms and are standing around in a half circle watching us, some with eager smiles on their faces and some who look like they'd rather be anywhere but here. Eh, I can relate to that. I use to hate PE except when it was field hockey day. Our teachers did this all the time when I was a student here so why shouldn't I get to have the same sort of fun.

I turn a look on those from my class who are already standing there and ready to play. They all nod an enthusiastic yes. "Fine. Soccer it is."

Nathan's grin grows wider. He calls out two boys from the group, one from his class and one from mine, to help him get the balls from the sports locker. "We'll meet you out there," he calls as he walks towards the gym, the two boys trailing behind him.

When they're out of sight, I look at the group of kids standing watching me and realize he left me here to lead both classes to the sports fields… on the other side of the school. Asshole.

"Alright guys, line up in two lines, please, and no shoving. If I see it, you'll be sitting this one out in Mrs. Morton's office."

One by one I see backs straightening as the threat of sitting in the principal's office begins to settle. I nod at the two girls in the front and let them take the lead up the mini-ramp and through the doors, down the hall, and out the doors on the other side into the bigger, middle courtyard that separates the lower grade classes from the higher grades. I walk beside the two rows of kids down the pathway, pass the buildings to the big, open sports field. As soon as I get everyone split up into their respective classes again, I look up and notice Nathan walking towards us with one netted bag of soccer balls while the two boys are each using two hands to carry the other bag.

"Exactly how many balls do you need?" I ask him when he gets closer and then immediately feel my face flame red with what I just said.

Nathan laughs, but thankfully none of the kids are in earshot of us. "Just two," he says with a mischievous grin. Then motions to the bags. "The rest are for warm up drills."

I duck my head, my face still hot at the innuendo I stupidly made, and then turn to do a headcount of both classes while Nathan calls out instructions.

"Alright, listen up. We're going to have a bit of a competition going on. My class versus Ms. Carter's class…"

My heart seizes at the sound of my surname. When I introduced myself to my class this morning, I told them to call me Mrs. C. But hearing that name fall from Nathan's mouth again, it just… I blink back the tears that threaten to spill. I thought I was moving on from wanting to cry every time someone said Jack's name, but I guess I'm not, at least not as much as I thought.

I don't hear the rest of what Nathan says then the two classes break off to do running drills.

"You okay?" Nathan asks, once he's made sure everyone is doing what they're supposed to be doing.

I nod. "Mhm, it's just still a little weird to think of myself as a teacher." I slide my hands in the pockets of my dress pants, making a mental note to keep a pair of track pants or shorts at work, and survey the groups of kids.

"What did you do back home?"

It's an innocent question but I think somehow, being the wife of Navy SEAL, isn't the right thing to say right now. "Website design mostly. I mean, I had my teaching license but… things happened, and it was just easier to do something that didn't require me to go into school every day. Easier to travel and still work, I guess."

I don't mention the fact that after Jack died, I couldn't leave the house. I had somehow built up such anxiety about stepping foot outside the condo we shared that it would sometimes take me a full day to psych myself up enough to go out and get groceries, or hell, even to get into the cab to go to the airport and catch a flight to Cape Town. So yeah, a few months after Jack died, I quit my job at the elementary school and made website designing my full-time job. I was pretty good at it before, so it wasn't all that hard to find more clients to help fill the financial gap.

I didn't want to do that here though, especially not after my mom went through all that to get me an interview with Pam Morton. Well, interview wasn't the right term. It was more like a sit-down tea where we discussed what I had been up to since leaving P.N.P.S. after grade six. We still talked about my teaching qualifications and experience, but it was almost like an afterthought. Like Pam knew she was going to hire me before I even stepped foot inside her office.

After a few minutes, Nate instructs them to get into smaller teams of three or four, with one person from each group running up to grab a ball. When each group has their own soccer ball, they begin practicing kicking the ball back and forth, using the inside of their feet like they've been taught, and not their toes.

"Have dinner with me tonight."

"What?" I ask, not sure if I've heard him correctly.

"If my class wins, have dinner with me tonight."

"And what if my class wins?"

He grins, and it's boyish and youthful and it makes me want to say yes. Yes, to dinner. Yes, to anything. "Then we'll have drinks to celebrate the win."

I laugh. "So, I'm either having dinner with you or drinks with you tonight."

"Awesome. I'll pick you up at seven. School night and all," he says then walks away to divide the kids up again so they can start playing.

It's not until we're halfway through the game, with my kids kicking ass by the way, do I realize that he tricked me into seeing him tonight. I never did agree one way or another, and he never stuck around long enough to hear my answer, and whenever I would get close to him during the game, he'd run off again. The bugger. I'm not really torn up about it though. Nervous, maybe. I haven't been on a first date since I was sixteen. Wait, was this even a first date?

Chapter 6

AFTER THE KIDS HAVE left and I've packed away the last of the science books, there's a knock on the classroom door and then Nathan strolls in wearing dress pants that look like they were stitched together around him. The sleeves of his blue dress shirt are rolled up, revealing a tattoo on his right arm, and the first three buttons are undone. This man is sexy.

"So, after your class thoroughly kicked our asses, which I expect a rematch by the way, I realized that seven seems a long time to wait," he grins sheepishly.

"Oh?" I ask, carrying the books back over to the shelf. When I turn around to grab the rest, Nathan is standing behind me, the remaining science books in his hands. "Thank you." I take them from him and finish putting them away.

"I've decided that we should just go now. We can drop off your car on the way there. No sense in taking two vehicles," he says as if we've already decided.

"Is that right?"

He grins, leaning back against my desk, the sleeves of his shirt pulling tight against his biceps when he folds his arms over his chest. I have a better view of his tattoo now. How I missed it before when he was at my house or earlier this morning on the field I'll never know. But it looks like a black and white realistic tattoo of a lion.

Actually, it looks so real I feel like it may actually be looking back at me when I stare into its eyes.

"Where exactly are we going?" I ask, snapping my eyes away from the lion and up to Nathan's.

"I know a place," he shrugs, looking around at my desk behind him. "Are you almost ready to go?"

I take a quick glance around the classroom. The kids did a surprisingly good job at cleaning up their craft projects earlier and aside from a few stray pencils, there's not much more that needs to be cleaned. The cleaning staff will get the tiny loose paper shreds on the floor when they come in to vacuum later.

"Yeah, just let me put away some of the pencils and gather my things."

I can feel Nathan's eyes on me as I move around the classroom, gathering the pencils that were left behind and putting them in the holders in the middle of the round tables. I notice one of the kids left their blazer on the hook with their name and I make a mental note to remind them to grab it before they leave tomorrow.

"All ready," I say, after I've slid the math assignment into my bag and grabbed my purse and coat from the chair.

True to his word, Nathan follows closely behind me until I pull into the carport. He's still sitting behind the wheel, his car idling at the bottom of my driveway when I walk out and close the garage door behind me. It's still one of those old doors where you have to physically push up to open and pull on the string to reel it down to close. I shake my head as I thread the lock through the handle at the bottom and secure it. I really need to bring this house into the twenty-first century. An automatic garage door that opens and closes with a click of a button would be so awesome. Then I begin thinking of how much something like that would cost me here and I'm suddenly okay with the manual way of doing things.

"Do you plan on telling me where you're taking me? I feel like I need to send a text to a friend just in case I go missing or something," I say, when we've hit the N1 freeway.

Nathan chuckles, wiping a hand down his face. I can't help but stare at his arms as the muscles pull with each movement. I was always an avid lover of arm porn. A man's arms - and eyes - say as much about him as I need to know upon the first meeting. I'm drawn to arms that could make me feel safe and protected, while still lifting me up and slamming me against a wall as he kisses me like his life depends on it, amongst other things. And eyes I could look into and have the eerie sense that I know what he's thinking. Nathan has both of those and more. Like a perfectly round ass that looks bitable in a pair of jeans. His hair is thick and full, and I can definitely picture running my fingers through it before tugging. I haven't seen his chest yet, but if the way his shirts mold to his body are any indication… my mouth waters at the thought of running my hands up the hard ridges.

"It's a surprise, but don't worry there'll be plenty of people around."

It feels so good to be able to spend time with a guy again that isn't Xander or Caleb. The last man I felt this comfortable around was Jack. It still hurts to think about him, but I'm at the point now where I realize he wouldn't want me to become a cat lady, too overridden by anxiety and fear to leave the house. He'd want me to meet new people. Hell, maybe he'd even want me to fall in love again, but that is something that feels so far off.

My head rolls against the headrest and I watch Nathan as he drives. One hand casually slung over the steering wheel as his thumb drums out a beat to the music flowing from the radio while his other hand rests on the gear shift, ready to change gears at a moment's notice. I wouldn't mind if anything happened with

Nathan. If we're both single then who does it hurt? I mean, I don't know about him but I'm not looking for anything serious right now. I just moved countries, bought a new house, and started a new job. I don't have time for anything serious. Nathan turns his head to me, and I lazily match his smile. Yeah, definitely not looking for anything serious... but something casual with him might just be what I need.

"We're here," he says forty minutes after we've left my house.

I glance out the windshield to see a small parking lot just off a small strip of beach with mountains on both sides. I recognize the mountains and beach farther down on the right side as Nathan parks the car, but I've never been this far down.

"Is that Hout Bay?" I ask.

He looks out his window to see where my gaze is pointing at. "It is. Technically, we're still in Hout Bay. Fish on the Rocks is down that way. So is the Hout Bay night market," he replies, gesturing to across the way to the harbour.

I feel like such a tourist. I should know that, but whenever I think of Hout Bay I think of Fish on the Rocks restaurant as well as Snoekies, two of the best fish and chips places in Cape Town. My stomach growls at the thought of fresh fish and slap chips.

"C'mon, let's eat before that monster decides to break free," Nathan says, and I can see he's trying to hold back a laugh.

I huff but follow him up the sandy steps and onto the restaurant's patio. When a server comes to seat us, Nathan asks for one of the couches on the patio. It's not too long until we're seated, both of us facing out to the ocean with the restaurant behind us.

"This is incredible," I say, taking in the water and the mountains.

Dunes Beach Restaurant & Bar is what's printed in a circle on the drink coasters on the table in front of us.

"I seem to always forget this place exists until I feel like going somewhere for a drink. They have one of the best sunsets in Hout Bay."

I glance at my watch, noting that it's only now six 'o clock and the sun is still going strong. I haven't been paying much attention to what time sunset has been since arriving back in Cape Town. It's almost like the sun is shining one minute and the next it's dark outside.

"We can stay to watch it," he says, having seen me glance down at my wrist.

I sigh, leaning back against the couch. "I don't think I've watched a sunset since I've been back."

Nathan thanks our server when he comes back with our drinks and orders us a calamari starter.

"How long has it been since you've been back?" he asks when our server has left.

"Oh gosh, I don't know. I had just turned thirteen when we left so about fourteen years."

"Did you ever think you'd be back here?"

I sip at the gin and tonic I ordered, squeezing a bit of the lime into it, then take another sip before I reply. "For a vacation? Sure. To live? Not really. I didn't know how much I missed it until I was back here, but it was never really in the cards before. Heck, I was surprised when my parents decided they were moving back. I never thought they would."

"Why did they?" Nathan asks. His dress pants and shirt look so odd against his casual pose of sitting back against the couch with an ankle resting over the other knee, a beer in hand.

"My ma isn't doing so well so I guess Dad wants to be close to her. My pa passed away several years ago so Dad's all she has left now, and I guess he feels guilty for not being here after Pa died."

Nathan hums. "Guilt is an interesting one," he says, sipping at his beer, his eyes trained on the ocean in the distance.

"How so?"

"Guilt makes us believe we're responsible for how someone else feels but we can no more control that than the setting of the sun."

"Aren't we, though?" I ask, squeezing lemon juice over the newly arrived calamari. "Responsible for how someone feels," I add.

Nathan drops his other foot and scoots forward on the couch to put his beer down on the table before picking up a piece of the battered fish. "We can only be responsible for ourselves and how we feel. If someone makes us angry, it's not their fault that their actions inspire such emotion. We choose to feel the way we do."

"I have a bookshelf full of romance novels that say otherwise."

Nathan grins. "Love is different. You don't see that shit coming until it's hitting you over the head with a shovel."

I laugh. "That's some description."

"Blame it on the reruns of CSI."

We lapse into a comfortable silence after that when the server brings by our dinners and refills our drinks. He's right though. We do choose the way we feel or how we react to situations, but I also think it's human nature to feel responsible for having a hand in how someone feels. He's also right that it's an interesting one. I wouldn't feel guilty for making someone happy, but I would if I had inadvertently made someone angry or upset.

"Dessert?" Nathan asks, drawing me out of my head.

"Don't mind if I do," I say, looking over the menu.

Nathan orders the ice cream with chocolate sauce and I go for the chocolate brownie when the server comes back to collect our dinner plates and ask if we want refreshers. I order another drink but Nathan switches to water since he has to drive later.

"What made you decide to be a primary school teacher by day and carpenter by night?"

"Ah, the superpower," he jokes but then his expression turns serious. "The man that used to own the company before I took over was a close friend of the family. So close in fact that he was my father. My mother died when I was a year old and left me to my grandparents. Apparently my mom never told my father that I existed. He only found out when he came back and discovered she had died."

"Oh, wow."

Nathan nods. "I guess it was my grandparents' way of punishing him, by not telling me he was my father. He could've told me himself when I was old enough, but he chose not to. He left me his business instead."

"Did you… were you two…" I trail off not really sure what I want to ask.

"He was allowed to come by the house. When I got older he brought me to his workshop and let me play around with the leftover pieces of wood. He helped me build a jewelry box for my gran and a spice rack for their kitchen." A slow, sad smile spread across his face. "I think by the time I was sixteen, they had a storage room full of little things I had made."

"They were proud of you."

"Anyway, when he died and left his business to me, I couldn't say no. I love my job at the primary school, but I also love fixing and rebuilding things. I kept on the guys who were already working there and made the decision to help out as much as I could on weekends and school holidays. I guess Pete had started giving them more and more of the work the sicker he got so they already had things covered, even if I wanted to take a more hands-off approach with the company."

"And you sleep when exactly? Don't you coach the U-13 boys' field hockey?"

Nathan grins around his spoon. "I sleep. Probably not as much as I should, but I sleep." He gathers the dessert dishes and piles them up in the middle of the table before pulling open out his wallet. "Ready to make like a banana and split?"

I groan.

"What? Don't like that one? How about, make like a tree and leaf?"

As soon as the server comes to take the payment, I start walking back to the car trying to ignore Nathan's corny one-liners and laughter behind me.

"I was going to hit up Lion's Head this weekend if you want to join," Nate says as he pulls up in front of my house.

"Yeah, that sounds good. I was planning on a quiet weekend at home, but I wouldn't mind the hike and fresh air."

"Great. I'll pick you up Saturday morning. The earlier we can get up there the better. Before it gets too hot."

I gather my purse up from its spot at my feet and then pause to look back at him. "Thank you for dinner. I had a great time."

"Glad I could be of service." His eyes drift down my face to linger a little longer on my lips and for a moment, I think he's going to kiss me. For a moment, I want him to. But then he pulls back and says he'll wait here until I'm safely inside.

Disappointment swirls inside my belly as I step out of the car and make my way up the front steps of my house. I just have the key in the lock when I hear a car door slam behind me and then footsteps running up the driveway. I turn around just in time for Nathan to grip my hips and pull me into him.

"I tried being a gentleman," he says, his breath ghosting over my parted lips.

"And?"

"I've decided it's overrated." He kisses me, gently at first like he's trying to make sure I'm okay with this, but I so am. I wrap my arms around his neck and pull him closer at the same time I deepen the kiss. His tongue dives into my mouth as soon as I open for him and I moan at the taste of beer and calamari and Nate.

"Definitely overrated," I whisper against his lips when he pulls away. "Do you want to come inside?"

Nate kisses me again, pushing my back up against the front door, but all too soon he pulls away again, taking a step back this time and I whimper, wanting to pull him closer.

"If I go in there, we both know I'm not coming out until morning."

"Is that so bad?" I ask, leaning back and allowing the door to hold me up. I don't think I can stand even if I wanted to, Nate made my legs go weak.

He cups my face in his hand and runs the pad of his thumb lightly over my lips. "It's only our first date. I already broke one first date rule." His eyes cloud over with lust the longer he stares at my lips. I press a kiss to his thumb and feel a flash of heat when his jaw ticks.

"And what's that?"

"Never kiss on the first date." His voice sounds raw and I imagine it's from the sheer force of will of holding himself back.

"That's too bad then. Goodnight, Nathan," I say, turning back to the door and pushing it open.

"Goodnight, Annika," Nate replies, and I close the door before I do something stupid like invite him inside for the second time. I hear his vehicle start back up several seconds later and then he's gone.

Nate's invite for a hike over the weekend has another hike bubbling up from the depths of my memories as I set my purse on the table and kick off my shoes.

"So, how long is this hike exactly?" I ask after we're both showered, dressed, and pulling on our shoes.

Jack pulls out his phone and it looks like he scrolls through something for a bit before putting it back and standing up. "Says about three miles downhill to get there."

I blanche. Three miles downhill to get there means it's three miles uphill to get back to the car. I stand, hands on my hips and face my husband. "Remember during school when they'd have to test how many miles you can run in a certain time frame?"

"Yeah."

"And remember how I was always conveniently sick during those days?"

Jack turns to me, eyebrow raised. "Where are you going with this?"

"Three miles, Jack. Three miles uphill."

He grins, throwing an arm around my shoulders and leading me out the front door before I have a chance to dig my heels in. "You'll be fine, Princess. We'll take it slow on the way back."

I sigh, following him down the hall to the elevator and then out to the car. "Fine, Mr. Navy-man, but if you have to carry me back, consider it part of your training."

He laughs. "Deal. Now get in. I already got a permit for us, but I want to hit up an outdoor store and grab a couple of those hydration backpacks."

"*I love my husband. I love my husband. I love my husband,*" I *mumble under my breath as I get in the passenger side of the car and try to remind myself that he has to go back to base in the morning.*

Jack pulls into the parking area and parks in a spot close to the entrance of the trail. There aren't many vehicles here which makes me think we may have a chance to have the watering hole at the falls to ourselves. The thought causes a grin to split my face as I step out of the car.

Looking around I can't help but feel blessed to live in such a beautiful state. It's the middle of November and while it's a cloudy day, we're still able to go hiking and if the water temperature is right, we'll be able to go swimming too. I mean, who else can say they're able to do that? Aside from the other southern States, that is.

"*Ready?*" *Jack asks, rounding the car and handing me one of the hydration packs we bought less than an hour ago.*

"*For the hike down? Yes. For the trip back? No.*" *I shrug on the backpack and then join Jack where he stands waiting at the entrance.*

"*C'mon, Princess.*" *Jack slides his hand into mine and we begin down the trail.*

I breathe in the fresh air and allow Jack to lead me down the trail as I take in the view around us. Hills covered in trees and lush bushes surround us on either side. We cross a flowing stream and then another and another, and before I know it three miles have passed and Jack's leading us up a giant rock and in front us is a beautiful waterfall and watering hole. I snort. Watering hole. Like Timon and Pumba from The Lion King. *Jack turns and raises a questioning eyebrow at my outburst, but I shrug it off and climb up next to him.*

"*Want to go swimming? Looks like there's a rope swing over there.*" *Jack tips his head towards the far right side of the falls and sure enough, there's a rope swing attached to a tree in the corner.*

I climb over the other rocks without answering him and once I'm at the water's edge, I slowly zip down my sweater, little by little revealing the black bikini and my bare skin underneath, inch by slow inch.

"Please tell me that's not the only thing you're wearing under there?" Jack groans, but I don't miss the subtle way he tries to adjust himself in his shorts.

"Okay." I grin, turning around to give him my back. "I won't," I say over my shoulder, hooking my thumbs in the waistband of my shorts and pushing them down to my ankles.

Strong arms wrap around my waist and I squeal as I'm lifted in the air. Jack slides down the last rocks and into the pool. As soon as our chests are submerged something brushes up against my leg but when I glance down it's too dark to see anything. I somehow manage to turn in Jack's arms and wrap my arms and legs around him.

"Uh, babe, is there something in the water... other than fish?"

Jack chuckles, cupping my neck in his hand and holding me to him as I try to climb higher when something else that definitely doesn't feel like a fish, brushes against my foot. "I don't think you want me to answer that."

"What's in the water, Jack?"

He kisses my temple, moving us further into the pool. "Just don't think about it, babe. Let's just swim, yeah?"

I exhale hard, looking over his shoulder ready to give in and just enjoy being in the water with him, but then I see a shadow swim behind him, and I just can't let it go, especially if what I think I saw is what I actually saw.

"What's in the water, Jack?" I ask again, scrambling to get closer to him, not really caring if I'm choking him by holding on for dear life.

Jack sighs, gripping me closer as he turns and swims us back to the rocks. After I've climbed up on the rock and completely out of the water, Jack follows, sitting with his feet still skimming the surface. "There might be snakes in the pool," he says so nonchalantly I almost don't believe him except for the fact that he's not smiling, there's not even a hint of amusement in his eyes.

"S-Snakes?!"

Jack hangs his head. "You're fine, Annika."

"You're telling me that was a snake that brushed up against my leg and then my foot?" I shriek not listening when he tries to calm me down.

Jack stands and moves in front of me, cupping my face and forcing my gaze from the water to his face. "Annika, breathe," he instructs, taking a deep breath and slowly releasing it, watching me do the same. We do it a couple more times before he pulls me into his arms. "You're okay, babe. I wouldn't have let anything happen to you."

"Did you know there'd be snakes in there?" I ask, wrapping my arms around his back.

"If I had, I wouldn't have made you go in the water. I only figured it out after I felt it against my own leg and saw it swim by."

I take another deep breath and hold it for a few seconds before letting it out, refusing to release him from my arms.

"You ready to get out of here and get some food?"

"God, yes. Get me away from those things."

I pull away and scowl at the pool. Jack laughs, handing me my clothes before pulling his shirt back on. I can see he wants to say something else but wisely keeps it to himself. Good, because if he was about to tell me that there were probably snakes along the edges of the trail I'd make good on him carrying me back to the car. I hate the slithering creatures. I shiver and pull on my sweater ignoring the fact that my body is still wet from the water. There was a reason why the devil masqueraded as a snake in the garden with Adam and Eve. They're evil creatures.

We make it three quarters of the way back up the trail before I have to stop and catch my breath. Jack hands me a protein bar and encourages me to drink more of the water from the hydration bag, but even after all that, it's like my legs refuse to move. Seeing my fatigue begin to grab a hold of me, Jack offers me his back and I don't hesitate climbing on and wrapping my limbs around him, letting him carry me some of the way. As I feel his back muscles work against my front, I know I hadn't imagined him getting bigger *and stronger when I saw him yesterday. We make it back to the parking area in less time with Jack carrying me than we probably would have if I had continued walking on my own. And he doesn't even look like he's broken a sweat! Meanwhile, I'm counting down the minutes until I can jump into another shower, preferably with my husband... my naked husband.*

I squirm in the passenger seat and clench my thighs together as memories from last night and this morning begin to play in my head. Jack directs us back towards the apartment and I try to keep my eyes on the scenery in front of us and off the bulge in the front of his pants. But when he drapes an arm over the steering wheel and the other one over the gear shift, and I see the muscles of his arms stretch and pull with the movement, I can't stop from leaning over and running my nose up the curve of his neck and across his jaw.

"Baby, I'm driving," he groans.

"I know." I shift closer in my seat, pulling the seat belt to give me more room. "Better keep your eyes on the road then," I say, skimming a hand up his thigh. I stop when I feel the bulge under my palm and give it a squeeze.

Jack curses, his grip on the steering wheel tightening. I nip at the sharp edge of his jaw. He tastes like Jack with a hint of something else, the water from the waterfall maybe. Rubbing my palm up and down his length, I continue nipping and sucking down his neck and feel him harden against my hand.

"Don't tease me, Nika."

I grin. "Then you better keep your eyes open and on the road. I don't feel like dying today, Jack."

I pull the drawstring of his swim shorts and tug until it opens, his cock springing free of its confines. The head red and angry with a bead of pre-cum already glistening on the top. I spread the pre-cum around the head of his cock before running my thumb nail along the slit and grin when Jack hisses.

"I can't wait to get my mouth around this cock," I whisper in his ear, closing my fist around the soft steel and sliding down to the base. "To run my tongue under the head until you curse and grip my hair in your clenched fists." I moan, my hand still gliding up and

down his length. I add a little twist on the upstroke and watch as his Adam's apple bobs with a hard swallow. "To suck one of your balls while I glance up at you towering above me, trying not to come." Jack groans and his hips buck up slightly causing his length to slide through my closed fist. "To take you to the back of my throat until you're coming, and I have no choice but to swallow."

"Fuuck!" Jack throws his head back against the head rest. Spurts of cum shoot from his dick and land on his shirt and my hand. I make sure he's looking at me before I gather up what I can on my fingers and sucks them clean one by one. It's not until I'm done that I tear my eyes away from a panting Jack and glance out the windshield to realize that we're stopped in traffic.

Jack pinches my chin between his thumb and forefinger when I move to settle back in my seat and forces me to look at him. "When we get home, you're going to be waiting for me in the bedroom, naked and on all fours with your ass up," he commands. His eyes turning a stormy grey and all I can do is nod.

"Does this ever get any easier?" I ask, standing with my arms wrapped around Jack at the door to our apartment.

He's due back on base to complete the rest of his training this week and he's not sure if he'll be able to make it off base next weekend again.

"God, I hope not. I don't want saying goodbye to you to ever get easier, Annika," he replies, pulling me closer, his chin resting against the top of my head.

This past weekend didn't even come close to filling the gap that was made by not seeing him for five months. And I know I should just be grateful that I at least got a weekend with him during training, but when you've grown dependent on seeing someone almost every single day for seven years then to not see them for months at a time, it's... hard.

"I know," I sigh, looking up at him. "It's just… I feel like this weekend went by far too quickly. It feels like I was just getting off a plane yesterday and seeing you for the first time in months."

"I know, baby. It'll get better when I'm done training." Jack leans down to kiss me and I have to hold myself back from trying to deepen the kiss. He's already in danger of running late.

"Until you go wheels up," I murmur.

"Until I go wheels up." He tries to give me a reassuring smile, but it falls flat. Instead he just kisses me again. His tongue licking along the seam of my lips, wanting entry.

I forget about the Navy and his training, and everyone waiting for him to get back to base, allowing myself to enjoy my husband. Until the sound of a car honking on the street below invades our little bubble. Jack pulls away, picks his bag up from the floor, and plants a chaste kiss on my lips before reassuring me that he loves me, and then he's gone.

Chapter 7

THE REST OF THE week went by incredibly slow. The only saving grace was getting to know the kids in my class better and seeing Nate at work every day. Our classes joined together for another PE class on Wednesday morning, this time it was warm enough to get the kids in the pool. They were so cute in their maroon swimsuits and swim caps. Wednesday was all about getting them used to the different strokes and jumping into the water. By the end of the class, some were even diving. It was awesome seeing them progress throughout the ninety-minute class.

On Friday morning the classes met back on the sports field and we had a rematch of the soccer game from Monday morning. Nate's class kicked our asses this time, but it was all in good fun and by the end of it, the kids were begging for another rematch. Of course, Nate and I said we'd be discussing it and would probably divide the classes up into mixed teams next time.

By the time Friday afternoon rolls around, I'm eager for the last bell to ring and the kids to be dismissed. I'm hoping I can catch Nate on his way out and convince him to have a drink or two with me at Dunes, and maybe go explore the night market in Hout Bay. I need a couple of pieces for my house anyway, and what better way to collect art than at a local market.

"Hey, got a minute?" I ask, stepping into Nate's empty classroom after the kids have left.

"For you? Always." He grins back, beckoning me closer. "What can I do for you, Ms. Carter?" he asks, stuffing papers into his messenger bag.

"I was wondering if you wanted to accompany me to Dunes for a drink. Maybe some dinner?" I add, bowing my head when I feel heat begin to spread across my cheeks.

"Why, Ms. Carter, are you asking me on a date?" He feigns shock and I roll my eyes.

"You did win the rematch after all."

His grin blooms into a full smile. "Yes. Yes, we did."

"Alright, no need to get cocky. So, dinner and drinks?"

Nate glances down at his watch and I think he's going to tell me thanks, but no thanks. What comes out of his mouth instead is, "Give me about two hours and I'll pick you up at home. I have a field hockey meeting but then I'm all yours."

My mouth opens to tell him that it's okay and I'll just see him tomorrow for the hike up Lion's Head but then his words register, and my mouth snaps closed. *Huh, I kind of wasn't expecting that.*

"S-sure," I stammer, running my palms down the legs of my grey slacks. "That gives me time to go home and change into something more comfortable."

Nate groans, and I lift my head in time to see him close his eyes and his Adam's apple bob with every hard swallow.

"You okay?" I ask, concern marring my voice.

"You're going to slip into something more comfortable?"

"Yes…"

His eyes pop open and he gives me a pointed stare until my words begin to sink in.

61

"Oh…" I say, and then grin at the pained expression still present on his face.

Memories from Monday night flash through my head. Nate running up behind me, pushing me up against my front door, and devouring my mouth like it was his last meal. A warmth blooms in my belly and spreads up. I look away to avoid his gaze, afraid that if I don't, I'll see the same heat reflected back at me.

"I'll see you in a couple of hours."

"Yeah. Sure, sounds good," I say and then turn and hurry out of his classroom and down the hallway that leads to the staff parking lot.

I'm so screwed.

18 months ago

Loud banging on the front door draws me out of the memories of the life I shared with Jack. I wipe away stray tears with the back of my sweater sleeve, my eyes already feeling puffy, and shuffle towards the door.

"Shit," Caleb curses, pulling me into a bear hug as soon as the door opens. "I thought I would've beaten them over here. I'm so sorry, Nika."

My hands curl into the back of his shirt, and I grip the material tightly, sobbing into his chest. "Were you…?"

Somehow Caleb manages to manoeuvre us into the apartment and shuts the door. "I wasn't stationed at the same site as him. We only got the call that he was MIA a few hours later but by that time, it was already too late." He sniffs and clears his throat, and I realize this may be as hard for him as it is for me. "I'm so fucking sorry, Annika. I should've been there. I should've had his back."

"It's not your fault, Cal," I say, moving into the kitchen to grab us some drinks. I need to keep busy or I am going to crumble under the weight of it all.

I hand Caleb a beer and then plop myself back down on the sofa, bringing my feet up to rest on the edge and bending my knees. It feels like someone else is steering my body and I'm just going along with it, afraid that if I try to take back control I'll lose myself to the darkness blackening the edges of my vision. Caleb comes to sit beside me and pulls me into his side. It's like we both need the contact to ground us and keep us afloat.

"I'm always here for you, Nika. I know we didn't get much time to get to know each other, but going through that training together like Jack and I did…" He pauses and I have this feeling he's trying to find the right words to say. "What I'm trying to say is, our team… we're like family. You were Jack's family which makes you my family. Always."

I let the truth of what he says settle around me. I have no idea what they went through during training, but I have heard stories and seen the small snippets of videos on YouTube. To me it seems like it would be insane to go through that entire process from start to finish with someone and not form a tight bond. I lean up and plant a soft kiss against the short stubble lining his cheek.

"Thank you," I say, and resume burrowing into his side. There is nothing sexual about cuddling on the sofa with Caleb in the apartment I shared with Jack. I sense we both just need the reminder that there is someone there for us when we start to crumble. I need to hold onto this reminder now more than ever.

"If you need help with the funeral or anything, the guys and I are here," he says, rubbing a hand up and down my arm.

My vision becomes cloudy with fresh tears and I have to bury my face into the soft material covering his chest, squeezing my eyes shut against the onslaught of fresh pain. Jack's funeral is the last thing I want to think about right now, but I know it needs to be done.

"I haven't even called his parents yet," I say, sitting up suddenly and wiping away the tears with the back of my hand.

Caleb hands me my phone from the coffee table. "Do you want me to go?"

"No." I reach out for him and he wraps his arms around me again. "I'm sorry. I just… I feel this need to hang onto him as long as possible and you…" I look down at the phone in my hands, feeling guilty about using him to keep somewhat of a connection to Jack.

"It's okay," Caleb says running a soothing hand up and down my forearm. He nods towards the phone. "Call them. I'll be here."

The conversation with Deb and Ron goes as I thought it would. I wasn't expecting them to openly sob on the phone, but some emotion from my in-laws would be nice. Or something to prove to me that they aren't completely heartless. All these years I held out hope that they would come around and reach out to Jack. To show him that they still love him and are at least trying to accept the fact that we are married and have been for years now. But it never happened. The next conversation I had to have was going to be the hardest, though. After hanging up with my in-laws, I start pacing the length of the living room with the phone in one of my hands.

Caleb had run out to grab us some dinner after I hang up with Deb. He hasn't returned yet and I know that now is the perfect time to call Xander. Well, not perfect. Nothing about this is perfect, but I need to make this one call by myself.

I blow out a breath and dial. Closing my eyes against a new wave of tears as I bring the phone to my ear. Xander answers on the second ring. He sounds so happy and refreshed after his recent vacation when he answers, and I hate to be the one who brings him down. Despite being the older brother, Xander took it hard when Jack enlisted and had to move across the country, and when Jack was deployed he called every day, sometimes more than twice just so that I didn't feel like I was alone.

"Xander?" I ask, after there'd been silence on the other end of the line for some time. I know he hasn't hung up because the call is still going, and I can hear him breathing on the other end.

"I'm here." His voice comes out rough.

THEN THERE WAS YOU

"Okay." I don't know what else to say, or how to comfort him. If he were here, I'd plant myself in his arms while I wrap mine around him and we'd hold each other while we cried. While we mourned Jack.

People say men can't feel emotions as deeply as women. I say they're fucking wrong. I think men can feel just as deeply but they've been so conditioned since they were kids to hide it. To be this picture of infallible strength. But strength doesn't mean that you don't feel. It means that you feel everything so strongly, but still continue to fight, to push through, to hold up those around you who can't hold themselves up.

I hear his throat clearing on the other side once... twice before he speaks again. "I'll be there in the morning." His tone brokers no argument, and honestly I don't know if I have the strength to fight him on it right now. It would be nice to have him here.

"Okay," I reply. "Send me your flight details."

"I'll get an Uber."

"Send me your flight details, please," I repeat. Two can play the stubborn game.

"Yes, ma'am." I can hear the sad smile in his voice.

We hang up with promises of seeing each other in the morning. I manage to call my parents and Londyn as well, before Caleb comes back with food for dinner and two other guys from Jack's team with their wives. I sigh, hanging up with Londyn and pinching the bridge my nose. Caleb shrugs when I shoot him a look, but I can't really be mad at him.

I am grateful, though, when no one lingers around me after each one gives me a hug. I don't think I can take the sympathetic looks right now, no matter how much the company may be nice.

"Go lay down for a bit," Caleb says, tipping his head in the direction of the bedroom. "I'll come wake you when dinner's ready."

I glance behind him and into my kitchen where the two wives are opening and closing the pantry cupboards and fridge and freezer while the guys raid Jack's liquor cabinet.

I shoot him a grateful smile and then disappear into the bedroom I used to share with Jack, and curl up in the middle of the *bed, dragging the light comforter over my head to block out the rest of the world. I don't even have the energy to feel guilty about being a crappy hostess and taking a nap instead of entertaining the guests in my condo.*

When I wake up hours later, there's no one in the living room, but the fridge and freezer are stock full of dishes, and Ziploc bags are filled with meals for the next week or so.

There's a note from Caleb attached to the fridge with a picture magnet of him and Jack in uniform

Didn't want to wake you. Jill and Meg made you meals for the next week. Eat them! Will call you later.

- Cal

Chapter 8

DINNER GOES JUST AS well as it had on Monday evening. Nate and I lapse into an easy conversation like we've known each other for years instead of just days. I find myself overthinking everything less when I'm around him. It's refreshing to be able to just be in the moment. That doesn't mean that I'm not going to overthink the whole date once I'm alone at home and trying to get some sleep, though. It's almost a guarantee that I'll be wide awake at two a.m. cursing myself for something I said or did today.

He tells me more about coaching the boys U-13 field hockey team this year and what projects his carpentry business has going on. And I tell him more about what it was like spending half my childhood in Cape Town and the other half in Miami, Florida. I also tell him about Jack, and it surprisingly feels okay to tell someone else about my best friend and husband. To share pieces of him with somebody who never knew him.

Nathan shakes his head, running a hand down over his mouth. "I can't imagine losing a significant other like that. Hell, I'll probably be single until I die," he jokes but it seems to cover something else.

"A sexy man like you? Nah, I'm sure you probably have women falling over themselves to get to you."

Nate scoffs. "If they are, they're doing a shitty job of making it known." He laughs but it feels forced. "I think my ex messed me up for other women."

"What do you mean?"

He's quiet for a while, staring out across the harbour. "She was the only woman I truly fell for. I mean, I had dated other girls in high school and college, but Vanessa... none of them compared to her. I was going to propose to her on our two-year anniversary."

"What happened?"

"She, uh..." he clears his throat and turns to look at me. "Turns out she was already married. She had this whole other life I didn't know about."

"Oh, shit." The words slip out before I can reel them back.

He chuckles. "Her husband wasn't happy. He blamed me for her cheating and all their issues."

"What a bitch." I slap a hand over my mouth. "Sorry," I flinch.

Nate just laughs, throwing back the rest of his drink. "No need to be sorry. Looking back on it now, I realize there were a lot of things in our relationship I overlooked or brushed off. I had blinders on when it came to her."

He changes the conversation back to me then and I'm happy to give him a reprieve from talking about his ex. I tell him about Londyn, and he seems to get a kick out of the crazy ass shit she used to make me do in high school, like cover our grade eleven English teacher's office in sticky notes with various Shakespearian quotes printed on them. It took frigging forever to write out the quotes. Covering the office hadn't taken as long as we thought it would, but we had help from some of the other kids in the class. The two-day after-school detention was worth it though.

"Feel like checking out the market?" I ask after I've paid for our food and drinks, and we're back in Nate's car.

The street the market is on is lined with cars by the time we make it to the other side of the bay by the harbour, but Nate manages to find a spot not too far. When we get out, he reaches for my hand and clasps it in his as we walk down the closed off street to the building that looks like a warehouse.

The first things I see are hand-carved wooden statues of a giraffe, elephant, and lion. All the animals one thinks of automatically when they picture South Africa. As we move farther into the low light of the building, the pieces of art change from wooden sculptures to big and small painted canvases, shirts, hanging glass terrariums, and jewelry. In the back of the building is a pub style eatery with local beer and a large wooden table so shoppers can eat in a family style setting.

Nate and I do a loop of all the vendors until a shop catches my eye and I veer off the path to get a better look. As soon as I step up to the booth, a sterling silver necklace catches my eye. It's a map of South Africa with a heart cut out at the bottom where Cape Town would be located.

"Do you want it?" Nate whispers in my ear, coming up behind me.

I turn it around and look at the price before sighing and putting it back on the stand. "No, that's okay."

Nate snatches it back up again and before I can protest, he's pulling out his wallet and handing the lady the cash.

"You really didn't have to do that."

"I know I didn't have to, but I wanted to," he says, handing me the little gift bag containing the necklace.

A blush crawls up my face as I accept the gift and thank him.

All too soon after leaving the market, Nate pulls back into my driveway at home and I'm almost disappointed that the night's already at an end. Although… I turn in my seat to look at him as he puts the vehicle in park and shuts off the engine. As soon as his arm moves out of the way, I unbuckle my belt and climb over the middle to straddle his lap. Nate chuckles when my ankle gets stuck on the gear shift, but he helps me get it free and then his hands are gripping my hips and pulling me closer. I cradle his face between my palms and kiss him. I can feel him growing harder beneath me with every rock of my hips. I moan into his mouth.

"You sure?" Nate asks when we finally come up for air.

I nod and go back to kissing him, his hands snake up the back of my shirt to unclip my bra and when he accidentally hits the middle of the steering wheel, sending the horn blaring, I can't help but untangle my lips from his and bury my face in the crook of his neck and giggle. *Frigging A*, totally forgot we were still in his car.

"Let's take this inside."

I push open the driver's side door and scramble off Nate's lap, narrowly missing doing a face plant on the bricked driveway. He manages to catch my arm and helps steady me until I have both feet planted firmly on the ground.

Nate adjusts himself then steps out and sets the car alarm before following me up the front walkway. As soon as I have the front door open, he pushes my front up against the wall and kicks the door closed, locking it and setting the deadbolt. All without letting me up from the wall. Then his front is pressing against my back. Nate grips my hips and pulls my bottom against his hard length.

"This ass has been driving me crazy all week." His one hand lets go of its hold on my hip and roams up the middle of my back and around my throat, pulling me up and back into him.

Nate nips and sucks up the curve of my neck. His teeth graze my ear, sending a shiver down my body.

"You're so sexy," he rasps, punching his hips forward and causing his length to slide along my ass cheeks.

I freeze as Jack's face appears in front of my face. It's so clear I can see every line creasing his forehead.

"You okay?" Nate asks, his lips no longer ghosting over the curve of my neck.

"I, um." I take a deep shuddering breath and shake my head.

Nate immediately let's go of my hips and takes a step away so I can turn around. I keep my eyes focused on my feet as I slump back. "I'm so sorry," I sob, covering my face with my hands.

"Hey, hey," Nate whispers, rubbing his hands up and down my arms. "It's okay. I can wait."

"Are… are you sure?" I hiccup, lowering my hands.

His hands move up to cup my neck, his thumb running over my top lip. "I'm sure. I'll see you tomorrow to get those shelves up."

"Okay."

Before he can move away, I curl my fingers into the front of his shirt and pull him to me, kissing him before he can protest. Nate groans, planting one hand on the wall beside my head and the other around my hip.

"See you tomorrow," I say, my voice low when we break apart.

Nate nods and then heads for the door, pulling it closed behind him.

Chapter 9

"MOM! DAD!" I CALL as I remove the key from the front door and shut it behind me.

The small two-bedroom house is quiet. Unusually so for a weekday evening. Normally Dad's in the kitchen preparing dinner while Mom sits at the dining room table with her laptop, working on her most recent cases.

"Dad?" I call out again. I know he's here; I saw his car in the driveway when I pulled up.

"Hey Peanut," my dad answers, rounding the corner from the hallway and slipping on his reading glasses, but not before I notice him wiping at his eyes.

"Everything alright?"

He smiles as he walks towards me and gathers me in his arms for a hug, but the smile doesn't reach his eyes. There's a sadness there that I can't quite understand.

"Where's Mom?"

"She had to go out for a little while. I'm sure she'll be back soon," he says, waving it off. "Have you eaten? I was going to put on a pot of lamb curry."

My stomach lets out a loud growl. I never can resist a bowl of my dad's famous curry. It's so good. Mouth burning hot, but delicious, nonetheless.

"With homemade roti?" I ask, my mouth already watering remembering the aromatic smells and taste of all the spices blending together.

Dad laughs with a slight shake to his head. "The things I do for you. Okay, grab everything for the dough. You can help me make them this time."

After I help Dad make and fry the rotis and we've eaten dinner, Mom still hasn't returned home which sets my warning bells off. I don't remember a time, whether in Florida or here in Cape Town, where either one of my parents missed a dinner. That coupled with the fact that when I called her earlier her phone went straight to voicemail. But I don't question him while I watch him make a plate for Mom and wrap it before putting it in the fridge.

When I've helped him clean up, Dad and I move to the couch in the living room to watch the cricket match. I wage a war with myself if I should bring up my uneasiness about Mom now or wait until the match is over. It is never a good idea to try and have a meaningful conversation with a South African man while he's watching a cricket match… or rugby for that matter. If the Springboks were playing, any conversation ceased. So, after I hand him another beer, I take up the seat beside him, trying my hardest to act normal.

After a while, Dad must sense my uneasiness because he leans forward and clicks the volume on the remote to mute the TV, sighing as he sits back.

"What's going on with you?"

"What?"

"Peanut, usually you're yelling at the TV. You're never this quiet during a match."

"Just worried about Mom is all." I keep my eyes on the screen, willing myself to pay attention. India's up to bat.

"Your mother's fine. She's at Granny's."

"She's what?" I sit up straighter. My mom hasn't talked to her stepmom in years. I guess they had a falling out ages ago and neither one have gotten up the courage to apologize or admit to being in the wrong. If my mom was at her parents' house then something big is happening. "What's going on, Dad?"

He sits forward, pulling off his glasses to pinch the bridge of his nose between his thumb and forefinger. "We had a falling out. She left last night and called to tell me she would be spending the night at your grandparents."

"You what? What happened?"

Through my entire life my parents were always the pillar of what a loving, successful relationship should look like. Sure, it wasn't like your traditional relationship where the wife stays home with the kids and cooks and cleans. My dad was the one who decided he wanted to stay home when I was little. He's the cook in the family and thank God for that because Mom would've burned the house down with her cooking. Dad works and has worked in web development, so it was easier for him to work from home and stay with me. Plus, it saved them from having to find a suitable daycare for me until I was old enough to go to school.

"Nothing you have to worry yourself about, Annika. You have enough on your plate as it is with the new job."

"Dad, tell me," I insist.

He drops his head, so his chin is resting against his chest. "Your mom… found out something from my past that I had neglected to tell her. Honestly, Annika, it's nothing and will blow over soon." I can tell the words are just meant to placate me and he doesn't believe them himself. He's scared.

I push up from the couch and stand facing my father. "I'm not a child anymore, Dad. Whatever is going on between you and Mom… I can handle it."

"This isn't something a daughter should find out about her father," he argues, and I can see a little of myself in him. We always want to protect those we love from our problems. Never wanting to burden them.

I will not relent though. Something is going on with them and I want to know what. Not because I need a distraction from my own love life, but because I care deeply for both my parents. Things with Nate are good. We're still in the stage of navigating this new relationship while working together but things are... good.

My dad's shoulders drop, defeat shimmering in his eyes and I know his resolve to leave me in the dark is crumbling.

"Do you remember Uncle Dave from before we moved to America?"

I nod. Uncle Dave isn't really my uncle but he and Dad went to college together and became close friends. From what I can remember, that's how Dad met Mom. Mom was friends with Dave's sister, and they met one day when Dad went over to Uncle Dave's house. His sister and my mom were there.

Dad clears his throat before he goes on. "Dave was more than just a friend, Peanut," he says cautiously, gauging my reaction.

I cock my head in confusion wondering what the hell he means when suddenly the lightbulb goes on. "He... You... oh," I stammer trying to find the right words.

"I'm not about to go into details with my daughter, but back then it was a sin to be seen a moffie, so we kept it quiet. Then I met your mother..."

Dad turns to look out the window that faces the neatly cut front yard and I swallow hard, not sure if I want to hear the rest of this story.

"We knew we could never have a future together, and I really do love your mom."

When he turns back to face me, there's fear and uncertainty swimming behind his eyes, but also loss and maybe regret?

75

"Anyway," he says and clears his throat again. "It was stupid of me to have kept that from your mom all these years and I regret it."

"Did you ever cheat on her?" I know it's a stupid question as soon as the words leave my lips. My dad has always been devoted to my mom.

His posture stiffens. "I deserve that after what I told you, but no. I have never cheated on your mother. The thing between Dave and I ended before I pursued Rebekah."

"How did… how did Mom find out?"

"Dave came over for a braai last night. He had too many drinks and let it slip that something had happened between us in college."

An incredible sadness clouds his eyes and I can't hold back from throwing my arms around my father's neck and hugging him.

"She'll come back," I whisper, hoping against all hell that I'm right. I can't see my mom holding his sexual orientation or what he did in the past against him and I'm almost positive that it was the hurt of knowing he had kept something like that from her that sent her running to my grandparents.

Dad pats my back. "I hope so." He wraps his arms around me, and we sit there for a while. Me absorbing the strength that comes from a father's hug and him coming to terms with the fact that not everyone will abandon him because of his secret. After a while he pulls away. "Come help me make some koeksisters. It'll be a welcome surprise for when she comes home, ne?"

He stands from the couch and offers his hand to help me up. I gladly accept and follow him back into the kitchen ready to make my mom's favourite dessert.

"You think she'll come around?" Nate asks, his fingers lazily caressing up and down my exposed arm as we lay tangled up on the couch watching *Sons of Anarchy*.

"I hope so," I sigh, drawing imaginary pictures on his chest. "I always thought my parents were the image of what the perfect couple looked like. They met in college and got married before graduation. One year later they had me. They've been through almost everything. I can't imagine them not coming back from this."

"Lying is a pretty big deal, but I get it." Nate shifts slightly, tucking a hand behind his head. "Cape Town isn't the most progressive of cities. North America may have made it legal for gays to marry, and the rest of the world may slowly become more accepting of it, but that doesn't mean it's accepted by everyone. Hell, it wasn't even thirty years ago that we were still under apartheid."

"That's true. I guess I just don't see what the big deal is. Love is love is love. Why should it matter if that love is between a man and a woman, or a man and a man, or a woman and a woman?"

"Because it doesn't fit in with their ideal picture of what the Bible tells them a relationship is supposed to look like. To them, it's one of the ultimate sins," Nate says.

I snort. "Being gay is not worse than committing murder."

"No, but to them it's still a sin."

"Well, they're a bunch of hypocrites. Jesus said those without sin should cast the first stone, and I'm pretty sure no one is without sin." I feel my body begin to stiffen in preparation for a fight, but Nate just pulls me closer.

"I agree with you. Jesus also said, love thy neighbour. But that doesn't change what the rest of the population have been told to believe their whole lives."

I blow out a relieved breath and relax against him again. "I just... I would hate to be told that I wasn't allowed to fall in love because the person was another woman."

Nate hums and when I glance up at him there's a dreamy look on his face. I can only image what he must be thinking.

"Shut up," I laugh, playfully backhanding him on the chest.

Nate catches my wrist and pulls. Planting my knees on either side of his hips, I sit up and straddle him. His jean-covered cock is hard, trapped between his belly and my heated core. Nate groans, lifting his hips and causing his cock to slide against me. I moan and drop down to kiss him. Nate's hands stray to my hips, guiding me back and forth over his hard length.

"Wait, stop. Stop," I breathe out.

Nate blows out a frustrated breath and drops his head back against the couch. "Fuck. I'm sorry."

I rest my forehead against his. "I should be the one who's sorry."

He cups the sides of my face. "I'll wait... for you."

A sappy smile spreads across my face and I kiss him again. I don't stop kissing him until Nate groans against my lips.

"Sorry. Sorry," I grin and move to take a seat on the couch beside him.

Chapter 10

DEAN

"THIS ISN'T WORKING, DEAN," Rebekah says, her eyes are downcast as she sits at the table where we just ate dinner. The corners of her lips turn down and her chin wobbles slightly.

"Rebekah don't do this," I plead, looking at the woman who's been my heart for the last thirty years.

"I've tried, Dean. I've tried looking past it. I've told myself that I can forgive you for your lie, and maybe I really have but I can't sit here and pretend that everything is okay again when I know... I know you're still in love with him. That you always have been." Her breath hitches and I rush to her side. Dropping to my knees beside her, I take her hands in mine.

"I love *you*. You're my wife," I say.

"Am I just... Was I just... a substitute for him?" Her eyes begin to water when she looks down at me. And that's when I know that I can't lie to this woman anymore. I can't keep doing this to both of us.

"You were never a substitute," I whisper, glancing away. Grey clouds have begun rolling in, in preparation for the storm we're expecting tonight. Appropriate. "But you're right. I've always loved him. I've always been *in love* with him."

She gasps, ripping her hands out of mine and pushing to stand. I have to stand too or topple over in her rush to put as much distance between us as possible. Rebekah backs up towards the wall separating the dining room from the guest room and folds her arms across her middle, curling into herself. Her pain palpable in the cool evening air.

"But I've always loved you too," I add because it's the truth. I grew to love Rebekah so much over the years we've been together, and I can't even fathom not having her in my life at all.

"Is that why you were so excited when I suggested we try moving to America?"

I slide my hands into the pockets of my jeans and nod. "It wasn't right that I felt these things for my best friend. We were both married and weren't teenagers anymore. I thought if there was more distance between us that the feelings would just go away. It's one thing to experiment in college. It's another when we had lives, careers, and a family. I'm so sorry, Becca. I never wanted to hurt you."

"Why couldn't you just have told me all this before we got married?"

I look over at her then. Really look at her. The last few months have aged her. There's more grey around her temples and the top of her head, the wrinkles on her forehead are more pronounced, and the smile lines that used to be around her eyes are... well, it doesn't look like she's truly laughed in a long time. And it's all my fault. She's still the most beautiful woman I've ever seen. If I had just been man enough to come clean maybe I could've saved us both the heartache, but I can't bring myself to wish we had never gotten married because then we wouldn't have Annika. And she's my world.

"Would you have still agreed to marry me if I had?"

Her mouth opens and closes, opens and closes like she's trying to find the words but can't exactly grasp onto them. Finally, her shoulders fall and she drops her head. "I don't know."

"I really am sorry, Becca, but I won't feel guilty about our relationship because it gave us a beautiful family. I only wish that I had come clean to you sooner."

She nods, and when she does finally lift her head and her eyes meet mine, I feel another punch to my gut. Her beautiful brown eyes are red from the tears streaming down her face.

"I want a divorce."

The four words are like an explosion in the quiet room.

"Please, Dean. You owe me this." Her eyes bore into mine as she pleads for me to give her the only thing she's ever asked of me.

I do the only thing I can think of and nod. I owe her this, and she deserves to be happy with someone who can be their full selves with her. I won't fight her on the divorce if this is what she truly wants.

"I'll, uh… I'll stay at a hotel," I say, walking by her to gather some of my things, yet when a sob rips free from her throat, I can't help but wrap my arms around her. I breathe out a sigh when she wraps hers around me and sobs into my chest. I really do love this woman, and I wish I could be everything she deserves, but I'd be lying to myself and others again if I say the prospect of being with Dave didn't send a thrill down my spine.

"We have to tell Annika," she says between broken breaths.

"I know."

81

Annika

"I'm ready," I rasp against his neck. It's been a month of pure agony falling asleep beside Nate on nights when he's stayed over late and been too tired to drive home. But that changes now.

Nate stops, dropping the knife and half cut pepper on the cutting board before giving me his full attention. "You sure? I can wait."

I grin at how he knew exactly what I was referring to without me having to spell it out for him. I shake my head and step closer. "No. No more waiting. I want you."

He takes a minute to move over the knife and cutting board he's been using to cut up vegetables for the pasta salad. Nate grips my hips and lifts me until I'm sitting on the counter with my legs dangling off the edge. The corners of his lips tip up into a half smile before they descend on mine, warm and seeking. His tongue traces the seam of my lips demanding entry and I willingly give it to him. His hands tighten around my hips, pulling me closer to him, then glide over the globes of my ass. His fingers dig into my skin as he drags me closer still.

Nate groans, stepping in further until I feel the solid outline of his cock against the material of the denim between my legs.

"Need this off." I manage to say between kisses, pulling at his shirt in an attempt to rid him of the offensive material. I need to feel his skin against mine.

"Yes, Ma'am." He grins but reaches back and drags the shirt over his head.

I groan as my palms skim over the hard ridges of his abdomen, tight pecs, and over his shoulders. I gulp down a harsh breath at the realization that this is the first time

I'm allowing myself to really touch him knowing that I won't be pulling back before it has a chance to go too far. I need this. Need him.

Nate grabs a fistful of my hair and forces my head back, exposing my neck to his roaming lips and tongue. With his hand still secured in my locks, he hurriedly undoes the button to his jeans.

"I want to see your lips wrapped around me," he demands, tugging my earlobe between his teeth, but it's not forceful.

He lets go of his hold around my hair allowing me to slide off the counter and drop to my knees in front of him. I look up at him from under hooded eyes and watch him shimmy the waistband down enough for his cock to spring free, standing up straight against his belly. A slight pressure at the back of my head forces me forward until my lips graze the underside of his cock.

Nate curses, dropping his head back between his shoulder blades when I lick up his shaft, running the tip of my tongue along his slit. When he increases the pressure on the back of my head I wrap my lips around him and take him to the back of my throat. Nate's hips buck and while he fucks my mouth, I slip a hand down the front of my pants and under the waistband of my underwear. I'm already wet for him.

"Enough," he grits out between clenched teeth, yanking me up by my hair.

I whimper when Nate lets go of me and takes a step back. Not because of the hold he had around my hair, but because of the sudden coldness I feel without his body pressing against mine.

"Strip," he orders, and before I can think too much of it, I obey and quickly shuck my shirt and unclasp my bra. My pants and underwear follow soon after as well as my flip-flops.

Then suddenly I'm being pushed up against the wall. Nate's hand slides over my body to curl around my ass and then he's lifting me. My legs automatically wrap around his waist.

"You like it a bit rough?"

My teeth sink into my bottom lip as I nod.

"Christ. This first time is going to hard and fast, baby, but then I'll give you the sweet loving after."

I groan, dropping my head back against the wall with a thud. My nails scraping over his shoulder blades. Nate grunts, curling a hand around my throat. His hips snap forward and then he's sliding into my wet heat. "Fuck."

My eyes roll back with every thrust of his hips. His cock pushing deeper with each forward motion. My nails find purchase in his shoulders, causing him to curse and I have little doubt that I managed to draw blood. My heels dig into the cheeks of his ass to keep him close.

He's here.

He's here and he's alive, and he's mine. And even though I have him in my arms and between my legs now, the weight pressing down on my chest tells me that he won't be for long.

As Nate ruts into me, I tighten my legs around his waist, bury my face in the crook of his neck, and sob at the same time my orgasm crashes over me.

Please, God, don't take him away from me. Not another one. I've just learned how to love again.

Chapter 11

"**DUDE, YOU STOLE MY** éclair." I turn narrow eyes to where Nate's leaning against the kitchen counter, a grin on his face as he licks whipped cream off his fingers. I swallow back a whimper remembering the way he looked not even an hour ago when he fucked me with those same fingers and then sucked my wetness from them.

"I can see why you love those," he says pointing to the now empty Tupperware container that used to hold my mom's baking. "They were so good."

"Bastard," I mumble under my breath and pout when he draws me into his arms and kisses my forehead. The knock on the front door has us reluctantly pulling apart. "Let's pretend we're not home."

Nate chuckles, running his thumb over my bottom lip that's stuck out in a pout. "That's pretty hard to do with both vehicles in the driveaway." He leans down to lick along the shell of my ear causing me to shiver. "And we left the music playing in the carport."

I groan in frustration and pull away from him. "Fine, but if it's your sisters then I'm sending them packing."

His deep laugh follows me to the front door. "Deal."

I pull open the door, the smile I'm wearing because of Nate slowly recedes when I get a good look at the person on the other side. It's definitely not Nate's sisters. My heart races, my breaths come faster... too fast. *Oh*

God, I can't breathe. This can't be real. I must be dreaming. Memories of his funeral come flooding back.

Every funeral I've ever seen on TV or in the movies, always have the weather match the somber mood. Overcast skies, light rain or in some cases heavy rain depending on the impact the death of the character had. The abundance of black umbrellas making their own Rorschach test from up above.

Not Jack's though.

On the day of his funeral, the sun beats down with such an intensity it almost feels wrong. There's not a cloud in the sky and the birds continue singing their happy songs. St. Andrew's Church offers a cool escape from the unending heat. I move somberly towards the front pews and take a seat on the left side, beside my parents and Xander. The front rows are empty except for the three of us. His own parents refused to come to San Diego for his funeral and somewhere deep down the atrocity of that registers, but all my energy is focused on the dark wood of the casket covered by the flag sitting in front of the church. Jack's military buddies, including Caleb, take up the two rows behinds us.

Father John begins the service but I'm not paying attention. My eyes roam over the crucifix high on the wall behind him, then to the organ in the corner, and over to the stained-glass windows at the end of our pew. For an instant, I feel guilty for not being more in the moment, so I try to force a tear, but when nothing happens I go back to gazing around the old church. My mom gently slips her hand over mine in what I'm sure is supposed to be a comforting gesture, but I don't feel it, and if I wasn't looking down at her hand clasped over mine, I would've never known that it was there. Is it normal to feel so detached at a funeral for a loved one? I am not sure it is, but no matter how hard I try, I can't make myself feel anything appropriate.

When my eyes land on the picture of Jack set in a black frame atop the dark mahogany casket, I don't recognize him anymore. The man we are burying today is so far removed from the man in that picture. I fell in love with the man in the picture. With his weirdly coloured sea-foam green eyes, his bright smile, and infectious laughter. The man who could make anyone feel like he really saw them when he interacted with them. I could no longer reconcile that man with the one I shared the last few years of my life. Every time he came home from a mission he had changed somehow. He became more distant, harder. Some would say he simply grew up and became a man. I didn't buy it though. War changed him and then it killed him.

I shake my head and the memories clear just as Father John asks if any of us would like to say a few words about Jack. I glance back down at my mom's hand over mine and feel her gently nudge my shoulder, but I can't look up. I can't make eye contact. There's nothing I want to say. Nothing I can say. I shake my head again and keep my eyes averted, feeling the crushing weight of the silence begin to settle over my heart.

Disappointment soon follows like a heavy rain follows a storm cloud. Disappointment in myself that I can't muster up two words to say about Jack. But mostly disappointment that our relationship had hit such a bottom that there is nothing I want to say about him. Nothing I could say would bring him back. We started out as two people in love but by the time his most recent deployment came around, we were simply just... roommates. Jack hadn't touched me in months before he was sent away, we hadn't talked beyond the superficial how are you? Or anything you want on the grocery list?

I stand when I feel my mom's gentle touch on my shoulder and see they're both already on their feet. I dart a quick glance to the priest and offer a clipped nod in thanks before scurrying out of the pew, down the aisle, and into the blazing heat of the Californian sun. I don't wait for my parents or Xander to catch up before bolting towards the back of the church and to the parking lot. I feel like I am suffocating under all these conflicting emotions. This would all be so much fucking easier if someone just told me what the hell I am supposed to feel. If someone just told me that it is okay to feel relieved, that it is okay to still mourn and grieve the distant husband.

"Annika, honey," my mom's voice sounds behind me as I stand in the middle of the parking lot with my arms hugging the folded flag and my head tilted back feeling the sun warm my face. "We're going to get some food. Are you hungry?"

I take a deep breath and count to five before letting it out in a rush. Focusing on a bird taking flight from the high tree top across the parking lot, I allow it to calm me down even more.

"No. I, uh, think I'm just going to head home and maybe start packing up some of his stuff."

"Peanut," my dad says, approaching me with concern in his eyes. "That can wait until tomorrow. Your mother's right you need to eat something."

Xander steps up to my side then and wraps an arm around my shoulders in a side hug, pressing his lips to the side of my head. "How about we go get a drink and meet your parents back at the house?"

I relax into his side a little more and nod my agreement. I look over at my parents just in time to see them exchange a look before my dad pulls out his keys and says they'll meet us back at the house in a couple of hours. Xander and I stay standing just as we are until their car turns out of the lot and then disappears down the street.

"I can't believe they didn't come," I whisper, turning into him for a proper hug. My cheek pressing against his hard chest.

He lets out a harsh breath, his arms wrapping tightly around my back. "I can. Mom and Dad… they've changed since Jack joined the navy."

I tighten my grip around him when I feel his breath hitch, reassuring him that I'm here but giving him time to feel whatever it is he's feeling. After all, Jack was his brother.

"C'mon," he says, stepping out of the embrace and tugging my arm towards his truck. "I feel like getting drunk and there's a good bar not too far from here."

"But, you're driving," I say, climbing into the passenger seat.

"Yeah, but we can call an Uber or whatever. I think we can both use a couple of drinks… or more," he adds under his breath as the engine roars to life.

"Just don't let me anywhere near vodka," I say and Xander laughs, nodding his head. No doubt remembering that one time in high school when he was a senior while Jack and I were sophomores and how we showed up to a house party and I got absolutely hammered on vodka.

As soon as we remember what we just came from, we both sober up fast, our smiles slipping from our lips like they were never there. I slump back in the seat and slide down a bit. What is wrong with me? We just left my husband's funeral and here I am laughing about old memories with his older brother.

"Hey." Xander places a reassuring hand on my knee, removing it a second later. *"It's okay,"* he says, swallowing hard. His eyes are still trained on the road ahead of him as he drives us to the bar. *"Jack would've wanted us to remember the good times."*

Maybe, but I still feel guilty. Why should I be able to remember the good moments when he isn't here to remember them with us? There are so many other bad people out there, people who deserve to die. Jack didn't deserve to die.

As Xander pulls into the parking lot of the pub, I realize that I'm still angry at Jack for signing up for a career that put his life in danger constantly and for people he didn't know. For people who didn't appreciate the men and women in the military.

The pub is dark when we enter. A large wooden bar takes up the entire left side. There are three small steps leading down to another level with four booths against one wall and a fireplace against the other. On the same level as the bar are several high-top tables and chairs. There are a few patrons seated in a booth and a couple at the bar but, other than that, it's a pretty slow afternoon.

The bartender motions for us to choose our own seats and Xander leads us to a booth in the corner, away from the other bar-goers. When we're settled in our seats, Xander orders two of the shot samplers. I have no idea which shots it comes with, but I trust *him... at least when it comes to alcohol. Either way, I know I'm safe with Xander and he'll get me home safely. But also, I'm a little afraid to ask what kind of shots those samplers come with.*

"Did Jack ever tell you about the time I almost broke his arm?"

"What?" I ask, shocked. "No, he never mentioned anything like that."

Xander nods, a sad smile pulling at his lips as he plays with the little candle in the middle of the table. "Can't remember what we were arguing about. All I remember is that he made me so mad, I chased him up to his bedroom and pushed him into the wall. I grabbed hold of his arm, pulled it against his back, and tried to push it up as far as it could go. Man, he screamed so loud. If Mom hadn't been home, I probably wouldn't have stopped until it snapped." A pained look crosses his face and his Adam's apple bobs when he averts his gaze to the big fireplace across the room.

Our waitress picks this time to drop off our samplers. A paddle board of six shots is placed in front of Xander and then a second is placed in front of me. As soon as I get a good look at the various shots, I'm not so sure anymore if I trust Xander with choosing the alcohol. Is that? I peer down closer to the one of the shots in the middle to get a better look. That is cinnamon.

I don't notice the waitress leaving but then Xander nudges my foot under the table and when I snap my eyes up at him from the shot, he's holding one of the end ones in his hand. The liquid inside a weird mix of blue and purple. It looks like a mini lava lamp.

Xander raises the glass. "To Jack," he says.

I hold up the matching one from my board and clink glasses with him, whispering, "To Jack."

Then we're both slamming back the shot. I wince at the immediate bitter taste, but then it changes to something sweeter and it is actually not that bad. I find out later that that particular shot is called a Pornstar, and I'm not even going to begin wondering why someone would name a drink that. Nope, don't want to know. Not at all.

Xander and I continue working our way down our boards while retelling stories about Jack. Note to self, the shot with the cinnamon sprinkled on top is called an Apple Pie and it is so fucking good. I make Xander order me a couple more of those and when our waitress brings them over, I hand the rest of the shots on my board to Xander, perfectly content with doing Apple Pie shots for the rest of the night.

Right around the seventh… or eighth shot, I'm not really sure which, Xander's phone begins to ring non-stop. We both freeze when my mom's number appears on the screen.

"Shit," he says.

I giggle. "I guess we should probably call that Uber now."

While Xander settles our bill up at the bar, I put in a request for an Uber and am surprised when one pops up just around the corner from the bar we're in. I stumble a little after sliding out from the bench seat and have to shoot a hand out on the table to help steady myself, but then Xander is right there beside me and we lean on each other as we make our way out into the parking lot.

"Thank you for today," I say to him. My head resting on his shoulder.

"Don't thank me. We both needed it. Jack would've liked it better than that funeral at the church."

I snort. "Jack would've hated being in that church."

Jack believed in God, he prayed regularly, but he hated how judgmental the Church was. Especially the Catholic Church. He couldn't reconcile his belief that everyone should be treated as equals regardless of race, gender, sexuality, etc. with what the Church preached about homosexuality being a sin. Especially when one of his best friends came out after we graduated high school. He hated that so-called Christians preached about God being the only one who can judge but then turning around and then judging people who didn't conform to their beliefs of right and wrong. I tended to agree with him. I believe in God too, but I couldn't care less about someone's race, gender, or sexuality. It's not my place to judge anyone, especially since I'm not without my own sins.

"Yeah," Xander says, laying his head on top of mine. "He would've."

We thank the driver when he drops us off outside the house I shared with Jack, then we both pause just before the front door. Xander and I glance at each other and then burst into a fit of laughter at feeling like we're teenagers again, coming home drunk from a house party.

God, I needed this so much. Xander reaches over and squeezes my hand in his as he pushes open the front door. A wave of warmth washes over me and I pray that Xander will continue to come around even now that Jack's gone. I couldn't bear to lose both Carter brothers.

I probably had too many glasses of wine and passed out on the couch because there's no way that my husband is still alive. But when he says my name in that voice that sounds familiar, with worry blurring the edges, I start to wonder if maybe this is all very real. And when he reaches out just as my eyes roll back in my head and my body collides with his very not-ghost-like body, I know it's not a dream.

Fate couldn't be so cruel to have ripped him away from me only to deliver him back when I had finally begun to move on. When I had just given my heart and my body to someone else. Could it?

Standing there, looking as alive as ever is Jackson Carter... my husband. My husband who I had buried two years earlier.

"Annika." Jack's voice is gentle, his fingers grazing down my arm until he slips his hand in mine. "Annika," he says again, this time his voice sounds so close to my ear, like he's pulled me into his arms.

He lets go of my hand to wrap his arm around my waist, his other coming up to cup my face, his thumb running lightly over my parted lips. "I forgot how beautiful you are," he whispers, his lips brushing over mine, but he doesn't kiss me. "God, I love you so much," he says, right before capturing my lips in a kiss.

"Annika!" His voice sounds panicked now. I move to pull away from him but when I open my eyes, we aren't standing toe-to-toe like we were. I'm lying on my back on the couch while Jack sits on the edge, the back of his hand resting against my forehead like he's checking my temperature.

It's at that moment I realize that while opening my front door to discover Jack on the other side wasn't a dream, kissing him; however, had been. I groan, bracing my hands on either side of me and try to sit up.

"Easy," he says and grips my arm to help steady me until I'm able to sit up on my own.

"Jack?" My voice comes out hoarse, like I haven't drank anything in days.

"Here," another voice says behind Jack before a glass of cold water is thrust into my hand. My brows furrow as I try to remember what the fuck is happening.

I look to Jack, still not computing how he's kneeling in front of me right now, and then over his shoulder to the person the other voice belongs to. Nate.

"What…" I clear my throat and take another drink of the cool water, trying to wrap my brain around what I'm seeing.

"You fainted, babe," Jack says, running a hand up and down my thigh.

My eyes snap to Nate when a low growl sounds from his side of the room. I don't even think he's aware that he's growling like a wolf because his gaze is securely fixed on Jack's hand skimming up and down my bare skin.

This is all too much. I place the glass as calmly as I can on the side table and push up from the couch, effectively disconnecting Jack's hand from my body.

"You-" I begin, pointing at Jack but my eyes keep bouncing between him and Nate, hoping my boyfriend will be able to fill me in on what the heck's going on. That's a foolish thought on my part though. Almost laughable, really. Looking to my boyfriend to fill me in on why my husband is now pushing himself up from his knees and standing in front of me.

"Nika, who is this?" Nate asks, arms crossed over his chest as he stares Jack down.

"I'm her husband."

"No." I shake my head, trying to make the pieces fit. "You're dead." I motion widely between us. "We're not... You're not... I'm-" I try to swallow down the burn from the tears threatening to spill.

Nate's eyes bounce between me and Jack, but he doesn't say anything. His body goes from seemingly relaxed before Jack showed up to rigid in the blink of an eye.

"Fok," he mumbles under his breath.

I want so badly to go over to him and feel the security of his arms wrap around me while he reassures me that everything is going to be okay, but I don't. I fight the urge and keep my feet firmly rooted to my spot in the middle of the living room.

"They told you I was dead?" Jack asks, a frown decorating his face.

I nod, still at a loss for words for what exactly is going on. I mean, I have a pretty good idea and I know my eyes aren't deceiving me. My husband is one-hundred-percent standing in front of me and alive as ever, but my brain is still having trouble catching up and trying to figure out how exactly this is possible. His teammate, Caleb, even believes him to be dead. Unless. No. *Cal wouldn't lie to me, would he?*

Jack's hands curl into fists at his side, his lips working between his teeth as he stares up at the ceiling.

"I'm going to go," Nate says, running the back of his finger down my cheek.

"You really don't have to."

He glances at Jack who has his eyes narrowed at the spot Nate is touching me. Nate turns to lock eyes with me again, a mix of an apology and loss swimming in the whisky coloured depths.

"You have a lot to talk about. A lot to figure out." He leans down placing a soft kiss to my forehead. "Call me later?"

"No, stay." I want to plead while gripping his wrist, but I nod instead, and try to fight back the tears that are closer to the surface.

Nate drops his hand from my face, taking a step back. He gives a clipped nod to Jack before collecting his jacket and car keys, and walking out the front door. My feet are frozen in place until I hear the rev of his bukkie and then slowly, with a hand pressing over my heart and an ache in my chest, I turn to face my husband.

"So... not dead then?"

"It appears not," Jack replies eyeing me warily. I can tell he wants to question me more about Nate but doesn't. And in the moment I'm thankful. There are more important things we have to discuss than my boyfriend... for now.

Jack follows me into the kitchen while I grab us a couple of Castle Lagers. He nods a thanks when I hand him one and then trails behind when I go and retake my seat on the couch. After a couple of pulls of the bitter liquid and some heavy eyeballing on both our parts, the questions begin to fall.

"What ha-" I pause, clear my throat and start again. "Where were you?" I flinch when it comes out sounding more of an accusation than I planned.

Jack leans forward, resting his elbows on his knees. The dark beer bottle dangling between his fingers. "What exactly did they tell you?"

"Not much. Just that you had been killed in the line of duty. Caleb said you had gone MIA but by the time they found out where you were, you were already dead."

Jack curses, brings the bottle to his lips, and drains the rest of the beer. He shakes his head when I offer to get him a new one. "It was supposed to be a simple mission; get in, get out, and be home in time for dinner."

He hangs his head, his shoulders hunching forward. Jack clears his throat once... twice then says, "Maybe I will take that second beer after all."

Unfolding my legs, I go and fetch us both a second round and grab a couple more just in case. I pop the cap on one and hand it to him when he mumbles a muffled thanks. After I'm sitting beside him again with my second beer and a leg pulled up underneath me, Jack continues with his story but never looks over at me. Instead his gaze focuses on the white tiles between his feet.

"I don't want to go into details about what happened, but I will tell you that it was a shitshow from the beginning." He looks over his shoulder at me this time. Tears pooling in his sea-foam green eyes, but he swallows them back before they have a chance to fall. "I was a prisoner of war for two years, Annika," he says, clarifying his last statement as if I wasn't sure what he had meant.

"What?" A prisoner of war?

I want to go to him. I want to go to him and wrap my arms around him and whisper in his ear that he's safe now, that he's home, but all I find myself doing is bringing my bent knees into my chest and curling my arms around them. "No. No, they said they found a body. They said it had your dog tags. They… They…" I hiccup and tighten my arms around my legs, refusing to believe that the U.S. Navy… the government who Jack put his life in danger for every time he went wheels up, would lie to me.

"I didn't have them on me when the team found me several weeks ago. I guess they must have gotten ripped off or something."

His voice changes with that last statement. It's subtle, and if I hadn't known him as long as I have, I wouldn't have caught it. He's keeping something from me. I've seen the gear the team suits up with when they go wheels up and if Jack had tucked his dog tags inside his shirt and under all that gear, there's no way it would've just been ripped off but having lived as a Navy SEAL wife for years, I learned when not to question orders, so I let it go. I think he's already told me more than what he should have anyway.

This time, I unclasp my legs and scoot closer to him until I can wrap my arms around his shoulders and press my cheek against his back, content to just breathe him in and feel him solid between my arms. Jack catches my wrist in his hand and pulls, forcing me around and to straddle his lap. I rest my arms over his shoulders and run my fingers through his too long hair, wondering when was the last time he's gotten it cut. He nuzzles my neck, pressing hot open-mouthed kisses along my jaw.

"I've missed you," he says, kissing the corner of my mouth and then his lips are ghosting over mine, coaxing me to open for him. When I do, Jack wastes no time in sliding his tongue inside, enticing mine to dance with his. His lips hard against my own.

He slides his hands down my back and over my ass, gripping a cheek in his palm and pulling me closer. My arms tighten around him when he stands and begins moving towards the bedroom. Not bothering to kick the door closed, Jack lays me down on the bed and follows me down, blanketing me with his body. My legs stay wrapped around his waist and I lift my hips, seeking any sort of friction.

Leaning on one arm, his fingers leave a trail of fire as he caresses down my side and then up under the navy blue tank top I threw on after my shower. I lift up enough for him to remove the offending fabric but once it's gone, his mouth is right back on my body. His tongue tracing the line of my collarbone. Jack moves down my body, his lips pressing wet kisses down my middle that's now exposed, and over my belly button.

He hooks his fingers in the waistband of my shorts, and yanks them down my legs, throwing them behind him once they're clear of my feet. My underwear follows soon after. I'm completely naked and bare to him, my legs bent at the knees. I squirm when Jack licks his lips and prowls towards me after ditching his jeans and t-shirt. A groan escapes us both when we're finally skin to skin with nothing separating us. I wrap my legs back around his waist and Jack reaches between us to guide his head to my entrance. There's no foreplay, but I'm already so wet for him that it doesn't matter. He slides in easily and my back bows off the bed, pushing my breasts in his face. Jack chuckles but sucks a nipple into his mouth. I tighten my hold around him and moan when his hips begin to buck. Long, slow thrusts at first that soon turn hard and fast.

No more words are exchanged as Jack peers down at me while he fucks me. The sound of skin slapping skin, the only music in the room. Jack curses when my nails dig into the skin of his muscled back. My own arches and my release crashes over me. Shudders still wrack my body when he stiffens above me, and liquid heat fills me. I try to ignore the feel of raised scars as my palms skim up and down his back.

It's not until Jack pulls out and goes to clean up in the bathroom does the realization of what we just did… of what *I* just did comes crashing down around me. I turn over on my side facing the wall and drag the soft sheets over my body, the sheets that still smell like Nate, and cry.

Fuck. I screwed up so badly.

Chapter 12

ME: I NEED TO SEE you
Me: Please
Nate: Just name the time and place, baby
Me: Café Caprice? An hr?
Nate: I'll be there

It feels wrong to not meet him at Dunes where we had our first date and subsequent dates thereafter. It quickly became known as our spot, but the conversation I know we are about to have requires somewhere more neutral. And truth be told, if things go south between Nate and I, I don't want the sour memory to taint the restaurant that became such an important place to me. To us.

It takes me about forty-five minutes to drive from my house to Camps Bay and find parking. The beach is still crowded with people and that doesn't really surprise me. There'll be locals and tourists on the beach until at least sunset. After all, Camps Bay is the perfect place to catch a beautiful sunset while having a drink on one of the numerous patios lining the street.

I ignore the guys on the pavement selling locally handcrafted objects and painted canvases and look both ways... twice before crossing the street. In Cape Town, you never know when a taxi full of people is going to come barreling down the road. *I do not want to get run over today*. As soon as I clear the street and turn in the direction of the restaurant, I see him.

The sun glinting off his black hair and mirrored aviator sunglasses. I'm kind of miffed that they hide his eyes from me. I love seeing his love for me shining back through them, now they're covered. The rational side of my brain says he's wearing them because it's bright as heck out, but the irrational side is saying that maybe his feeling towards me have changed since witnessing my husband's return from the dead yesterday.

The irrational part shuts up as soon as I'm close enough for Nate to pull me into the tight circle of his arms. Time ceases to exist as he holds me. I inhale his scent of coconut and spice and let out a relieved sigh. I used to always joke with him that he smelt like Malibu rum. But I love the smell, it reminds me of summer days spent at the beach and cool drinks afterward. Of sipping Pina Coladas by the pool.

Nate moves to pull away, but I refuse to lessen my grip just yet. I need a little bit more of this. I need to imprint his scent and the feel of his arms around me if this is the last time I'll ever get the chance. He obliges by pulling me closer. I sense someone moving up beside us, but he asks them to come back because I hear the faint sound of footsteps disappearing farther inside the restaurant.

"I'm sorry," I whisper into his chest, feeling like we must look quite a bit odd standing on the patio of a very popular restaurant just hugging.

"Never feel sorry. I'll hold you for as long as you'll let me."

"Hmm, forever," I hum before I can stop myself.

Then Nate lets me go. Stepping around me he pulls out a chair and gestures for me to sit. I do and watch as he takes the seat across from me. Not beside me like he always did before. I squirm in my seat, feeling the void already growing between us. A void that's growing bigger than the square table we're seated at.

My head spins as everything happens in fast forward motion. The waitress comes back to take our drink order and Nate goes ahead and orders dinner for both of us. *Well, at least that part hasn't changed.* We somehow fall into a comfortable conversation discussing everything but what happened at my house yesterday. I know I should be glad that at least we can still talk, but we aren't talking about the important things. It's all superficial crap and what I really need to know is what Nate thinks about this whole fiasco.

"Do you believe we only get one true love in our lifetime?" I ask after our waitress has come to collect our plates and refill our drinks. Then to bring the tequila shots I order.

"If you're asking me who you should choose. I can't tell you that. If you're asking me if it's possible to love more than one person then yes, I believe it's possible."

I sigh. My fingers playing with the still-full shot glass in front of me. "That doesn't help me."

"Look," he says, reaching over to take my hand in his. "I'll always love you whether you decide to choose me or him. He's your first love, your husband. I get that, but I won't lie and say I wish I was your last. No one can make this decision for you, Nika."

"Am I a bad person for thinking this was so much easier when I thought he was dead?"

A small smile tugs at the corners of his lips. "You're not a bad person, but he's not dead."

"No," I say, before taking the shot. The alcohol burns on the way down. "He's not."

Nate stands, gathering my light jersey and purse from the back of my seat. "Go home, get some rest. No good decision ever came from the bottom of a tequila bottle."

Pouting, I slide off the stool and step impossibly close to him, pressing my palms against his chest, leaning in until my lips brush against the skin below his jaw.

"But it can be lots of fun."

"Annika," he groans. His fingers wrap around my biceps and gently push me away from him. "Baby, there's nothing I want more than to take you home right now, but you have a big decision to make and no matter how much I want to be the asshole that takes you home and tries to convince you to choose me, I'm not going to."

"So, you're just not going to fight for me? For us?" I ask, feeling the alcohol start to take hold. *I probably shouldn't have drank so much.* "Did you mean it at all when you said you loved me?"

"Don't," he warns, a hard edge to his voice as he rakes a hand through his clipped hair. "You know I'd give my fucking life for yours, but you're married, Nika. To him."

"But I thought he was dead! They told me he had died on deployment! I planned his damn funeral, Nate."

Memories of finding out the man I married straight out of high school, the man I vowed to spend the rest of my life with was dead, and the years of pain and mourning that followed threaten their way up again, but I push it all down. Nathan came into my life at a point where I was finally ready to move on, when the pain of losing Jackson wasn't the first and last thing I felt every day. He made me remember what it felt like to fall in love again, and it was all being threatened because it turns out my husband isn't really dead and is currently waiting for me at the house while I make my decision. I want to scream that it's not as easy as they think. I love them both equally.

"Have you slept with him?"

The question takes me by surprise and all I can do is look up at Nathan as his eyes cloud over and his features darken. I can practically see the hurt begin to transform him, but what the hell do I say to that? *I was caught up in the moment of my husband being back so yeah, I did fuck him, but I felt so guilty afterward that I practically cried myself to sleep thinking about you while my husband snored beside me.*

This was all so fucked up.

"Nathaniel…"

Something flashes in his eyes but then it's gone. I can just imagine what he must think of me now. He reaches out, tracing a line down the side of my face from temple to jaw with the back of his finger before pushing a strand of sun-lightened brown hair behind my ear. "I refuse to come between a husband and his wife again."

My heart clenches at this being goodbye. I grip his hand tighter in mine when he turns to leave. "I love you, Nate."

His whisky-coloured eyes dance in the light of the setting sun as he leans in and presses the softest kiss to my lips. "You love him too."

A tear slips down my cheek when he turns to leave, his hand slipping through mine until our fingers are barely touching and then nothing. For the second time, I watch a man I love walk away with no idea if he'll ever come back.

He will if you choose him.

What the fuck am I going to do now? Jack and I have been together since we were high school sophomores. I've only just met Nate several months ago. Is it possible to love someone this much after only six and a half months? Or is what I am feeling lust? I don't think it is. Nate and I shared some pretty deep conversations over the time we've spent together. If it's lust, I'm almost positive we would've spent ninety percent of that time fucking, but we hadn't. Nate knew me almost as well as Jack did.

Chapter 13

"HEY BABE." JACK'S DEEP voice greets me as soon as I step through the front door of my house.

Our house? I don't know anymore. The whole situation has my head spinning and I have no idea how to make it stop. I want off this merry-go-round.

His arms slip around me from behind when I toss my keys on the dining room table. I immediately shrug out of his embrace without much conscious thought. I don't even make it a few seconds before the guilt begins to settle in my gut again. He's my husband for pete's sake. I shouldn't feel guilty about him showing me affection.

My mind instantly goes back to Nate and his words from the bar earlier tonight.

Of course, I love Jack. He's technically still my husband, isn't he? Even if he isn't, he's still my first love, my first boyfriend, my first kiss... my first everything.

The memory of the first time we made love comes rushing back. We were sixteen.

"Come on, X! Let me just take the car for one night." Jack begs his older brother, Xander, while I sit at their kitchen table and pretend not to hear the conversation going on down the hall in Xander's bedroom.

"No, Jackson. Mom and Dad will kill me if they found out I let you drive without an experienced driver not two weeks after you got your license."

"They don't need to know," Jack argues. "Plus, they're out of town this weekend. Who's going to tell them?"

"The cops if you get caught."

"Then I won't get caught."

"Look, bro. I'd love to help you out. I really would, but if I let you take the car and Mom and Dad find out then I get my keys taken away, and if I get my keys taken away then I won't be able to take Kelly on a date next week,"

I picture Jack rolling his eyes when he responds with, "Like Kelly will ever agree to go on a date with you."

Something hits the wall with a dull thud, and I imagine Xander throwing something at Jack's head, but Jack ducks, sending the item into the wall.

"She will," Xander says with a confidence I've never heard from him before. "I'm so close to getting her to agree. I can almost taste it."

"Dude, please," Jack begs again. "It's our first official date. Would you have wanted a chaperone on your first date?"

"Fuck no," Xander groans.

"Exactly."

There's a beat of silence, followed by a bed creaking, the sound of a drawer being opened then closed, and finally a sigh.

"If you get caught, I will deny ever having known that you took the car. You're on your own then, baby bro."

"Deal," Jack says excitedly.

"And for God's sake, make sure you pack a rubber… or two."

We did the standard date; dinner and a movie, but neither one of us was ready to go home and call it a night after the movie let out, so we went for a drive, parked at the beach, and went for a late-night stroll along the shore.

When we got back to the car one thing led to another and let's just say, the back seat of a Corolla was not the way I pictured losing my virginity, but it was still everything I imagined it would be. I think Jack had everything to do with that.

We weren't always in love and inseparable. There was a point in grade eight, my first school year in America, where I hated his guts. He was in my class and also lived in the house at the end of the street.

He was the boy who made fun of my accent and the way I pronounced certain words, but he was also the boy who would run to defend me if he saw anyone else try to bully me. He was both my tormentor and my protector. I was grateful Florida had relatively similar weather patterns to Cape Town, but Jack always made sure I was warm when it got cold... well, cold by Cape Town standards. Floridians would look at me weird when I'd be bundled up in a long-sleeved shirt and a hoodie while they were in t-shirts.

When we entered freshman year of high school, we were no longer in the same classes and it was weird, but it somehow brought us closer together.

He and I would walk to school together in the mornings then he would drop me off at my first class and he would always be there to walk me to my next class. It became this unspoken ritual between us, one I think we both grew to rely on whether we admitted it or not. There were times - which were rare - when he was sick and wouldn't be waiting for me outside of every class. I hated those days. Loathed them, actually. Everyone knew that Jack was sick because I would inevitably become bitchier.

It wasn't until our sophomore year that we finally decided if it looked like a duck and acted like a duck then it must be a duck. Meaning, if we looked like were dating, acted like we were dating, then we may as well be dating. And that was the beginning.

I became known as Jackson's girl, and Jack... he became known as mine, and there wasn't a soul in that school who dared to threaten that. It helped that he was the quarterback of the football team and towered over the guys in our grade. Standing at a whopping 6'3" and 220 pounds at only seventeen years old, he was the tallest and biggest male in our junior year.

"You're still mad." Jack accuses, heading into the kitchen for a beer.

"I'm not mad. I have no reason to be mad," I defend. "Just…" I sigh, leaning a hip against the wall that separates the kitchen from the rest of the house. "It's going to take some time to get used to. It's a lot to process."

He gathers me in his arms, his chin coming down to rest on the top of my head. The fresh pine scent of his body wash surrounding me in old comfort.

"I know. It's weird for me too. I never thought I would live long enough to get out of there, let alone see you again. When I found out you weren't in Florida anymore I thought it was too late."

"How did you find me?" I ask, my fingers curling into the belt loops of his jeans.

"I managed to get a hold of Londyn. She said you had moved back to Cape Town about two years after they told you I'd died on deployment. She said you wanted to be closer to your family."

I hum, thinking about my friend back in Florida. "How is Londyn?" I ask.

Jack's hands slide up and down my back in a comforting movement. "Kyle really messed her up but sounds like she's found some pretty great housemates. Their new neighbour is driving her nuts," he laughs, explaining Carson - Londyn's new neighbour - who also happens to be the cousin of one of her housemates. From what Londyn has said about him, Carson is close to completing his commitment to the Canadian Navy.

"So-" Jack clears his throat.

I squeeze my eyes shut and pray that he won't ask me what I know he's about to. I won't deny that Nate means something to me, but I cannot… will not choose between my legal husband and my… boyfriend? Plus, how do you admit to the man you promised to spend your life with that you managed to go and fall in love with another man two years after you thought he had died.

"Who was the guy that was here the other day?"

I inwardly curse, not sure why I hoped that he wouldn't bring up the subject. It's only natural.

"He, uh, he's my… carpenter." I shrug nonchalantly.

Jack stands in front of me, his eyes pinning me to the spot. His arms cross and he leans a shoulder into the doorjamb. He doesn't look convinced and I know I'll have to admit that I fell in love again; That he's no longer the only man who holds my heart. I take a deep breath, close my eyes and count to five before I open them again, and square off with my husband.

"He's also the man I've been seeing," I say, my voice small and unsure.

Jack's eyes flame and for a moment I'm scared he'll go off on me. Instead, he uncrosses his arms and straightens off the door, running a hand through his already mussed hair.

"How long?" he asks.

"Wh-what?"

"How long have you been seeing him?"

"Um…" I shuffle from one foot to the other, avoiding meeting his gaze. "Six… seven months."

"Do you love him?"

I blow out a frustrated breath. "You can't ask me shit like that, Jack. I thought you were dead. D-E-A-D. Dead. We had a funeral. I watched them lower your coffin into the damn ground. So, you can't stand there pissed off that I somehow managed to move on two years after your death!" It's not until Jack gathers me in his arms that I realize not only was I yelling at him but there are tears streaming down my face.

"Shh, it's okay." He soothes, running a hand up and down my back in the way he knows calms me down.

"This is all too much, Jack. I don't know what to do," I sob into his chest, my fingers curling around the fabric of his t-shirt.

"I can leave. Go get a hotel and let you have a few days to get your mind wrapped around everything."

Just the thought of watching him walk through the door again with no idea if he'll come back this time, has my heart beating faster. I curl into him more, tightening my fist in his shirt. "Don't leave," I whisper.

Jack grips my shoulders and pushes me away until he can see my eyes. "This has been a lot for you to take in, Nika. I can see how overwhelming it would be to suddenly be faced with the reality that the husband you thought had died is actually still alive. You need time to process and I'm not sure if having me stay here will allow you to do anything you need to."

"But I just got you back." I'm acutely aware of how whiney I sound but I don't care. My world was just flipped on its head for the second time in as many years.

"I won't be far. There's an Airbnb close to Muizenberg Beach. I can crash there for a few days then when you're ready, we can talk and see if we can work all of this out."

"But you don't know the city," I say, trying to get him to change his mind.

Jack grins like he knows exactly what I'm trying to do, and I guess he does, seeing as how we have been together since we were kids. "When you've had time to process all this maybe you can show me around. Take me to all your favourite places as a kid."

"Yeah, I'd like that."

Jack dips his chin in approval. "Can you give me a ride to the Airbnb? I've seen your taxis here and…" he shivers, "I'd like to make it there in one piece."

I laugh. "Good call. The locals are usually the only ones taking the taxis and even then it's sketchy."

"Is that even legal? The one I saw was so overcrowded. There were people hanging out the windows."

I lift a shoulder in a half shrug. "I'm not entirely sure, and if it's not then they don't give a fok. The more people, the more money."

I walk over to the dining room table to grab the car keys while Jack fetches his bag.

"Have you ever ridden in one?" he asks.

"Once." I turn to lock the front door behind us. "When I was little, my dad and I took a taxi. I can't remember why or where we were coming from but I'm pretty sure that was the first and last time my dad ever took one with me or otherwise."

Jack shakes his head in disbelief as he attempts to get in on the driver's side. I smirk at the confused look on his face when I stop beside him.

"You plan on driving?" I ask with an eyebrow raised.

He tilts his head in question, not sure what I mean until he catches a glance at the steering wheel through the window.

He barks out a laugh as he moves in front of the car to the passenger side. "I'm going to be doing that a lot here, aren't I?"

"Yup, pretty much," I say with a grin, starting up the car.

"You guys couldn't have made it easy and put the steering wheel on the left side like the rest of us?" he jokes.

"And where would the fun in that be? I mean, if it had been on the left-hand side then I would've missed moments like this."

"That sass is going to get you in trouble one day."

Jack and I fall back into an easy flow of conversation while we drive closer to the Airbnb. It begins feeling almost... normal. Like we haven't stopped being a couple. But the more comfortable it becomes, the more guilt I begin to feel.

Guilt that I shouldn't be feeling this comfortable around a guy that isn't Nate. Then guilt that I shouldn't be feeling guilty because Jack is my husband. Oh man, this is getting a shit-ton more complicated as the days go on.

As we get closer to the beach and the strip of road with the Airbnb, I roll down my window and inhale a lung full of salty ocean air, immediately feeling my body relax. All the guilt and uncertainty is washed out with every inhale. This is where I have always belonged. At the beach.

Once I have dropped Jack off at his Airbnb with a promise to call him on his temporary Cape Town number, I pull into the parking lot of the beach down the road, ditch my flip-flops in the back seat of the car, and take off down the sandy path to the shore.

Despite the windy day, there are still quite a few people lounging on their towels on the beach with their umbrellas anchored in the sand to keep them out of the sun. That's the thing about Cape Town, it can be an overcast day like today, but spend enough time outside and you can still end up with a nasty sunburn. Trust me, I know. It's happened to me on more than one occasion.

I dodge kids running back and forth from the tide and the sandcastles they're building, as well as a couple walking their dog, and a group of guys playing frisbee. As I zigzag between all of them, I wonder how they can all go about their lives as carefree as they are while completely ignoring the fact that my heart is in a vice while simultaneously being ripped in two. I'll enviably hurt one of the men I love. There's no way around that.

112

I sigh, kicking at a random rock buried in the sand while fighting the growing urge to pack up and take off for a week… or two. I'm not a child anymore, though, and my problems won't solve themselves. This isn't something I can simply run from. Or have my parents take care of, no matter how tempting that sounds.

When I come to the colourful changing rooms along the beach, a woman catches my eye, sitting by herself on a beach chair, her sunglasses perched on her nose as she reads a book. There's no ring on her finger as far as I can see from where I'm standing and there doesn't appear to be anyone with her. She's looks so at peace, and for a brief moment I envy her.

What if.

What if I don't choose either of them? What if I focus on myself and put me first? I stop at one of the cafés across from the beach while I allow myself to ponder it for several minutes.

Ever since I was old enough to date, it had always been Jack. After he died, I stayed single for two years but I didn't focus on myself. I was just trying to get from day to day without the man I had relied on for half my life. Then there was Nate. Did I even really know myself as an individual?

I shake my head again as the guy behind the register places my iced coffee on the counter. It's a ridiculous thought. Of course, I knew myself. Didn't I?

The house is eerily quiet when I push open the front door and deposit my keys and purse on the entryway table. After I kick out of my flip-flops I make a beeline for the kitchen and the bottle of red wine that has been waiting for me. I sigh with relief at that first sip, some of the tension already melting away.

My FaceTime rings just as I'm sitting down at the dining table and open the lid of my MacBook. My best friend's concerned face stares back at me when I accept the call.

"You look like shit."

"Gee, thanks, Londyn. Nice to see you too, asshole."

Londyn grimaces. "Sorry, habit. How are you holding up?"

I shrug and take a long sip of the Two Oceans Shiraz. It isn't my wine of choice, but it was free courtesy of my mom.

"That well, huh?" Londyn asks.

"Why didn't you tell me, Londyn? Jack says you knew. That's how he found out I wasn't in Florida anymore." I can't keep it in anymore. The fact that Londyn had known that Jack wasn't really dead, had talked to him, told him where I was but never bothered to give me a heads-up, isn't sitting well with me. She's supposed to be my best friend, supposed to have my back. So why not in this?

Londyn's eyes water and her lip begins to tremble when she responds. "He asked me not to, Annika. God, I wanted to. I really did, please believe that. But he said it was something that should be done in person."

I nod, realizing that I do believe her. This is too big for Londyn to willingly keep from me. I take another drink until there's nothing left in the glass. Holding up a finger to tell Londyn to give me a second while I go refill the glass. On second thought, I grab the bottle and bring it back to the table with me. The tequila shots from the restaurant having worn off already.

"How did my life get like this, Londyn?"

"Oh, honey, I'm so sorry."

"I thought he was dead. I mean, they didn't ask me to identify a body or anything, but they said the body had his tags. How could they screw that up? And now he's here. Like, here in Cape Town. And then there's Nate," I rant to my best friend, realizing that I need to just unload everything that has happened in the last two days.

"Did Jack say what happened? Where he had been for the last two years?"

I pause, taking the time to think about it. "Yeah," I say. "He said he was taken prisoner."

"Jesus," Londyn says on a sharp exhale. "What are you going to do, Nika? Do you need me to come there?" Genuine concern mars her voice, and not for the first time I feel incredibly lucky that I have a best friend like Londyn.

"I couldn't ask you to do that. Tickets aren't cheap and it's a long trip. Plus, you have your job to think about."

She waves me off. "I haven't taken a day off in two years, I have some vacation time owed to me. Plus, if I tell them it's a family emergency they have to give me some time off. And don't worry about the ticket or the long trip, you know I love travelling and I'd do anything for you, Nika. You're my family."

I feel my eyes begin to well with tears and try to discretely wipe them away when a few decide to fall.

"No. Nu-uh. None of that," Londyn says, wagging her finger at the camera. "No crying."

"Sorry," I sniff. "God, I'm such a mess."

"I think you're allowed to be with everything you've found out in the last forty-eight hours. Where is Jack anyway?"

"He thought I needed some time to myself so he's staying at an Airbnb close to one of the beaches for a few days. What am I going to do Londyn? I don't want to end things with Nate, but Jack is my husband and I'm pretty

115

sure our marriage is still legal even if he has been dead for two years. But then I don't know if I want to divorce Jack. I still love him so much and if this is an opportunity for us to be together again then I should take it, right? I mean, how often does one's dead husband come back to life? But I can't stand the thought of hurting Nate."

"You're talking yourself in circles, babe. Why don't you work on just processing the fact that Jack is back. Then, when I get there, we can figure out what it is you really want." Her expression changes to one of weariness making me wonder what else she wants to say but isn't.

"What?" I ask.

"It's just a suggestion… but you're allowed to choose yourself." She continues on without giving me a chance to reply. "Listen, I managed to find a flight for three days from now flying out of Orlando. I won't get there until the evening of the seventh, though. Will you be okay until then?"

"Yeah," I say. "Yeah, I should be."

"Good." I watch as she goes about booking her flight online and when her eyes light up, I assume she got a good look at where her layovers will be. I'm proved right when she exclaims, "Paris! I get a layover in Paris!" Then her head ducks closer to the screen, leaving me with an up close and personal view of the top of her head since Londyn still has the old school webcams. "Oh darn! It's barely a two-hour layover."

I laugh. "If I make it through this, I'll go with you on that European trip you've been dreaming about since we were in high school."

Her head pops up and I have to hold back the giggle that threatens to come out when her eyes round like a cartoon character. "Really?!"

"Hells yeah! We could even take the train from London to Paris. I've heard it's pretty neat."

"Okay, flight is booked. Should I have booked a hotel too?"

I scoff, "Really?"

"What?" She holds up her hands, palms up in a shrug. "I don't know if you plan to get busy while I'm there and I'd rather not hear my best friend's sex noises… again, thank you very much."

"One time. You forget your best friend is sleeping on the floor one time."

Londyn shivers at the memory as I shake my head and take another sip of the wine realizing why it is I never indulge in red wine. The shit goes straight to my head. Do not pass go, do not collect $200. I go from zero to fucked up in less than two glasses. Eh, and the shots may not have worn off like I thought.

"And anyway." I stop and clear my throat when my words begin to slur already. "There will be no 'getting busy' until I figure out what the fudge to do."

Londyn laughs at my use of air quotes… or it could've have been my slurring, I'm not quite sure.

"How many glasses of that have you had?"

I glance from the empty glass to the screen and back again before I shrug. "Uh… no idea." I'm pretty sure it was only two glasses but when I go to lift the bottle to pour more it's surprisingly light for only missing two drinks. *Huh, so maybe I did have way more than two.*

"Annika, you know you and red wine are not friends." Londyn groans. "Am I going to have to call your mom to come babysit you until you sleep it off?"

"What?" I shriek. Seeing my mom is the last thing I want right now. I mean, I get along with my parents really well but neither of them have seen me drunk, let alone drunk and going through a crisis. "No! I'm fine. I swear. I'm going for a nap after this so there'll be no trouble getting into."

She snorts. "Will turning off your phone be happening too?"

I tilt my head in confusion wondering why I should be turning off my phone when an image of me drunk texting during a house party our junior year comes crashing back. Oh, it had been bad... so bad. It was also the first big fight Jack and I had. He was furious and I thought he was going to end it between us for sure, but then he found out that the guy I was texting was gay, and he calmed down a bit. He still wasn't happy that I was texting Leo about Jack and my sex life. I groan, resting my forehead in the palm of my hand. "So bad," I murmured.

Londyn laughs. "Yes, yes it was. But oh, so entertaining."

Without looking up I reply, "Phone's definitely going off." And then I give my best friend the finger which she proceeds to laugh off... and laugh and laugh.

Chapter 14

I HAD ALL THE intentions in the world to do as I told Londyn; I would and turn off my phone. But see, drunk me doesn't agree. Nooo, the bitch thinks now is the perfect time to message Nate. The only reason why I go along with the plan is because I don't think he'll be awake at oh… three o'clock in the morning. But surprise, surprise he is! Also, what the fuck is he doing that he's awake at three a.m.?!

Nate: Are you drunk?

I giggle.

Me: Nooooooo…..

My phone rings, Nate's handsome face smiling up at me from the screen. It's a picture I had taken during one our trips to Dunes. He'd just looked up from getting out his wallet to pay the bill and the sun was at the perfect spot. It's my favourite picture of him. I hit cancel.

Nate: Answer the phone, Nika.

Me: No. You'll just tell me that we can't be together.

Nate: I'm coming over. Answer the door.

Me: No. If I don't want to hear your rejection over text what makes you think I want to hear it in person? You hurt me, Nate.

Nate: Annika, baby.

Me: You hurt me and I'm horny. Hurt and horny. You suck.

I giggle again. No, that was me.

Nate: Shit, babe. You can't say shit like that.

Me: Suck. Suuuuck.

I reply just because I can, and I know it'll get him all bothered. *Good, then that'll make two of us.* I have no idea if he replies after that because as soon as I send the last text, the tequila shots and the bottle of wine I consumed by myself catch up with me. I pass out with my phone still gripped in my hand and resting on my belly.

"What the hell was that last night?" Nate asks, cornering me in the staff room at school the next morning.

My head's pounding like a sonofabitch, and I'm regretting the copious amounts of alcohol I consumed even while knowing it was a school night. I groan, popping a coffee pod into the machine and hitting start.

"It was nothing," I say, hoping he'll drop it. When I woke up this morning and saw the texts we had exchanged last night, I naïvely hoped that Nate would forget about it or that he'd decide to not bring it up while we are at school, but I should've known that this is Nate and he isn't the type of person to just ignore something. Plus, I wasn't at my greatest last night. I inwardly cringe at the memory of the texts I sent him. So childish.

Nate reaches out to grip my wrist, stopping me from removing my mug from the machine. I think he's going to spin me around so that he can get a good look at my face when he tells me again that this thing between us needs to stop, that we can't carry on. So, I'm surprised when he presses closer until I can feel the hard ridges of his front against my back, until my lower belly is sandwiched between the counter and Nate's groin. He releases my wrist only to grip my hip in one of his big hands. I shiver when his fingers brush a strand of hair back from my neck. Nate leans in, his lips brushing lightly against the curve of my neck.

"You have no idea how your words affected me, Annika," he says, rotating his hips forward, pushing his growing erection into the curve of my ass. "I dreamt about sliding my cock into that sassy mouth, of how those full lips would look wrapped around me, of how you'd look on your knees while you looked up at me and sucked me deep."

I groan, bracing my palms on the counter and drop my head back against his shoulder, pushing my ass against him. He moves back just enough to slip a hand between my legs and cup me through my dress pants.

All too soon his hand is gone and he's stepping farther away, taking all his heat with him. I blink over my shoulder at him confused until I hear the click clack of someone's heels as they approach the staff room. I use however many seconds we have left to close my eyes and take a steadying breath. When I open my eyes again, the rush I felt when Nate was pressed up against me begins to sizzle away and I reach for my coffee mug with steadier hands.

When I finally turn around to face the room, Nate's gone, and Ms. Kennedy's popping her food in the microwave. Part of me wants to shoot daggers at her for interrupting us, but the other sensible part wants to go over and give her a hug in thanks. It would've been stupid for us to do anything here at school, especially in the staff room, but I also can't deny the heat flaming my cheeks at the possibility of being caught. I nod a hello to Ms. Kennedy and then hightail it back to my classroom, pushing all thoughts of Nate and his dick out of my mind. I need to focus on math if I'm going to have a chance in hell of teaching these kids anything when they come back from lunch.

Cape Town International is packed. It takes me about half an hour to find parking and another ten minutes to make it from the car to arrivals, which is also packed. *Jesus, did everyone and their grandma decide now was the perfect time to fly into Cape Town?*

It's not long before I spot my best friend. Her blonde hair's piled high on her head in a messy bun and she's trying to tug off her sweater while simultaneously pulling a suitcase behind her. I laugh, and as soon as she crosses the invisible barrier into the arrivals, I rush towards her, throwing my hands around her after she's just barely slipped the material from her body. When I'm good and ready, I force myself to let her go and take hold of the handle for the suitcase.

"Let me help with that."

She scowls up at me after stuffing the sweater in the carry-on bag on her shoulder. "You didn't say it was going to be *this* hot."

I giggle. "Welcome to summer in Cape Town."

"Am I melting? I feel like I'm melting."

I roll my eyes. "Let's go drama queen," I say, leading the way out of the terminal and towards the parking lot.

"Sweet Jesus," Londyn says as soon as we've left the somewhat air-conditioned comfort of the building. "Are we in hell?"

I chuckle but keep leading the way down the path to the parking garage and towards the car. At least I had the sense of mind to buy a vehicle with air conditioning. I don't think I'd be able to survive the summers without. It's bad enough that the transmission is manual, which means I already work up a sweat just driving the damn car. I could not add no a/c on top of that. Three more days. Three more days and then my dad needs to trade cars with me to go up to Franschhoek since mine is better on petrol. But his bukkie has an automatic transmission.

Londyn helps me load her suitcase in the boot of the car, and then we're heading away from the airport and towards Northpine. The drive to my house is nothing special, just miles of freeway, but I'm planning on taking her to do all the touristy stuff tomorrow and the rest of the week. Actually, when my dad comes back from Franschhoek, I'm going to take Londyn up there to do the wine tram. I haven't done it yet, but my cousins have, and they said they loved it. A whole day of wine tasting and being taken from winery to winery by a tram? Yes, please. I figure we can maybe find somewhere to stay the night up there too since I won't be in the frame of mind to drive back to Cape Town.

"Oh my gosh, your house is so cute," Londyn says about the ranch-style house when we pull into the driveway.

I don't feel like opening and closing the garage door right now, so I leave the car parked in the driveway and attach the steering wheel lock.

"Thanks... I think," I grin. "Nate just finished the built-ins in the guest room and the office."

"You decided to keep the tile?" she asks when we step through the front door.

"Yeah. I thought about it and figured I'd keep it for now and see. It's already been a lifesaver since the weather's gotten warmer. Plus, if it does get really cold later on I can just put down an area rug or something. Nate said he'd help me install carpet if I decide that's what I want later on."

123

Just the thought of Nate has my mood souring. I try to play it off like it's nothing as I lead Londyn down to the last bedroom at the end of the hallway but nothing gets past her.

"Hey, none of that. At least not today. Let's pop open a bottle of wine and you can show me around the house. I'm assuming there's a backyard?"

"There is." I cock my head towards one of the windows in the room. "You can see a bit of it through there. Not much though."

Londyn pushes past me to glance out the window. Unlike me, she has to lift a bit on her tiptoes to see through the glass. "What's that bricked part over there?"

"That's part of the carport. When my dad built it, he wanted to leave some of it uncovered so that we could put the braai in that sandy part at the end but have the chairs sit on the brick. It was also meant for me to rollerblade on so that I didn't have to rollerblade in the street."

"I sense a but there," she says, dropping down from her toes and turning a knowing smile on me.

I shrug. "I liked rollerblading in the street better. I can go farther without having to turn around."

She laughs. "Why am I not surprised?"

I roll my eyes and throw an arm around my best friend. "You said something about wine."

Chapter 15

"MOM?" I CALL, PUSHING open the front door.

Little barks greet me as I step into the quiet house and close the door behind me. A mop of white fur comes barreling towards me yipping at my ankles.

"Hi Snowy," I say, bending down to pet the Westie behind her ears.

"Oh, Annika. Honey, I wasn't expecting you to come over."

I shrug, rising to my full height before giving her a hug. "I was in the neighbourhood and thought I'd stop by."

"You were in the neighbourhood?" Mom questions with a lift of an eyebrow.

I avoid her knowing look and head into the kitchen to raid her fridge. Mom always has something to eat and I'm starving. "I went for a drive up to Cape Point and figured I'd stop in before heading back."

Mom gently pushes me out of the way of the fridge door and then she goes about collecting different toppings for sandwiches. "What are they charging for that now?"

"Cape Point? I don't know. I didn't actually pull in there. I turned around right before the pay booth and came back. Pulled off a bit to watch the penguins."

Mom grins as she goes about putting the sandwiches together. "You always did love watching them. Even as a little girl."

When she's done assembling the plates and adding some potato chips to each, she motions for me to lead the way to the dining room table a few feet away. A plate is set in front of me after I take a seat at the dark, round table and I don't waste time digging in. I forgot to eat breakfast this morning so I'm even hungrier than I normally am.

About halfway through my sandwich and potato chips I realize my dad isn't here, which is odd considering he's always here unless it's a weekend and he's at Dave's house working on a car or some other repairs.

"Is Dad at Uncle Dave's?"

Mom stills, her half-eaten sandwich halfway to her mouth. Something I can't decipher passes over her face but then it's gone in the next instant. The silence stretches on for longer than is comfortable. My throat goes dry and dread crawls down my back.

"Mom?"

She places the slices of bread, cheese, and meat tenderly back on her plate then dusts her hands of the crumbs before sitting back in her seat.

"Where's Londyn? I thought she would've been with you?"

"She wanted to take a nap before we go out tonight," I say, waving it off but never removing my eyes from her face. "Mom, answer my question."

She sighs. "I didn't know you'd be stopping by today. Why don't we wait until your dad gets here and then we'll talk."

I have no idea what that means, and why is she being so cryptic? It was a simple question that should've had a simple answer. What the hell's going on?

"Why won't you just tell me now? Are you okay? Is he okay?"

Various scenarios begin playing through my mind. One of them has cancer and is dying. Mom lost her job. Someone hacked into Dad's computer. They're getting a divorce. Someone cheated. They're moving again. My heart starts racing with all the possibilities of what she could be keeping from me and my breathing begins to pick up.

Suddenly, Mom's kneeling in front of me. A hand resting on my clenched fist, the other cool against my heated skin as she cups the side of my face, forcing me to look at her.

"Breathe honey."

I can't. The events of the last few weeks are too much for me to handle. My throat feels like it's being squeezed by a professional body builder and no matter how many deep breaths I try to take in, it doesn't feel like enough.

Mom curses, forcing my head between my knees as she continues telling me to breathe. I don't know why she keeps saying it, it won't make me take deeper breaths.

"Annika, you need to slow your breathing, baby. Concentrate on my voice and count with me. Ready?"

I nod.

"One," she starts, inhaling deep and holding it for several seconds before exhaling. I follow her lead and do exactly the same.

"Good. That's good. And another. Two."

Deep inhale, hold for several seconds, then exhale.

I can already feel my racing heart begin to slow. We do this for a few more. Her counting each breath and holding it for a few seconds before exhaling, and me copying everything she does. Soon, my breathing is somewhat back to normal and my heart rate has slowed enough that I no longer feel like I'm going to pass out.

Just as I lean back in the chair and Mom moves to reclaim her seat, I hear the front door open and the jingling of keys before my dad appears around the corner.

"Hey, Peanut," he says with a smile, but it doesn't light up his face like it usually does. His eyes hold a sadness to them I've never seen before. As he moves towards us, I notice that his shoulders are curled in, like he's carrying a huge weight on them.

"Hi, Daddy," I say, getting up to loop my arms around his waist in a hug.

"She was in the neighbourhood and decided to drop by," Mom says from her seat at the table, catching my dad's eye. Something passes between them in silent communication until my dad gives a clipped nod and with a hand on my back, leads me back to my seat. He takes the seat between me and Mom. His hands are entwined together and resting on the table.

"W-what's going?" I ask, my eyes bouncing between him and my mom.

"Peanut, I-" Dad starts then stops.

Mom takes a deep breathe then says, "Your dad and I are getting a divorce."

I don't know what happens then. I can see their lips moving but no sound reaches my ears. Darkness begins moving in from the corners of my vision and the last thing I see before it all goes black is my mom's horror-stricken face and my dad reaching for me, then nothing.

I leave my parents' house feeling like a zombie. After I passed out, Dad ended up carrying me to the guest bedroom, where I guess I took a mini-nap before coming to in the empty room. When I finally got up the courage to face them, Mom and Dad were sitting in the living room. Mom sat on one end of the long sectional, her hands on her lap and a worried look on her face while Dad sat on the opposite side looking like he'd aged fifty years in thirty minutes.

At the sound of my flip-flops on the wooden floor, they both look up. Mom races over to me, gathering me in her arms and asking me if I'm alright.

"I'm okay," I croak out, untangling myself from her arms and taking a step back. I send my dad a small smile to let him know I really am okay. At least physically. I never could handle stress very well and I guess the events of the last few weeks coupled with the news that my parents, the couple I looked up to, were getting a divorce was too much for my body to take.

They sit me down between them and explain that it doesn't make sense for them to stay married. They're both holding the other back from being truly happy.

Finally, I can't take it anymore and tell them I need time to think and process everything, then I leave. I don't remember getting in my car, or the drive home. I don't even remember walking in my front door and Londyn asking me how my drive was. I walk past my best friend, down the hall to my bedroom, close the door, and then crawl under the soft blankets.

This is where Londyn finds me minutes... hours later. Time ceases to exist for me today.

"Annika, what happened?"

Rolling on my back, I scoot over, and flip open the blankets so she can crawl in beside me. Londyn lays her head down on the same pillow close to mine. Both of us staring up at the hideous popcorn ceiling.

"My parents are getting a divorce," I say, my voice barely above a whisper.

"What?" Londyn screeches and I flinch.

"Sorry," she says, laying back down. "What the fuck?"

"Apparently Dad has been staying at a hotel for the last few weeks. They were planning on telling me at Sunday dinner."

"Are you okay?" She turns onto her side and props her head up on a bent arm.

"I don't know. I don't think it's fully sunk in yet. They've been together thirty years, Londyn."

"I'm so sorry, Nika," she says, gathering me in her arms and it's only then do I realize that I had started crying at some point.

"I don't think I can handle any more surprises," I say when the tears have slowed down a bit.

"Now we should definitely go out."

"What?"

"C'mon," she says, slipping from the bed. "You need a distraction… at least for a night." She shrugs. "What better way than going out with your best friend for a night of drinking and dancing."

I stare at her as she starts swaying her hips to a beat only she can hear. I want to tell her no, that I'd rather stay home and eat a tub of ice cream while watching cheesy horror movies, but I can't deny that she may have a point. I try to think back to the last time I went out and had fun but the only thing that comes to mind is the house party we went to in high school were Jack proposed. God, my life is pathetic and so drama laden.

"Fine," I say, throwing the covers back and swinging my legs over the edge so I can sit up. "You win. We'll go to Cocoon."

Londyn starts doing this weird dance thingy. Actually, I'm not even sure if you can call it dancing. Then she pauses and straightens up. "Wait, is that the one you were telling me about that's kinda fancy and has a view of the city?"

"Yup," I reply, opening the armoire and digging through my clothes for something to wear tonight that's not my usual cut-off shorts or dress slacks that I wear to work. "That's the one," I say, pulling out a little red dress I forgot I had.

"Friggin' A," she says then I hear her feet pad away as she retreats to the guest room.

Chapter 16

"HOLY SHIT. THIS IS great." Londyn beams when the doorman lets us into the club after we've stepped foot off the elevator and onto the 31st floor of the ABSA building. Two throne-like chairs situated on either side of a round glass table greet us as we enter the club.

I turn to Londyn. "East or west?" I ask.

She cocks an eyebrow at me, her head leaning to the side as she contemplates my question. I can see the wheels in her head turning, but then something clicks as she glances from the left to the right of the club.

"Can't we move back and forth?"

"We can. East is more VIP seating and lounge feel. West is more dancing."

Londyn beams and I giggle. Her excitement is so palpable, you'd think this was her first time going clubbing. She hums, walking to the window behind the chairs and looks from right to left and back again.

"East. Let's do east. The view on that side looks amazing."

I grin, glad that I had put a call in to get on the VIP list before we left the house. It also doesn't hurt that my cousin is the owner.

"Annika!"

I turn to my left and see Kim, my cousin's right hand, strutting towards us with her arms already open wide for a hug. I always thought Kim would've done well as a model. She's tall, and lean with just the right amount of curves, and she has the sharp bone structure that most photographers salivate at. Her dark hair is pulled up into a ballerina bun and the kohl lining her eyes makes the gold pop even more than they usually do. The sleeveless emerald dress hugs her body like a glove.

"Hi, Kim." I allow her to pull me into a hug and kiss her cheek in greeting. Her flowery scent assaults my nose as soon as I lean in.

"Did your cousin know you were coming? I just saw your name on the VIP list, but Clint never mentioned anything to me." She frowns, scrolling through the electronic device in her hand I hadn't noticed before.

"It was a last-minute thing," I say, ignoring the eye-popping-cartoon like expression Londyn currently has.

"Hmm, well, the glass booths are already all booked up, but I can still manage to score you one of the regular VIP tables. If you're okay with that?"

I glance at Londyn to see that she's already nodding her head. If she nods any harder I'm afraid it might pop off and roll over the shiny floor.

Kim grins but doesn't say anything about Londyn's enthusiasm, for which I'm grateful.

"That's fine. Thank you."

"Great. Follow me. Your cousin should be around here somewhere. He'll probably come say hi later on," Kim says as she leads us to our own table.

The couches look more comfortable than the ones I have at home, and I briefly consider asking my cousin where he found them so that I can purchase a set for myself. When Kim leaves us to attend to some of the other club goers, Londyn and I take up a seat across from each other. My eyes almost roll to the back of my head as my butt hits the soft fabric and I sink back. I definitely will be asking him where he bought these.

"I'm going to go get us a bottle. What do you want?" I have to raise my voice and lean in close to her ear for Londyn to hear me above the DJ's music.

"What do they have?"

I list the different bottles of alcohol available that I remember seeing on the website. When Londyn begins worrying her lip at all the different brand choices I tell her that I'll take care of it and leave to walk across to the white marble bar. It doesn't take long to get one of the bartenders' attention. I order a bottle of Patrón Silver, slipping my credit card from its resting place in the side of my bra when he goes to retrieve the bottle.

"It's on the house, Don," a deep voice says behind me.

Don nods, placing the bottle he just opened within my reach, then goes off to attend to another patron.

"Seriously, Clint. You don't need to do that," I say, turning to face my cousin.

His green eyes dance with amusement while his lips tip up in a lopsided smile. "Nika, I know what a primary school teacher makes. Let me do this for you."

My brows pull together in a frown as I stare him down, but when several seconds go by and it doesn't seem like he's going to budge, I sigh and give up. If the comment about my career choice had come from anyone else I would've had something to say about it, but this is my cousin. I know he didn't intend for it come across as the dig it sounded like.

"Fine. You can buy me booze."

Clint laughs, pulling me into a side hug. "A thank you would work too."

I nudge him in the side with my elbow, dislodging his arm from around my shoulders. Clint chuckles, moving to lean an elbow on the bar and effectively ignoring the hungry looks all the women are giving him.

134

"Thank you," I say. "It's… it's been hard." I'm not sure why I say that, but it just feels right. He was always the one I could confide in when we were little. Maybe that's because we're only two years apart in age, I don't know. Moving away from Cape Town wasn't hard. Moving away from Clint was.

"I know," he says, sobering. The smile slipping from his face and concern taking its place. "We should get all the cousins together soon. I think we can all use the family time."

"Sounds like a plan." I reach for the bottle of Patrón on the bar. "I should get back to my friend though before she sends a search party."

He laughs. "Alright. I'll come check on you ladies in a little bit. Anything you need is on the house."

"Thanks, Cuz," I say, slipping an arm around his waist and then head back to Londyn.

"Who was that hottie you were talking to?" She asks, raising her voice above the music as I pour us each a shot glass of the tequila.

"That's my cousin, and whatever you're thinking the answer is no."

I hand Londyn her shot and we clink glasses before throwing them back. This shit burns the back of the throat but because it's so flipping expensive, the burn is almost worth it.

"I wasn't thinking anything."

I glare at her and she giggles.

"Okay, I wasn't thinking *much*."

"Not going to happen, Londyn," I warn.

Londyn's a great girl. I wouldn't consider her my best friend if she wasn't. And I love my cousin, but the two of them together would be like sparking a match too close to gasoline. They'd destroy each other and I love them both too much to see that happen. If it were any

135

one of my other cousins… my *single* cousins, I'd gladly try to set her up with them, but not Clint.

After a couple more shots, Londyn convinces me to join her on the other side for some dancing. Clint comes over just as we're getting up to go over and he assures us that no one will tamper with our bottle while we're gone. He'll even put it behind the bar himself and one of the bartenders will bring it over when we return. I practically have to drag Londyn away from him, but I don't miss the way his eyes travel down her body either. I inwardly groan. This is supposed to be my night to let loose and not worry about shit. Instead, I'm having to play babysitter to my best friend so that her and my cousin don't sneak off somewhere to jump each other's bones.

About three or four songs into the night, I think I see a man leaning against the bar who looks eerily similar to Jack, but I shake it off. Jack was never really into the partying scene, even when he was home between missions. And if he was, Cocoon wouldn't have been the place you'd catch him. It's too expensive for his taste. When I glance back towards the bar again, the man is gone. Londyn grabs my hands and pulls me closer when "Piece of Me" by Britney Spears begins blaring from the speakers. This was our jam during our senior year of high school, and still holds so many memories for us.

Hours and a bottle of Patrón later, it's three thirty in the morning and the bartenders have just called last call. My feet are killing me, I'm sweaty, my hair's a mess and I'm pretty sure I have someone else's thong in my clutch. I'm not entirely sure how that happened and I'm beyond the point of asking questions.

I plop my ass down on one of the comfy couches and sink down until my head's resting on the back. Londyn's still dancing away, and I make myself promise to get up and go get her after one more song. She looks so happy and carefree on the dance floor though, even if she is the only one left. I vaguely realize that I may envy her endurance and her ability to still look good after hours of dancing and drinking.

"You look like you've had a hard night," my cousin says, sitting down beside me.

I nudge his dress shoe with my bare foot having lost the battle with my heels hours ago.

"Pretty sure that counts as one of those things you're supposed to think but not say out loud."

He leans forward to rest his elbows on his knees and grins over his shoulder at me. "Pretty sure that doesn't apply to family."

"Asshole," I murmur.

Also, how the hell does he still look so put together at almost four in the morning and after a full night of work? Minus the rolled-up sleeves and the undone top buttons, he still looks good. His gold watch shines in the lights of the incandescent chandeliers when he runs a hand through his wavy hair.

"Should you go get her?" he asks, tipping his head towards where Londyn is doing some sort of weird remake of the sprinkler.

"Yeah, probably." I stand, wincing when my feet send a jolt of pain up my calves in protest.

"C'mon," Clint says, helping me gather up my heels and purse. "I'll give you ladies a ride home."

It takes me a little longer than I would've liked to coax Londyn from the dance floor but once she catches a glance of Clint standing at the throne chairs waiting for us, her mood instantly changes and suddenly she's more than happy to leave the club.

"Don't you have to stay and close up?" I ask my cousin after we've wrestled a very drunk Londyn into the back seat of his car.

"Kim's staying to close up tonight," he answers, reversing out of his parking stall.

Clint helps me bring Londyn in from the car and even stays to help put her to bed. A fact that I refuse to examine right now. Maybe not even in the light of day.

After seeing him out and promising to keep in touch more, I lock the door behind him and shuffle my way back down the hallway and into my bedroom. Not even bothering to take off my dress, I fall face first on top of the covers and swear that it's the last time I'll be drinking. My inner voice laughs, calling me a liar as I succumb to sleep. Somewhere in the distant land between being awake and asleep, I hear my phone beep with a new message.

Chapter 17

"Umbrella, ma'am?" One of the men asks as Londyn and I pad our way over the sand to a spot on the beach.

"Please. Just over here," I say, pointing to the spot in the sand we're heading too.

He walks ahead of us in his board shorts and springbok t-shirt to dig the pole of the umbrella in the sand and make sure it's steady enough that the wind can't blow it away. I thank him and hand him a ten rand for the umbrella.

"I can't wait to get into the water," Londyn says, already pulling off her tank top and shimming out of her shorts to reveal her barely there white bikini.

"I'm glad we got here when we did. We may not have gotten a spot if we had come later." I fluff out my towel and lay it on one side of the pole, leaving the other side for Londyn to put her towel down.

Clifton 1st Beach isn't normally on my list of preferred beaches to visit in the city. It gets crowded fast because it's so popular and there are a slew of houses that use it as their personal beach, even though it's public. But after hiking Lion's Head Mountain this morning and showing Londyn the view on the way to the top, she insisted we stop and swim for a bit before heading back home to shower before dinner. I'm glad I had the sense of mind to have us both pack our swimsuits and towels in case this very thing happened.

Crossing my arms over my belly, I pull my own tank top off and work my running shorts down my legs until I can kick them off to the side. I wave Londyn off when she asks if I'm coming in and settle on my back on the towel, pulling out my copy of Dani Rene's latest novel. The model on the cover is so hot. He's got that older 'I'll call him daddy' vibe going on. And I've heard that there may be some man on man action within the pages. I'm excited to find out since I've been on an m/m kick lately when it comes to books. I devoured Lucy Lennox' series in a matter of a few days. It's like I can't get enough of them.

I'm brought out of the world Dani has created after a few chapters when my phone buzzes with an incoming message.

Jack: Dinner tonight?
Me: Londyn's in town.
Jack: She can spare you for a few hours.

"If you keep frowning so hard you're going to get wrinkles," Londyn says, dropping to her knees and stretching out on her stomach on her towel.

"I already have wrinkles," I reply with an eye roll. "Jack wants to have dinner tonight."

"So? Go."

"I can't just leave you. You're only here for a few more days."

"Annika," Londyn starts, turning onto her side and leaning up on an elbow. "This is the reason why I'm here. To help you figure out this thing with Jack suddenly being alive and Nathan. If you want to go have dinner with your husband, then you should go. Plus, I'm a big girl. I can handle a night to myself." She turns back on her stomach, folding her arms under her head like a pillow. "I can just call up that cousin of yours."

I groan. "Stay away from my cousin. I mean it, Londyn. He's… he's not right for you."

She pops up on her elbows and glares at me. At least I think she's glaring. It hard to tell with her reflective sunglasses covering her eyes. All I can see is my own reflection staring back at me.

"Are you saying I'm not good enough for him?"

"No." I roll over onto my front and slide my own sunglasses up my face to rest on the top of my head. "I'm saying he doesn't have the greatest reputation and I don't want to see you get hurt."

Now it's her turn to roll her eyes. "I'm only here until the end of the week. Nothing serious is going to happen between us. Plus, I'm not looking for anything long distance."

"I know. It's just-"

"You should tell Jack that dinner sounds great," she says, effectively cutting me off and pulling her phone out of her bag.

I huff in frustration but do exactly what she suggests and text Jack that I'm looking forward to seeing him tonight.

The dim lights of the restaurant greet us as Jack pulls open the door for me. The lights are turned down so low I feel like I'm still outside, about to dine under the moonlit stars. The hostess greets us when Jack steps in behind me and places a warm hand on the small of my back. His hand stays there as he gently guides me to follow the hostess to our table, only removing it when he goes to pull out my chair for me. Such a gentleman.

I vaguely hear her tell us about tonight's specials when Jack takes up his own seat across from me. The candlelight from our table does nothing to soften his sharp features, if anything it just makes him look more ethereal. He's let his dark hair grow out a bit on the top. It's still short enough for me to run my fingers through, but there's just enough length I can grab hold of it and tug. His usually bright sea-foam green eyes look darker in this light. There's a general air of mystery surrounding him tonight and I'm not entirely sure how I feel about that. I used to pride myself on knowing this man inside and out, but now... now I'm not so sure I know him at all.

Jack orders a drink for himself the second our server walks up the table, but I don't think too much of it. He's always enjoyed a drink or two with dinner especially when we've gone out to a fancy restaurant like this one. But when one drink turns into two then four then six, I begin to worry. This isn't like him at all, and the more he drinks the more animated he becomes. Almost hitting the guy sitting at the table beside us in the head when Jack flings his arm out.

"What's going on with you tonight?" I ask, keeping my voice low so that only he can hear me.

"Nothing. Why would something be wrong?"

Okay, that's not quite what I asked. I narrow my eyes at him and have to hold back the gasp of shock that threatens to escape. How could I have been so blind? Beyond the soft light of the candle and the dim lighting of the restaurant, there are dark circles under Jack's eyes. But even beyond that, his eyes hold something that looks a lot like... defeat? Exhaustion?

I reach out across the table and lay my hand on top of his, feeling guilty that I haven't exactly been there for him since he came to find me in Cape Town and especially after finding out that he spent the last couple years as a prisoner of war.

"Talk to me," I plead, giving his hand a squeeze.

It's like that one gesture is enough to bring the wall he built around himself to come crumbling down. His expression turns pained when he flips his hand over so we're palm to palm, and squeezes mine back.

"I, uh, I haven't been sleeping all that well," he says like it's not a big deal.

"Nightmares?" I ask, having remembered that was something that was pretty common among POWs. I didn't do a ton of research and I mostly just skimmed what I had found, but that one stood out to me.

"It's nothing I can't handle." Jack slips his hand out from under mine and slams back the rest of his drink, ordering another when our server comes around to collect our dinner plates and offer us dessert. We both decline the sweet treats.

"Jack, please talk to me. Tell me what I can do to help. You're my husband."

He snorts. "I'm glad you acknowledge that I'm still your husband."

"What's that supposed to mean?"

Jack takes a healthy sip of his newly refilled drink and leans forward with his elbows on the table. "Have you been fucking him while I've been back?"

I start to tell him that it's not that simple, but I stop before the words have a chance to leave my lips. Nate and I haven't been alone except for that time I met him for dinner the day after finding Jack on my front doorstep. So, it should be easy for me to tell Jack the truth that I haven't been seeing Nate, but I just... can't. I'm not sure what it says about me that I just slump back in my seat and stare at my husband without defending myself against his accusations. Nate means something to me and I'm not about to deny it.

I lift my clutch from the edge of the table and stand, smoothing down my dress in the process. "Take me home, please." I don't make eye contact with Jack as I utter the request, choosing to stare straight ahead with my chin held high. The moment I see him stand from the table and pull out his wallet, I head in a straight line for the door and walk out into the cool night air.

"Annika!" I hear Jack call and then running feet sound behind me before a hand slips around to grip my arm and he halts my progress to a waiting Uber. "Jesus, babe. I'm sorry. I'm such an asshole. I know you'd never do something like that."

My throat burns with the tears I'm struggling to hold back because he's wrong. I would do something like that. I have been doing that ever since I moved here and met Nate.

"It's just… the nightmares. They really fuck me up, you know?" He blows out a harsh breath, running both hands through his hair. "I can't fucking sleep. The damn pills they gave me have stopped working. I can't even close my eyes without seeing-" His voice hitches in a choked sob and I find myself pulling him into my arms and holding this huge man as he breaks apart.

I can't even begin to imagine the things he's been through and seen over the last couple of years especially.

"Would it help if you talked to me about it? About what you went through?"

His warm breath ghosts over my neck and I shiver. "Not allowed to." His speech is so slurred now, I think the amount of alcohol he drank is beginning to catch up with him.

Jack starts pressing open mouthed kisses up my neck and I groan.

"Come on, big guy. Let's get you home."

"I want you so much, Nika." He grips my hips and pulls me against him.

"You're drunk," I say, trying to disentangle myself from him and lead him to the waiting Uber.

"Not that drunk," he replies, stumbling into the car. "Alcohol is the only thing that helps," is the last thing he says before falling asleep as soon as the driver pulls away from the curb, his head resting on my shoulder.

Without giving it much thought, I pull out my phone and send Nate a text. In a perfect world, we would've had this conversation face-to-face, but the world isn't perfect and seeing him again, seeing the look of hurt in his eyes will be my undoing. I don't think I can go through with it then.

Me: I have to choose him. I'm sorry.

The three little dots appear almost immediately but then stop, and it isn't until the Uber is pulling up to my house do they appear again before Nate's message comes through.

Nate: I understand.

My thumb hovers over *delete contact* but I can't bring myself to make it that official no matter how much I know I should.

Chapter 18

AFTER STRUGGLING TO GET a very drunk Jack into the house and to bed while trying not to wake up Londyn, I collapse on the couch with a mug of rooibos tea and prop my feet up on the edge, curling my hands around the round cup and resting it on my bent knees.

This was the third night in a row that I've had to wrangle a drunk Jack into bed after he indulged in one too many drinks while we were out. I know he said that it was the only way he could get some sleep without the nightmares returning but it's not healthy and I'm really starting to worry about him.

After that first night out with Jack, I told him that he should just move in to the other guest room. There was no point in him continuing to rent the Airbnb by Muizenberg Beach. Plus, I kind of wanted to keep an eye on him and his alcohol consumption. I had to swallow hard against the lump forming in my throat when I got home yesterday evening and saw the stash of empty liquor bottles littering the side of the bed with a passed out Jack lying face down in a puddle of drool.

It takes me a while to gather up the remaining collection of bottles and throw them in the recycling bin and then clean up the kitchen. I'm pretty sure the bottles I pick up are a collection from the last three days' worth, but I'm too scared of the answer I may receive if I ask.

It's close to one in the morning but there's no way I'm going to convince my body to sleep right now. There's still too much stuff swirling around in my brain like a tornado looking for a spot to touch down.

Alcohol is the only thing helps.

Jack's mumbled words play on a loop in my head and no matter how hard I try I can't forget the look in his eyes when he uttered those words.

My phone beeps on the couch beside me with a new message and my heart dips at the sender. After texting Nate that night, we decided that it was going to be too hard to maintain a professional relationship outside of school. So, we cut all communication that wasn't related to our students. It almost fucking killed me, but I felt it was necessary.

Nate: Tell me again why we decided to cut all communication?

Me: Because it was too hard.

Nate: Right.

Nate: Guess I suck at it.

I smile. Little does he know he's not the only one feeling the loss right now.

Me: Nate?

Me: I miss you too.

Nate: Have a drink with me tomorrow night? Dunes?

I sink my teeth into my bottom lip and cut a glance in the direction of the bedroom where I set Jack up temporarily. It's too weird sharing the same bed with Jack that I shared with Nate, so I convinced my husband to stay in the guest room for now until we figure out some stuff about our relationship. Most wives would be ecstatic to learn that their husbands weren't really dead. Me? I felt like fate was playing a cruel joke on me.

My brain's telling me not to go, that I made a vow to Jack and to back out on it now would be wrong. But my

147

heart… my heart is begging to feel the comfort of just being near Nate again. Of feeling his arms wrap around me one last time. I blow out a frustrated breath. It would be nice if my brain and my heart could agree on something just once in my life.

Me: I'll be there.

Nate: Lekker.

I grin, easily picturing and hearing him say the Afrikaans word as if he were sitting beside me at this very moment, but it falls almost as fast it appears because I just lied to someone I love. I'm not going to be at Dunes tomorrow night after school. In fact, I'm not going to see Nate tomorrow at all. Or the next day after that or the next after that.

It's for the best I tell myself.

I pull into the staff parking lot of the school after dropping Londyn off at the airport. I'm grateful when I see Pam's car already in the lot. I grab my purse and phone as well as the envelope from the passenger seat, set the alarm on the car and head into the school. As I approach the front, I can't help but admire the building for the last time. If you'd seen this place from the road, you wouldn't have guessed that it was a primary school. A brick walkway is surrounded by lush bushes and greenery leading to a building with three archways, in the middle, a set of three steps takes you up to a patio area and a front door with glass tiles surrounded by dark wood paneling. To the right of the walkway is the expansive sports field and to the left is the high fence separating the Olympic-sized pool from visitors entering through the front gate. The entire building is shaped in a U, with the front entrance encompassing the bottom curve. Pam's office is immediately to the left after you enter into the foyer area.

Picture upon picture of past pupils decorate both walls of the foyer. It's still surreal seeing myself in one of those photos, wearing the old school uniform of maroon and white with the blazer that had the school logo embroidered on the left breast pocket in gold. To think that I had started out as a pupil when I was six years old and am now a teacher. Was. Was now a teacher because as soon as I hand this letter to Pam, I'll no longer be considered a staff member at Pinelands North Primary School.

"Come in," Pam's voice calls from behind the partially closed door after I knock. "Ah, Annika. How are you?"

"I'm fine. Thank you. How are you, Pam?"

She glances up at me from behind her desk, her short blonde hair glowing in the morning sun. "Is something wrong?"

I hate the way she can so easily pick up on my mood changes. She did the same thing when I was a pupil here. Like she could see something was bothering me but wanted me to come to her. It's a tone that begged you to confide in her even when you didn't want to.

I sigh, taking a seat in one of the plush chairs in front of her desk and hand her the sealed envelope. She takes it from me with a raised eyebrow and pursed lips but doesn't say anything until she's read through the long letter.

Pam mirrors my sigh, sliding her glasses off her nose and placing them on the desk in front of her. "I feared this was coming." Putting the letter on the desk, she sits back in her seat and folds her hands in front of her. "Can I ask you something and will you answer honestly?"

"Um… Yes?"

"Is this…" She points a finger at the letter without unfolding her hands. "Because of Nathaniel Walker?"

"H-How… um, what?" I stammer.

"Annika, I've known you since you were a child. Despite so many years passing, there's very little about your reactions that have changed. I know the two of you had something going on but in recent weeks that seems to no longer be the case. I had feared that you would hand in your resignation to keep it from getting awkward here at school."

"Well, I-" I start but she cuts me off with a raised hand.

"And while I appreciate what you're trying to do, I don't think it's necessary. You are both adults and I trust the both of you to keep it strictly professional when you're here."

"I appreciate that, Pam, I really do. But," I let out a fast breath, "I just can't continue to act like nothing's wrong anymore. It…" I pause, looking over at her and wondering just how much I can confide in her. When she gives me that soft, motherly smile I decide to just lay it all out there. "My, uh, husband… well, it turns out that he isn't actually dead, and he showed up here in Cape Town a few weeks ago. I ended it with Nate and hoped that things could maybe go back to the way they were before, but I've come to realize that they just… can't. It hurts every time I see him in the halls, or our classes do gym together. It would just be easier for both of us if I bowed out since he has been teaching here longer than I have. Plus, I don't think it's fair to the kids."

That motherly smile turns sad, and I have to swallow hard against the pang of guilt from disappointing yet another person in my life.

150

"Annika!"

The loud knock on the front door is followed by Nate's booming voice. I guess Pam must have told him that I had resigned from my position at P.N.P.S. and was not coming back. Either that or he figured it out after I stood him up last night and wasn't at school by the time the students arrived this morning.

In truth, I was. I saw him walk past Pam's office and down the hall towards both of our classrooms, but I made sure I was behind the door frame and that Nate didn't see me. Pam tried one last time to get me to stay before I pushed my way through the door, around the corner, and out the front door of the school. I didn't allow myself to breathe until I was in my car and merging onto the freeway that would take me home.

As soon as I walked through the door, I chucked my shoes and climbed into bed, fully clothed, pulling the comforter over my head. That's when I allowed the tears to finally fall. Now I am equal parts grateful that Jack isn't here, and wishing he was so that Nate would leave because hearing him call out desperately for me is breaking my heart even more than it was already.

This isn't the way I pictured us ending. In fact, I never pictured an expiration date for Nate and me, but it is how it has to be now. I couldn't keep seeing him, keep working with him, knowing Jack is waiting for me at home. It doesn't feel right, but neither does walking away from Nate.

After several more minutes of his insistent knocking and pleading going unanswered, I hear the rev of his car, the bass of his music kicking in and then fading in the distance as he drives away. *It's better this way* I tell myself as

I force my body to get out of bed and start dinner for when Jack gets home.

I tell myself the same thing as Jack enters me later that night and finds his release first.

"It's better this way," I repeat to myself, sinking further into the sofa where I moved after Jack rolled over and fell asleep, his snores now filtering down from the bedroom. I owe it to Jack. To our marriage. To our history.

Chapter 19

I EYE THE NEWLY refilled glass of beer in Jack's hand and mentally count back how many I think he's had since we sat down less than two hours ago. The pitcher is empty again and I am almost positive I had only one drink out of the two pitchers we'd ordered. Since there is still half of one sitting in the middle of the table, it means Jack drank almost one and a half to himself.

Jack waves his hands around in the air as he speaks sports with one of the guys sitting at the bar directly beside us. I have never seen my husband so animated before. Usually Jack likes to keep to himself when we come out to watch the game. Yes, he was the popular jock in high school and was at all the parties, but not like this. Never like this. I feel like the man sitting in front of me is a complete stranger. One who looks like and sounds like my husband.

The bruise on my bicep still stings whenever my sleeve brushes against it, and it hurts like a bitch when I accidentally bump my arm into something. That is the biggest change. Before he left on deployment, Jack would never have thought about laying a hand on me. Not in a way I didn't enjoy anyway. But the more he drinks, the more I feel the man I knew is slipping away and someone entirely different is taking his place.

Ever since he came back he's been different. I no longer see the boy who left for basic training all those years ago or the man who left for deployment several years later. I know they say war changes a person, but I didn't expect this much of a change. Maybe I am naïve, I don't know. Or maybe it is the stress of the last while finally catching up to me.

I think back to my parents and how thirty years of being together is about to be flushed down the drain all because my father felt like he had to hide who he really was. My heart breaks for him because I can't imagine having to hide such a significant part of yourself for so long, but I'm so mad at him too. How could he ever think it was okay to put my mother through that?

When Dad finally came out and told me the reason for the falling out between him and Mom, I wanted to hate him so much. I wanted to lay the blame at my Uncle Dave's feet. After all, if he had just stayed away maybe Mom and Dad wouldn't be going through this right now. If he had just minded his own business, those feelings Dad had for him wouldn't have resurfaced. God, I wanted to scream at all of them. How could they do this to me? Until Londyn reminded me that it wasn't about me. It wasn't about me at all. It was about them, and about Dad finally owning up to who he is, and I am being selfish by demanding my father continue to ignore that part of himself so he and Mom could continue being the perfect couple everyone thought they were.

I sigh. I feel bad for ending the FaceTime call with Londyn abruptly after that little come-to-Jesus moment. I know she is right. Of course, she is, but I am not ready to admit that... to myself or anyone else. I want to live in my bubble of anger a little while longer. My world feels like it is crumbling under my feet and that bit of anger gives me something to hold onto, something that anchors me because if I just let myself accept it, accept that everything I believe about my parents is a lie then I am going to lose it, and I can't lose it. I am the one who always has their shit together, dammit. My hand tightens around the glass and I take a long drink of the now warm beer.

So, yeah, a part of me is raging mad at my father, but I kind of get it. It sucks so hard that my mom is hurting through all of this. I mean, she's the one who had to find out that the man she loves isn't who she thought he was.

I look up at Jack. The low lights of the bar painting him in a soft glow. He has barely looked at me since the waitress set down that first pitcher in front of us. His gaze was locked on one of the TVs above the bar and then he began talking to that guy. I am pretty sure that I could slip out and he wouldn't realize I am gone until it's last call and he needs a ride home.

Is this the end for us too? It is a silly thought. He hasn't done anything to really make me consider leaving him.

Except put his hands on you, a little voice in my head says.

It was an accident. I hadn't been listening to him and he grabbed my arm to get my attention. So he grabbed me a little too hard causing finger shaped bruises to appear the next day. But it's not like he had ever done that before. Jack would never hurt me.

You never thought your dad would hurt your mom either.

That is different. My dad lied to my mom for thirty years. Thirty. Years. Jack has never lied to me, he just gets a little rough and that's all. And it was only the one time.

It only takes one time.

I mentally shake myself. I feel like a crazy person arguing with the voices in their head. What Jack does isn't intentional. I know it isn't intentional. But… I can't help but remember the way his eyes darkened when he yanked me around to face him, and the stench of beer that radiated from him.

From all the countless hours of research I had done on POWs the one thing that stands out is the fact that most of them turn to drugs or alcohol as a way to deal with some of the flashbacks they still endure and because they have trouble adjusting back to civilian life. So that's all it is. Jack is trying to adjust to being free.

Yup, it is all totally normal. Completely normal.

Now if only I could convince the annoying voice inside my head to believe the same.

"I'm going home," I say to Jack, picking my purse up from the ground at my feet. I fully expect him to go on not paying attention to me but as soon as I stand and begin turning away from the table, Jack pushes up from his seat and grabs my arm pulling me into him. I lose my balance a bit and stumble into the round table. My face heats as I glance at the surrounding tables and realize almost everyone has just witnessed what happened.

"Did I say I was ready to leave?" he seethes, spit flying and landing on my face. "Sit your fat ass down and be quiet while I finish my beer."

"Jack, please," I plead, ignoring the pain radiating from where his fingers are digging into my flesh.

"Sit. Down."

My ass has never hit a seat so fast in my life. Jack glares at me as he reaches for the pitcher and pours the remnants into his glass. I let out a relieved breath when his attention finally turns back to the game on the TV, the incident evidentially forgotten. Our waitress approaches and I can see that she wants to ask if I'm okay. I subtly nod my head before she can get the words out. She sends me a sympathetic smile, picks up the empty pitcher, and heads back to the bar.

A small part of me wonders what would've happened if I had told her I wasn't okay. Would she stand up against my husband for me? Would the bartender? Would the bouncers by the door? People like to think that they'd be brave enough to stand up for someone who they see is being abused, but the stark reality is that it's not true. People are too scared to get involved. They keep their heads down and continue in their naïve bliss, too engrossed in their phones to notice when someone is in pain.

"Don't you dare disrespect me like that again," Jack seethes, spinning me and pushing my back against the wall with his hand around my throat, as soon as we've entered the house.

"How did I disrespect you, Jack? I just wanted to come home. I'm tired." I claw at his arm, trying to get him to let me go but his grip tightens as he snarls in my face.

"We leave when I say we leave. I think I've been too lenient on you."

"What are-"

I don't see it coming so when his hand connects with my face. It comes with so much force that it sends me falling to the ground on my side. I gently cup my stinging cheek with my palm and glance up at my husband from under a curtain of brown hair.

The haze in his gaze clears and the anger that was there a second ago dissipates and morphs into sorrow and regret. Jack's brows pull together in a pained form and he crumbles to his knees where he was standing. His head is buried in the palms of his hands, his body shaking with the force of his sobs.

"I'm sorry. I'm so sorry," he chants.

Forgetting about my cheek, I move beside him and pull him into my arms.

"Shh, it's okay."

"I'm so sorry, baby. I don't know where that came from. That's never... I would never-" He takes a shuddering breath and now it's his turn to wrap his arms around me and pull me into his chest.

Jack sits back on his ass on the cold floor and I plant a knee on either side of his hips and settle onto his lap. He rocks us back and forth, tears still leaking from his eyes.

"Are you-" His words are cut off by a ragged breath, but I answer anyway.

"I'm okay," I lie.

We sit in stunned silence, Jack still rocking us back and forth for several minutes before my head rises and falls on his chest with the deep breaths he takes.

"We didn't know it at the time, but our mission was fucked before we even got there."

"You don't have to tell me this, Jack."

"I know, but I feel like I should. I've been so closed off since I got here, and I think you should know why. It'll also explain the nightmares."

I burrow closer into his chest and wait for him to continue.

"I still don't know how it happened, but our location was compromised almost as soon as we landed. They came at us from all directions with much more firepower than we were prepared for." He pauses. "It was supposed to be an easy mission. Get in, gather the intel, and get out. As soon as the shooting started we got separated. I think that was their plan all along. Separate us and drive us in different directions and towards the men they had hiding behind bushes."

"Seriously, Jack, it's okay if you don't want to continue. I know you didn't mean to..."

He silences me with a soft kiss. "I need to." After taking a couple more calming breaths, he goes on. "I didn't see them coming. Years of being a SEAL and trained to see things before they happen, and somehow, between all the chaos, I hadn't noticed I was walking into an ambush of my own. They took my weapons and my dog tags…"

"That's how your tags ended up on the dead body, isn't it?"

"That's what I'm guessing. I have no idea what they did with them after they ripped them off my neck."

"How… how long?"

"A year and a half. They weren't going to send someone in after me."

"What? Why?"

"America doesn't negotiate with terrorists," he says so calmly. "Not even for one of their own."

"Then how?"

"My team. When Caleb and Sam found out that what happened and that they weren't being ordered to go back in for me, they came anyway."

"I don't know much about the Navy, but isn't that frowned upon? Or going against orders or something?"

"It's more than frowned upon. It's cause for disciplinary action. But my team didn't care. *No man left behind.* Our CO was able to set up a mission close to where my last known location was and sent the guys in."

"So, he was in on it?"

Jack places a soft kiss on the top of my head. "He was, and if they find out what he did he could get jail time."

"Wait," I say, leaning back to get a better look at my husband. "How do they think your team found you?"

His lips twitch. "Another SEAL team found me. They were there on a different mission. Purely a coincidence."

I scoff, "That seems too easy to be a coincidence."

"I agree, but I'm not questioning whether they bought it or not, and neither are the guys. Hell, Caleb is retiring soon, and I doubt Sam will be relisting again either."

"And your CO?"

A sadness passes over his eyes. "I haven't heard from him since I was released from the hospital in the States."

"Do you think they pieced it together and went after him?"

Jack shakes his head, his grip tightening around my back. "I'm not sure, Nika. I'll have to ask the guys."

Jack doesn't tell me what exactly happened to him while he was held prisoner, but my imagination runs wild with the possibilities and I'm not sure if I want to know the truth. As the weeks tick by, that becomes the last thing on my mind, though.

I never understood why women stayed with their significant others after they hit them the first time because despite them begging for forgiveness and promising it won't happen again, it always does.

Now I understand.

High school Graduation

"I can't believe we did it! We're high school graduates!" my best friend screeches in my ear as we exit the building after the ceremony.

"I know," I answer. "It feels surreal."

"So, what should we do first? Go cage diving? Sky diving? Bungee jumping?" She bounces on the balls of her feet, an excited smile lighting her face.

"Or," I say, wrapping my arm around hers to try and dial down the crazy. "We can do what normal teenagers do and bribe

someone into buying us alcohol then going to an underage house party."

Londyn pauses, her lips purse while she contemplates my suggestion. "Deal. Oh! Jack's brother is over twenty-one. He could buy us booze." Her eyes light up at the thought and I can't help but laugh.

"Xander is twenty-three, yes. But I doubt he'll buy us booze."

"Why not?" She asks with a pout. "He let Jack take the car before he had his license."

I stop our advance to meet up with the guys and playfully smack her on the arm. "Excuse me, but Jack had his license. It is just his learner's at the time, but it was a license."

Londyn laughs. "Whatever you say, Nika."

"There's my girl." Jack slides off the tailgate of the truck the guys are sitting on and pulls me into a bear hug. "Congratulations, baby."

"Thank you. You too."

"That was a great speech, Nik," Kyle hollers from his spot on the tailgate.

"Thank you. I thought for sure that I would choke up," I answer.

I was surprised when I had been named this year's valedictorian. Surprised. Shocked. Terrified. I hate public speaking and have a fear that as soon as I get up on stage, I'll not only forget my speech but how to form words. I have nightmares of the audience where they point and laugh at me. To make it that much worse, during some of these dreams, I'm naked. But knowing Jack was somewhere in the audience helped me get through my valedictorian speech.

He stayed over late every night this past week to help me rehearse my speech until I had it memorized and wouldn't need to rely on my notes. And when my eyes connected with his part of the way into my speech today, I felt all the tension leave my body and I was able to get through it without mumbling and forgetting my words.

"Nah, you did good," Kyle says, and I thank him again.

"So, what's the plan for tonight?" Jack asks.

"Well." I side-eye Londyn. "Londyn wants to go sky diving or bungee jumping, but I think I talked her down to a good old-fashioned house party."

I laugh when Londyn sticks out her tongue at me before hopping up on the tailgate beside Kyle.

"Oh, thank God," Jack mutters feigning relief. He has no issues with sky diving. I know that because he has already gone a couple of times this year. He likes the rush of adrenaline.

"Not a fan of bungee jumping?" Trevor asks.

"Not a fan of seeing the ground rushing up to greet me while I'm only secured by a rope to my ankles," Jack corrects. "I like the security of a parachute."

I cringe, wondering how many people have died while bungee jumping. No thanks. "I'm with him on this," I say, pointing to Jack.

"Dude, are you even allowed to drink?" Kyle asks bringing us back to the party idea, but his question is directed at Jack.

"What does he mean, 'are you even allowed to drink'?" I look up at my boyfriend just in time to see the 'shut up' *look he directs at Kyle. "Jackson?"*

"It's nothing," he says, averting his eyes, running a hand through his shaggy hair.

I don't believe him.

"Dude, it's not nothing," Kyle chimes in, hopping off the tailgate of Jack's pickup truck. "You could be drafted into the SEALs. That's a big deal."

"Our little boy is going to be a Navy man." Trevor fake sniffs, drawing a line down from his eye to indicate a non-existent tear.

I don't move. I don't respond. I can't. I am speechless. Jack and I have plans. Well, had plans now I guess. Plans to get into the same schools, find an apartment off campus. One we can stay in after we get married, once we graduated college. None of those plans involve him joining the military.

*The shit thing about it is, if he had discussed it with me...
brought me into the decision-making process, I would've been fine
with it. I would have even encouraged him. But he didn't. And for
the first time in five years, I'm not sure if I even know the man who
stands in front of me now, worry clear in his sea-foam green eyes.*

*I don't realize I'm crying until Londyn quickly hops off the
truck and wraps me in her arms, turning us back towards the
school while telling the guys that we'll meet them at the party later.*

*The last thing I hear isn't Jack trying to get me to stop so he
can explain. It isn't the sound of him shouting my name or cursing.
The last thing I hear is the snick of the heavy school door as it shuts
behind us. A physical barrier between Jack and me to cement the
emotional one he just initiated between us.*

*This is not how I pictured my high school graduation day
going.*

*"He hadn't discussed this with you at all?" Londyn asks as
we sit against the wall of lockers in an abandoned hallway of the
school.*

*Everyone left as soon as the ceremony was over, so I am pretty
sure we are the only ones still in the building aside from the cleaning
staff and a few teachers. I don't care. Outside of these walls holds a
future I am not sure of anymore and the more I put off leaving the
school, the longer I don't have to face the unknown.*

*"Not at all," I reply, hugging my knees up to my chest and
resting my chin on top of them.*

"So, what are you going to do?"

*I sigh and shrug my shoulders. "I don't know, Londyn. I'm so
mad at him for not telling me he was even considering this, but I get
it, you know. We had this whole life planned out after graduation
and maybe it was too much for him or he thought he was
disappointing me by going against it." I pause, staring at the wall of
lockers across from us but not really seeing them. Our first date
plays on a loop inside my head and the words he spoke me that
night.*

*"I will always be the only one taking you home at night. The
one you fall asleep next to and wake up beside."*

I guess 'always' had an expiration date.

"I don't want him to go, but I can't hold him back. I won't hold him back."

Londyn's arms wrap around me from the side and she lays her head on my shoulder. "I'm sorry, Annika."

"It is what it is," I say in broken breaths and wipe away the fresh batch of tears sliding down my cheeks.

"Well," my best friend starts, "if this is the last time for the two you to be together then you should be making the most of it." She jumps up to her feet, pulling me up with her. "Let's go get you beautified so Jack can see what he'll be missing."

Chapter 20

DEAN

"**ARE YOU SURE?**" **DAVE** asks. I can hear the hesitancy in his voice. It's not every day that you come out to your adult daughter and have to tell her that you're dating a man she's considered an uncle her entire life.

"No," I sigh into the phone, pinching the bridge of my nose and willing the headache away. "But I have to tell her we're together."

Dave is quiet for a few beats before he says, "I wish I was there with you so we could do it together."

"Me too." I smile, picturing his smiling green eyes and instantly feel a wave of calm settling over me. "How'd Denise take everything?" I ask.

Denise is… *was* Dave's wife. Their divorce had been newly finalized the night before Dave came over for a braai, got sloshed, and spilt the beans to Rebekah about our past which inevitably led to our divorce because I couldn't deny that I was not only still viciously attracted to Dave, but that I still loved him. Maybe more so than I ever loved her, and didn't that just make me an asshole.

"She was surprisingly okay with it. You know her brother just came out as well? I think she hasn't properly processed it yet."

I can hear the underlining hurt in his voice. He's not telling me everything. I want to get him to open up to me but now is not the time, not when I'm pulling into Annika's driveway. I'll deal with Dave when I get home tonight. Our home. It's still weird to know that I can finally be with the man I've loved for more than thirty years.

"See you at home?" I ask, turning off the engine. My brows furrow when Annika doesn't step out onto the front stoop at the sound of my car pulling in. Ever since she was a little girl, she was always there to greet me when I came home. That never changed the older she got.

"Ja. I'll get us a couple of beers. See you," he says before hanging up.

Annika

I shuffle towards the front door and pull it open before the person on the other side can knock a third time. My ribs really hurt today and all I want to do is curl up on the couch with *Sons of Anarchy* and not move. But when I see my dad standing on the other side, that hope gets squashed. Especially when his eyes round in shock and then outrage. That's when I realize I may have forgotten to cover up the black eye and swollen lip Jack gave me last night.

My dad curses, pushing his way into the house and slamming the door so hard behind him that I flinch, and then wince when the movement sends a shock of pain up my side.

"What the hell happened?"

"Nothing. I'm okay." I move back to the couch and gingerly start lowering myself down when my dad appears beside me and helps steady me with an arm around one of mine.

"This isn't nothing, Peanut."

"I'm fine," I say, not wanting to tell my father that my husband, his son-in-law, is responsible for this.

Dad curses again and if I wasn't in so much pain, I'd laugh.

"Your mom's going to shit a brick when she hears about this," he says, turning to pace the length of the living room.

"No!" I reach for him and then gasp at the pain radiating from my side. "Fok," I breathe, collapsing back against the couch. "She can't..." I heave out a forced breath. "I don't want her to know. Please, Dad."

He stops his pacing long enough to study me and I cower under his gaze. It's the same look he used to give me when I was a teenager and did something he didn't approve of. I hated that look then and still do now.

"Did Jack do this?"

I flinch at the sound of his name and curse myself for my failure to not react.

"Jesus H. Christ. I'm going to kill him."

"Dad," I plead, scooting to the edge of the couch and trying to stand but then my father is there kneeling down in front of me and taking my face between his hands. His two thumbs lightly run over the bruises on my face. At the sight of his own tears pooling in his eyes, my breath hitches and I can't fight back the sob anymore.

My father pulls me gently into his arms, still paying close attention to where I may be hurting and holds me while I cry. I'm not sure how much time passes with us like this; me cradled in my dad's arms. It could've been minutes or hours but I'm not in any hurry to pull away yet. There's something about the comfort only a father's arms can provide that has me wishing I was a little girl again, when life wasn't so complicated.

"Why don't you come have dinner with Dave and me tonight? We can make up the guest room for you."

Shaking my head, I pull away and wipe the remnants of the tears away with my index fingers. "No. Jack should be home soon, and I really need to make sure he has dinner ready." I don't say that he'll be pissed if he comes home to find I'm not here. Which will inevitably spiral into him accusing me of sneaking around on him. Again. I'm not sure when he thinks I have the time to do that since I come straight home after work at the new school and am here making sure he has a hot meal for when he comes home. Not to mention that I haven't seen Nate since I handed in my resignation at P.N.P.S.

"Annika, I don't-"

"Dad, not now," I say cutting him off. "Please," I add.

He sighs and I can tell he wants to say more but refrains. I'm pretty sure if it wasn't considered kidnapping, he would carry me to the car and take me back to his house where he'll watch over me to make sure I don't sneak back over here. And honestly, I would probably let him. But every time I think about leaving Jack, guilt begins to coil in my gut and I just can't bring myself to pack the bag and leave. I settle a hand on my lower belly. At least not yet.

"Are you sure you're going to be okay?"

I nod. "Yes. It was an… accident." I want to hurl after the words leave my mouth. I swore I would never be one of those women who covers up the abuse with the word accident, but here I am. The funny thing is that I can't even blame it on falling down the stairs. There are no stairs in this house unless you count the two going down to the backyard or the three going down to the front walkway, there aren't any at school either. More than that though, I'm not even sure why I bother lying to my dad. I've never been good at keeping a poker face when it comes to him. "Jack's not…" I pause, "he's not this guy." I gesture to my face and ribs.

My dad's jaw ticks but he holds his tongue. His fists clench with what I can only assume is barely contained anger and trying to hold himself back from actually carrying me to the car and protecting me from Jack.

"I'm going to call you tonight. Make sure you answer it when I do. Please, Peanut. I need to know you're okay."

I wrap my arms back around his shoulders and pull my dad into another hug, inhaling the scent that has comforted me my whole life. "I will," I whisper against his neck.

He gives me a clipped nod then heads for the door and before I can change my mind and beg him to take me with him, he's gone.

Dean

It takes everything inside me to not march back through that door and gather up my little girl and protect her from the monster her husband has become. And if I knew I wouldn't get thrown in jail because of it, I wouldn't have hesitated, but the way she looked at me and pleaded for me to leave it alone. Well, I just hope she sticks to her promise of answering the phone when I call tonight. But I swear to Christ, if that piece of shit lays another hand on her, I'll kill him. Even if I end up getting twenty-five to life, it will have been worth it to protect my baby girl.

Forty-five minutes and a text to Dave later I pull up to the warehouse building. Various pieces of furniture in differing stages of completion are spilling out the garage doors. Nate stands over a workbench in dusty jeans and an even dustier t-shirt, holding a power sander. Not for the first time since discovering Jack wasn't really dead, do I wish my daughter had chosen this man instead. Jack may have been good for her when they were teenagers, but Nate… Nate was her other half.

"Dean," he says, turning off the sander and stepping away from the bench to shake my hand. "Wasn't expecting you around here today."

"I was around the area and figured I'd stop by. You have any new pieces I can check out?"

"Ja. Just let me put this away and I'll walk with you to the back."

Nate unplugs the sander from the outside plug and puts it back in its spot among the countless other power tools he's collected over the years, along with the ones he inherited from his uncle.

"Ready?"

"Lead the way," I say, stepping to the side and allowing him to take me through the warehouse. "Did you do all of these?" I ask, taking in the large reclaimed wooden dining room table that can easily fit ten people and maybe then some. Almost immediately my eyes tack onto a wooden coat holder that gleams in the rays of the setting sun coming in through the high windows, and then to what I'm assuming is a headboard. The designs carved into the wood are so intricate, I wonder how he was even able to achieve that much detail. When Nate remains quiet throughout my exploring, I turn back to see him rocking back and forth on the balls of his feet, his hands stuffed into the front pockets of his jeans.

"I, um… have a lot of time on my hands lately."

His unspoken words don't go unnoticed. Especially, since my daughter broke it off with him to stay with Jack.

Just the thought of that bastard has my hands curling into tight fists.

"Dean? You okay, man?"

I clear my throat and force myself to relax my hands. "I just came from Annika's."

A myriad of emotions flashes across Nate's face, but it's not the first thing I notice when I mention my daughter. No, it is the tick in his jaw and the way he averts his eyes that I notice first.

"I tried convincing her to leave Jackson."

Nate's head whips back around. I'm sure in shock that I, as her father, would be on his side rather than my son-in-law.

"She…" Nate pauses, running a finger over the top of the dining table. "She belongs with him."

I wonder how much it cost him to say that out loud.

"Jack is the last thing she belongs with."

My refusal to acknowledge Jack as a person doesn't go unnoticed, but I didn't think it would. The minute he put his hands on my daughter, he stopped existing as a human being in my eyes.

"What's going on, Dean?"

"She has a black eye and some bruised ribs."

Nate's nose flares and then he's swinging a fist through the drywall of the building. I wince when he pulls his fist back and I see the trail of blood oozing from his knuckles. Retrieving the first aid kit from where I remember it being the last time I was here; I get him to sit on a dusty stool while I clean and bandage up his hand.

"Did he?"

I nod.

"She's still at the house?" he questions, running his other hand through his hair.

"She wouldn't leave."

Silence descends around us while I finish patching him up and put the kit back. When I return, Nate is staring through the open door of the warehouse, but his eyes are glazed over like his body is here, yet his mind is miles away.

"Why are you telling me?"

"Because you care about her almost as much as I do as her father. Because you love her."

Slowly he turns to face me. His brown eyes staring into mine trying to assess what exactly it is I want him to do.

"How long has this been going on?"

I fetch us a couple of beers from the mini-fridge he keeps in the warehouse and hand one to him before popping open my own and leaning against a workbench. "Don't know. She's been avoiding contact with her mom and me for a couple of weeks. She's not our biggest fan right now."

"I heard about the divorce. I'm sorry, man."

We stand in quiet contemplation for a few more minutes before Nate tips his bottle back and drains the beer.

"Why do you still come around here, Dean? I mean, not that I'm not grateful for the business but-"

"But I can find cheaper furniture elsewhere?"

He moves to throw the empties in the garbage bin before retrieving two more beers and handing one to me which I gladly accept.

"Your uncle was a good man, Nathan. He would've been proud of what you've accomplished here," I say indicating the warehouse. I know it doesn't answer his question but I'm not sure *how* to answer him because I don't know why I still come around. I feel like maybe I owe it to Randall to check in on Nathan from time to time. Make sure he's not alone.

"You know he wasn't really my uncle."

I nod. "I know. He confided in me in one night when we got sloshed. He was a good man, Nathan."

He bops his head like he agrees with me but isn't sure how to continue talking about the one person he looked up to, even if he won't admit it.

"So, what are we going to do about Jack?"

"We?"

Nate shrugs, emptying his second beer and tossing it in the bin. "Like you said, I love her."

It should make me feel uncomfortable hearing him tell me how he feels about my daughter, but this whole thing is weird. Me coming to hang out with her ex included, but I've always thought of Nathan as the son I never had.

"I tried asking her to leave but she won't." I drain my beer and toss is in the bin along with his. "Maybe she'll listen to you."

"And what makes you think that?"

I begin walking back out into the newly darkened sky and pause beside my car. "Because she loves you. Protect my baby girl, Nathan," I say and then climb in and start the engine.

Chapter 21

Annika

"I'M SORRY, MOM. I think I'm just going to have a quiet night at home with a glass of wine. I have a lot of marking to catch up on too," I say into the phone, feeling guilty yet again that I'm cancelling on dinner with her, but I just can't let her see me like this.

The black eye has faded a bit but it's still noticeable even through multiple layers of cover up and foundation. It's bad enough that my dad unexpectedly saw me like this a few days ago.

I hear her sigh dramatically through the phone and brace myself for the guilt trip only a mom could pull off.

"But, honey, I haven't seen you in a few weeks and I'd really like to spend time with my only daughter."

Yup, called it.

"Look," I start when there's a knock on the front door. "I promise I'll come over on Sunday for breakfast and we can go shopping. I'll even stay for dinner if you're making mac and cheese."

"The one with the tomatoes on top?"

I nod, even though she can't see me, and move towards the front door. "That's the one. I gotta go, Mom. Someone's at the door. But I'll see you Sunday. Love you, bye," I say, hanging up and not giving her a chance to keep me on the line any longer.

When I finally pull open the door I feel like deja vu has hit me all over again. Except it's Xander, Jack's brother, staring down at me instead of Jack.

"What are... How are you...?"

Xander grimaces, running a hand through his too long brown hair and hikes the strap of his backpack higher on his shoulder.

"Jack never told you I was coming?" he asks, sheepishly. His gaze averted to his shoes.

"Uh, no, he never mentioned you coming," I say, quickly making sure my hair is covering the side of my face with the black eye before he looks up again.

When his head does pop back up to take me in, his eyes narrow and I try not to squirm.

"What are you doing?"

"What am I doing what?" I ask, playing dumb.

Xander comes towards me, dropping his backpack just inside the door but his steps don't falter until he's standing within inches of me. I don't look up, afraid that if I do, my hair will fall away from my face.

"Why is your hair all in your face, Nik?"

I shrug. "I've been trying out new hairstyles. Got bored," I say, trying to keep my voice even.

Then he's taking my chin between his fingers and tipping my head back. Xander curses when my hair does exactly what I fear it would and falls away to reveal the black eye and bruises.

"What the hell happened to you?"

I jerk my face from his fingers and turn towards the kitchen, giving him my back. "It's nothing. Got into a little... altercation," I say, hoping he buys it.

175

"Shit," I hear his footsteps follow me onto the tiled floor. "I'd hate to see the other guy."

My hand pauses momentarily at his words while reaching for a mug. A tornado of emotions swirling in my gut. I'm grateful that he's taking my excuse at face value, especially after the confrontation with my father earlier. But at the same time, if anyone should be able to call my bullshit aside from my parents, it's Xander. Even though I can't bear to see his face if he finds out his brother was the *other guy*.

"Yeah," I reply, going about the room making us both a mug of tea.

It's only when I'm handing him his, do I realize that I never actually asked if he wanted one. I give him an embarrassed smile but Xander laughs it off and thanks me after taking it from my hands.

"So, this is the house you grew up in, huh?" he asks, while taking in everything from the white tiled backsplash with strawberries in the middle, to the giant cookie jar in the shape of a strawberry in a corner of the counter, and finally to the red kettle I had used a few seconds ago, before his eyes settle back on me and he raises an eyebrow in silent question.

I laugh behind my mug. "What can I say? I like strawberries."

"Uh-huh." He grins teasingly.

"Hey," I backhand his arm playfully, forgetting the pain in my ribs for a few seconds. "At least it's not *all* red or strawberries."

He groans, "Thank God for small miracles." Then laughs, depositing his mug on the counter and pulling me into his chest. "I missed you," he mumbles into my hair.

"I missed you too, X." I slide my arms around his waist, careful not to spill the burning liquid from my cup on his back, and hug him back.

176

Xander and I hang out around the house, shooting the shit and catching up on things we've missed in each other's lives since I moved to Cape Town. I mean, we talked on the phone, but I always felt like it wasn't the same as having him close by. We also talk about how weird it is that Jack isn't dead, and if Xander notices my slight tensing at his brother's name then he doesn't let on.

At about four in the afternoon, I start making dinner so Jack can eat right after he walks in the door from the bar where he works under the table. Xander jumps in to help slice up the meat in strips while I slice the peppers and onion and grate the cheese for the fajitas.

I've just retrieved a couple of beers from the fridge, popped one open and handed it to Xander when the front door opens then snicks shut. Jack rounds the corner to the kitchen wearing a pair of new dark wash jeans and a white golf shift with the clothing company's logo on the right breast pocket. I hand him the second beer and go back to check on the chicken and peppers in the pan.

"Dinner's ready. We can eat at the table or outside if you guys like?"

"Smells good in here," Jack says, placing a hand on my arm and giving it a hard squeeze while pressing a soft kiss to my temple. He's standing so close that Xander isn't able to see the hand squeezing my arm through my sweater but can see the gentle, loving kiss. It's only when I turn and acknowledge my husband with a smile, does he let go and turn to his brother.

With a quick glance over my shoulder I start wondering that maybe I was wrong and Xander had seen the painful grip Jack had around my arm because he's looking at me. His eyes narrow into slits and his head cocks to the side. His attention on me is broken when Jack turns to face him and suggests they take their beers outside while I get dinner ready on the table. Because God forbid he has to make his own plate. I swear, this was not the man he was when I married him or even before he left on that last mission. Hell, this wasn't even the man he was when he first appeared on my doorstep again, but sometime between then and now something snapped inside him that turned him into this... this monster.

I sigh, dropping my head and half-heartedly stirring the mixture in the pan. That isn't fair to him. I know he's seen a lot of shit out in the world and he's just learning how to not be a soldier anymore.

Plating all three meals, I pick up two and walk them out to the covered carport where Jack and Xander are sitting around a folding table. Both of them are leaning back in their chairs, one ankle thrown over a knee, and a beer in hand. I place a plate down in front of each of them and then go back to fetch them more beers before picking up my own food, a glass of water, and joining them. Xander eyes the water but doesn't say anything, and I relax a little. It's not like me to not have a glass of wine or join the guys in a beer during dinner so I know the fact that I opted for water is a little suspicious but I'm not ready to answer questions about it yet.

The boys head back into the house after we've finishing eating and I grab up all the dishes from the table and head in after them. As I wait for the sink to fill with water and suds, I glance out at the picture window and see dark grey clouds begin to roll in. *Thank God, I had taken down the washing earlier in the day*, I think and then go about washing the dinner dishes.

I'm about halfway through when Jack comes back into the kitchen and opens the fridge, bending down to get a better look.

"Where's Xander?" I ask, thinking it's an innocent enough question. Man, am I wrong.

The door of the fridge slams closed and then Jack is crowding in behind me, his hands gripping my biceps hard enough to leave nail imprints in my skin even despite the sweater I'm wearing.

"What do you care where my brother is? You going to fuck him too?" Jack snarls by my ear.

"What? Don't be-" I stop myself before the words are out, but Jack doesn't miss it.

He spins me around to face him and grips my arms again, this time I whimper at how hard he is digging into my skin.

"You were going to call me stupid, weren't you?" He seethes between clenched teeth.

"N-No. I wasn't. I swear," I cry out, seeing his hand already rising in my peripheral.

He doesn't get a chance to swing though because suddenly there's another hand gripped around his wrist and pulling him back.

"What the fuck's your problem man?" Xander says, stepping between me and Jack.

"None of your goddamn business," he hisses. His face turns a red that rivals the kettle behind him and his hands clench into fists so tight his knuckles are turning white.

"Since when do you put your hands on her?"

"Since she's my fucking wife and I can do whatever the hell I want with her."

I freeze having never heard Jack talk about me like that before. Then I wonder if he's always thought of me as some property he owns but was just skilled at acting like a gentleman that I never noticed. I shake off the ridiculous thought. Of course, he was never like this before.

"You're drunk," Xander scoffs. He looks like a raging bull ready to ram his brother through a wall. I don't want either of them to get hurt so I tentatively reach out and put a hand on his arm, willing him to back down. Jack notices the gesture and his nose flares. I

179

immediately remove my hand, but the damage is done. I'm going to pay for that later when Xander leaves.

His eyes are bright when he half turns to me, still keeping his brother in his line of sight. "Did he give that to you?" he asks, nodding his head at the black eye.

I drop my gaze and my head. "N-No. Like I said, it was an altercation with one of the other teachers at work," I say because if I don't say anything, if I don't defend Jack somehow, then tonight is going to be infinitely worse than previously nights.

Xander pinches my chin between his thumb and forefinger just like he did when he first arrived and forces me to look up at him. "Don't lie to me. If he did this, I'll take you away from here right now, Annika."

I gulp in air and shake my head. Feeling tears begin to pool in my eyes but I blink them back. "He didn't do this," I lie, my voice so low in the eery quiet of the kitchen.

Jack steps up to us then, wraps an arm around my shoulders and pulls me back into him, away from Xander and his prying eyes.

"There you have it big bro. Now, get out." He tips his head to the side and I gasp. Certainly, he won't kick his brother out after Xander flew for hours just to come visit him.

Xander's green eyes ping pong between Jack and I. Anger is radiating from him in waves. I want to ask him, no… beg him to stay because Jack won't dare do something with another person staying in the house, but it's like my lips are Superglued shut and my feet are planted firmly to the floor when Xander turns and heads out. I hear him grab his backpack and other luggage from their place still by the front door and then a door opens and closes. He's gone.

"He has the hots for you."

"Fuck you," I roar spinning around and pounding my fists into Jack's chest.

He grabs my wrists with such force that I whimper, afraid he'll snap the bones. His face flames red as he grabs hold of a chunk of hair and pulls me alongside him. It hurts so much that I have to almost run to keep up with him or he'll pull a chunk out of my head.

When we get to the master bedroom, he pushes me through the door and I barely have enough time to brace myself before I land hard on my hands and knees. He's on me in the next second, flipping me on my back.

"You do not get to fight me, and you won't ever run from me," he snarls, his fingers tightening around my neck as I gasp for air. "But even if you did there's nowhere on this earth you can run where I won't find you."

"Jack," I wheeze trying desperately to draw air into my lungs. I can't pass out. If I pass out, I lose any chance of getting out of here alive and I need to live if only to tell Nate that I love him. I am so sorry for leaving him, for making him think that I didn't care about him.

Jack turns me around, pulling my arms behind my back and shoving me face first on the bed, wedging his knee between my legs as he binds my arms together with a shirt that was discarded on the floor last night.

"If you're going to go around whoring yourself out to my brother and that other asshole, I think I'm gonna have to teach you who you belong to."

He pulls on the shirt, drawing my arms even farther back until I scream in pain. I'm pretty sure he just dislocated one of my shoulders. The pain is unbearable, but I won't give him the satisfaction of reacting any more to him than I already have. I pray that if death is coming for me that it comes quick.

The sound of his belt being drawn through the loops of his jeans and his zipper lowering are the last sounds I hear before the leather material is placed between my lips and secured around my head. I mentally check out and take a trip back in time to Nate and I lounging on an outdoor sofa at Dunes Beach Restaurant & Bar.

Nate.

I'd give anything to be with him right now instead of living this nightmare.

When Jack's done, he crawls off me, leaving me laying on my stomach with my hands still bound, and cum running down my thighs.

"If you leave me I'll kill you," he says, and leaves me like this while he goes to shower.

Chapter 22

TURNS OUT THAT THE shoulder I thought Jack dislocated last night, is indeed actually dislocated. Or was. I've just thanked the doctor who immobilized my shoulder in a sling. I lean my head back against the raised hospital bed when Xander and Nate come barreling through the door.

My first thought is why the hell are they together? They've never met each other before. My second thought is that I don't really give a shit because the pain meds the nurse gave me has me feeling all giggly and light. Then my dad pushes through behind them and my first question is answered.

"Annika, what happened?" Dad asks, rushing to my side. The one not in a sling.

I roll my head to face him, a goofy grin on my face. "Hi, Daddy." Damn, these pain killers are sweet.

"What the hell did they give her?" Nate asks. At least I think it's Nate.

"Really strong pain meds, apparently," Xander chimes in.

My dad shakes his head and curses while I giggle. "They could've given her Tylenol #3s and she'd be just as loopy." He looks to Xander. "You don't remember what she was like when she was younger and had a cold?"

Xander's eyes widen before his lips tip up into a wide grin. "Shit. Yeah, I forgot."

"So, this is normal?" Nate asks, gesturing to me. I take hold of his hand before he has a chance to drop it back to side, and bring it in close to my cheek, rubbing it like I'm scenting him. Momentarily forgetting about the bruises on my cheeks from the belt.

"When did they say we could take her outta here?"

I'm so enthralled with Nate's skin against mine that I lose track of who is talking.

"We can take her now. Just have to keep an eye on her while she's on the meds, but the doc said they'll start waning off in a few hours."

That's my dad... I think. Shit, I should start paying attention but then Nate's other hand is in my hair and my eyes roll back. It feels so good to have his hands on me again. The more he massages his fingers across my scalp, the heavier my eyes become until sleep takes me.

Chapter 23

"SO YOU'RE STAYING WITH him out of some sick sense of obligation?" Nate asks, leaning against the brick wall of the house, arms crossed over his wide chest.

"Yes. No. I don't know," I huff feeling defeated. It's been a few days since dislocating my shoulder and he and Xander, along with my dad, found me in the hospital room. I had forgotten that mom and dad are still listed as my emergency contacts. I hadn't bothered to change it when Jack reappeared, and I'm relieved for it. I don't know what would've happened if Jack had come to get me at the hospital.

"Nika," Nate says, his voice softening. "You don't owe him anything. Not anymore."

"He's right, Annika. My brother isn't the same person he used to be," Xander chimes in.

I take a couple of steps back, my eyes bouncing between the two men. "What is this? Some kind of intervention? Look," I say, folding my good arm protectively over the sling holding my other, and effectively closing myself off. "I'm not going to be one of those wives who turns their backs on their husband just because he came back different after a mission. I'm not doing that to Jack."

Nate curses, turns, and begins to pace along the edge of the grass while Xander's eyes narrow into slits. I gave

Jack some bullshit excuse about my dad needing me to spend a couple of days at his house to help him out with a project. But I couldn't put off coming home any longer. Today is my first day back. Xander and Nate insisted on escorting me home, but thankfully Jack's still out. The mountain of empty bottles in the bedroom and along the kitchen counter doesn't bode well for me though, and this conversation proves it.

"And what if he kills you one day?"

"Well, I'll be dead so what does it matter?"

"Fucking Christ." Nate grips his hair, his head tilting up towards the cloudless sky. "That's the whole fucking point, Annika. You'll be dead. He's not just going to stop. One night he's going to come home so fucking sloshed that he won't know what he's doing. What if he doesn't stop? What if he literally beats you to death? What then?"

"Nate," Xander hedges.

"No," he says, his face flushing red as he stares me down and I try really hard not to cower under the weight of it. "She needs to hear this. It's not a matter of if he'll kill you, Annika. It's a matter of when."

"He won't take it that far," I say, my words barely above a whisper.

Now it's Xander's turn to curse. "You can't possibly know that, Nika. When the memories get to be too much and he can't distinguish between them and reality anymore, you'll just be another person who's in his way."

That's just it. Someone who's in Jack's way to get back home. Back to me. These guys don't get that though. Still, I have to believe that there's hope for Jack to become the man he was before he was taken prisoner. I know he's in there somewhere, I just have to keep fighting.

"I'm not leaving," I say, raising my chin and staring both men down.

Nate freezes in his pacing, his entire body going still at my words. Xander's face falls. I'm expecting them both to keep arguing with me over this, so I'm surprised when Nate just stands there blinking at me, until slowly he puts his hands on his hips and hangs his head.

"I can't watch you do this, Annika. I'm sorry," he says, giving me a pained look and then moving towards the door leading out to the driveway.

"Nate?" My voice hitches.

He doesn't stop. Nate pulls open the door and the whooshing sound it makes when it swings closed behind him feels like the final period at the end of our story. My chin trembles and I manage to cover my mouth with my hand right as a sob escapes and I fall to my knees.

"You know I love you, Nika. You'll always be my little sister," Xander says, kneeling beside me and putting his arms around me to help me up. When I'm standing on my own, he drops his arms and takes a couple of steps back. "But Nate's right. Seeing you like this. Knowing what Jack's capable of…"

"X…" I start, pleading for him to stay.

He drops his chin to his chest and shakes his head. "I'm sorry, Annika." And then he too is gone.

Chapter 24

"'ELLO."

"Xander," I croak. Wincing at the pain in my lower belly. I squeeze my eyes closed and try not to think too much about the warm liquid running down my legs as I lay curled in the fetal position in the middle of kitchen. Exactly where Jack left me.

"Annika?" His voice sounds hesitant and when I don't answer right away, it changes to worry. "Christ, Annika. Where are you? What's happened?"

The loud music I heard when he first answered the phone gets dimmed until there's no background noise.

"Jack…"

I don't say anything else. I don't have to. Xander curses and I think I hear him say that he's on his way but the darkness around my vision begins creeping in again and I can't hold it back this time.

"Hurry," I whisper into the phone before everything goes dark.

"Annika! Nika!"

The first thing I notice when I come to are big, strong hands cupping my face. The second thing I notice are Xander's wide green eyes filled with worry and concern as he leans over me, checking me over.

I'm still laying on the white kitchen tile -well, used to be white kitchen tile- where Jack left me after beating me and then kicking my stomach and head repeatedly until I passed out. I curl my arms around my middle, already feeling the loss somehow. I hadn't even made it past the first trimester. A sob escapes me, and I reach for Xander.

"I got you baby girl," he coos, sliding one arm under my knees and the other under my arms to lift me and cradle me in his hold.

I wrap mine around his neck and allow my head to rest in the curve, breathing him in and allowing it to calm me.

"You're going to be okay," he says, gently placing me in the passenger seat of my car.

Xander shuts the door then jogs around to the driver's side. The roar of the engine starting up a second later.

"Your parents are meeting us at the hospital."

I want to tell him that he shouldn't have called them. That they don't need to worry about this on top of their divorce, but I don't have the energy. Whether from loss of blood or just not having the energy to defend Jack anymore. Not after this.

I rest my head back against the seat and close my eyes. Preferring to drift off while Xander drives to the hospital than think about my husband or the loss of our child.

I refuse to think of it as a living being because somewhere deep inside, I feared this would happen. My throat burns when I try to swallow down another bout of tears. I've already cried too much where Jack is concerned. A thought niggles in my brain that it won't be the last time I have to choke back tears because of him.

"Where's Dad and Xander?" I ask my mom a little while later when I come to again.

I'm in a different room than last time, and am actually wearing those awful gowns they give patients instead of the t-shirt I was wearing when I came in with a dislocated shoulder.

"They went to get some food and coffee," my mom says, sitting in the visitors' chair beside the bed. "How are you feeling?"

I try to sit up but then instantly drop back down again, groaning in pain.

Mom gives me a small, sad smile and takes my hand in hers, careful not to jostle the IV.

"Baby," she begins. A line forming across her forehead. "Why didn't you tell me?"

About what? I want to ask since I'm not entirely sure of which thing she's referring too. She quickly reads my confused expression correctly and continues.

"About the baby…. And about Jack. The hospital called me when you dislocated your shoulder but when I called your dad he said it was an accident. That you were playing field hockey when it happened."

I drop my eyes from hers and turn my head to look out the window. The view is nothing speculator. Just a bunch of other buildings but further in the distance, I can see Table Mountain.

"It wasn't a field hockey accident, was it?" Her voice is low, almost a whisper when she says it.

I shake my head and then wince when it causes a headache.

"Was it… did Jack do that too?"

I nod, slowly turning back to face my mom.

190

"Oh, honey." Her voice catches on a sob and then she's leaning over me in a hug.

"I'm so sorry, Mom." My own tears start flowing as I hug her back.

"You have absolutely nothing to be sorry for, you hear? Nothing," she states pulling back and wiping away the tears on my cheeks before wiping her own. She takes up her seat on the ugly blue chair again and lets out a slow breath glancing up at the ceiling to gather herself a bit more before dropping her eyes back to me. "Do you remember what the doctor said? You were still pretty out of it when you first woke up."

I scrunch up my nose and try to think. "I think so. I have a concussion and a… broken rib?" And I'm no longer pregnant. I don't say the last part out loud, but it still hangs in the air like a heavy cloud.

She takes my hand again and gives it a gentle squeeze. "We'll help you get through this. They taped up your ribs. He said taking deep breaths is going to be painful for a while but he still wants you to do it a couple times a day."

She pauses and then opens her mouth like she's going to continue, but shuts it again. Looking unsure.

"What?"

"I want you to come stay with me while you're recovering. Both your Dad and I agree that we're not letting you go back to that house while Jack is still there."

I don't miss the way she braces herself for an argument, but she's not going to get one.

"Okay," I say.

Mom's quiet for several seconds and I think I've finally shocked her into silence.

"Okay," she repeats when she's found her voice again.

Xander

I'm still vibrating when Dean and I leave Annika's hospital room to go in search of food and coffee. But when we do find a little café a couple of blocks away, my stomach churns, not at the thought of food but at what my brother has done.

Even though I'm older, I always sort of looked up to Jackson. Everything seemed to come easy for him. Girls. Football. School. The Navy. I mean, yeah our parents practically disowned him when he enlisted but that never seemed to slow him down or discourage him. I knew that I still never measured up to him in their eyes after that.

I was the screw up. The bad boy. The son they had to bail out a couple of times because I couldn't control my temper. I'd had it fairly under control by the time I graduated high school. And by the time college rolled around, I wasn't fighting anymore. At least not outside of the illegal rings I'd attend on the odd Friday when I needed a stress release.

It fucking gutted me that I couldn't protect Annika from my own brother. Or that I couldn't protect my brother from himself. I should've known that he sounded different on the rare times he called after he returned. I just thought that he was still learning to adjust to civilian life. I didn't know his drinking had gotten this bad. Bad enough for him to beat his wife.

I have to stop abruptly on the sidewalk and bend over with my hands on my knees as I try valiantly to breathe in as much air as possible before I hurl.

She was pregnant.

Annika was pregnant with their kid, my niece or nephew, when Jack went after her. I don't think I can ever forgive him for what he did to her.

"Hey, you okay?" Dean asks, coming to place a hand on my back.

I nod and suck in another lungful of air. When I'm confident that my earlier lunch isn't going to make a repeat appearance, I straighten up to my full height.

When I take in Dean standing beside me with a concerned look on his face, I realize that I can't just let Jack get away with this.

Annika is like a sister to me. Dean and Rebekah have always treated me as more of a son than my own parents had. They still do after not seeing me for years. Seeing Dean and Rebekah again felt like coming home. I was always welcome in their house… in their lives, no matter where they were.

That sick feeling in the pit of my stomach is back. What if they want nothing to do with me now?

I convince myself that what I'm about to do is as much about Annika laying in that hospital bed all cut up and bruised, than it is about me needing to feel like I'm an accepted part of a family.

"Xander, I know that look."

"Dean, I have to. I can't let him get away with this."

He lets out a harsh breath, looking up and down the side walk we're standing in the middle of.

"I've always thought of you as a son, Xander. When I try to picture what Kody would've grown up to be if he were still here, I picture you. When you started fighting in those underground rings I was a little disappointed," he pauses, and I frown not liking where this is going. "But you seemed to thrive in your life, so I learned to be okay with it. I mean, I wasn't your father so I couldn't tell you what to do. But I also hoped that you knew I was always here for you."

"How'd you know?" I made sure nobody in my family found out about the fighting. That included Annika and her parents.

"I have my ways, Son."

That one word has the potential to rip me open.

He places a hand on my shoulder and squeezes. "You boys were always so protective over her. You more than Jackson." He studies me closely then. "And I can see how much you want to protect Annika now, even from your brother."

"No man should ever place his hands on a woman," I grit out, balling my hands into fists.

"I agree," he says. "And if I didn't have to go back to the hospital, I'd be right there with you."

I'm ready to tell him that I'm going back over to the house no matter what he thinks but then his words register, and all the fight drains out of me momentarily.

"What?"

He pats me on the back then drops his hand and steps away.

"Go do what you need to do. Call me if you need me to come get you."

I nod then turn to head back to the hospital parking lot where I left Annika's car.

"Xander?"

I pause, looking over my shoulder at Annika's father.

"Leave him breathing. I may know of someone else who may want a turn when he finds out."

I give him another clipped nod before continuing in my haste to get back to Annika's house and my brother.

Annika

"Where's Xander?" I ask my dad when he steps back into my hospital room without my brother-in-law.

"He had something to take care of. He'll be back to check on you later," he says, moving closer. But the way he avoids making direct eye contact makes me feel like he's hiding something from me.

"What aren't you telling me, Dad?" I ask, placing my hands behind me and trying to lift myself up. The reminder of my broken ribs comes screaming back when pain so deep it sucks the breath out of me, radiates from my side.

"Are you okay, honey?" Mom asks from my one side and I nod to try and reassure her, but I'm still having a hard time catching my breath, and the ones I am managing hurt like hell.

"He'll be okay, Peanut," my dad says from my other side and somehow with just those few words, I know.

For the first time in a very long time I close my eyes and pray. I pray that Xander doesn't get killed.

Chapter 25

IT TURNS OUT THAT prayer really does work.

Xander didn't make it out without his fair share of cuts and bruises. In fact, he was brought into the same room as me several hours later with what I'm assuming is a knife wound, with what I'm able to piece together from various whispers when the curtain is pulled between our beds. When I try asking, Xander says that he is okay and to not worry any longer. That Jack won't be bothering me anymore. I assume from the lack of police presence outside our hospital room or breaking news of a murder, he left him alive.

I'm released a few days before Xander when the doctor is convinced that I'm not going to develop a lung disease or something, but I'm once again relegated to the care of one of my parents since I'm going to need some help during my recovery. Since I stayed with my dad with my broken collarbone, Mom insists that I move in with her until I've recovered, and they've helped me figure out my next move with Jack. The doctor says that Xander is going to need just as much, if not more, care once he's released. Mom already sets out a plan to move him out of his hotel room and into her house. I think this whole situation has sent her info full mother hen mode. It's kinda cute right now, but I have no doubt that her hovering is going to get old fast. Especially because I've been so used to being independent since Jack and I got married.

"Really, Rebekah, I'm okay," Xander says to Mom as she fluffs the pillow beneath his leg again and asks if she can get him anything from the kitchen; water, a cool drink, a snack.

He's been out of the hospital for a couple of days and she's still hovering just as bad as she was the first day we were allowed to bring him home.

The two of us have been spending our days camped out on the couch, watching movies and playing video games. My cousin, Clint, brought over his PlayStation 4 for us to use as well as a couple of games including NHL 19. Xander squealed like a little girl – as much as he could with a knife wound in his side – and has been coaxing me into playing with him every day.

My dad has also come over a couple of times to check on us. At first, things between he and my mom were so intense it made everyone in the room with them uncomfortable, but it seems like the more he comes over, the easier it's getting between the two of them.

Just before Xander got released from the hospital, my dad sat me down and talked to me about him and Dave officially being in a relationship. He apparently had wanted to have this conversation when he came over that day and discovered my black eye but since then, other things have taken precedence over this conversation.

It's taken me longer than I care to admit to accept that the picture I had of my dad wasn't who he really is, but he's even better. I've always been wary of anyone who doesn't appear to have secrets. That one thing that makes them less than perfect. For the longest time, I couldn't find any flaws in my father. He was always just my hero. The one man in my life who I looked up to. The person who could do no wrong in my eyes. Knowing that he kept this secret from my mom and me makes him seem more human now. The act of keeping the secret not the actual secret itself. I couldn't care less if he was straight or gay, I still love him the same. If it's at all possible I think I look up to him more now.

It's not easy coming out anywhere in the world, but especially in countries like South Africa where acceptance isn't at the level it should be. Sure, things may be tolerated, but tolerance isn't acceptance. It's not loving someone despite their differences or flaws. It's like that friend you can't stand to be around, but you put up with them because you have to.

"What'd you do that for?" I gently nudge Xander in his non-wounded side, careful not to jostle him too much though. He may be healing nicely and acting like he's not in pain anymore but I'm not buying it. Plus, the bandage still wrapped around his side says he's far from being healed.

"You were sleeping on the game," he says just as his video game character takes a slap shot on the net.

"Fucker," I mumble when the puck goes in and Xander hoots and hollers. Well, as much as he can.

By the way he's acting you'd think we were playing an actual hockey game and not the PlayStation. Xander's team takes the lead and he eventually wins the game. His grin is wide when he sets the controller down on the coffee table and leans back against the couch, still favouring his right side.

"You cheated," I pout, setting my matching controller down beside his.

Xander chuckles. "I did not cheat. I don't even think that's possible with this game. I beat you fair and square."

I stick my tongue out at him which makes him laugh harder but then he winces and curses, his hand going to his side and I immediately flinch in guilt and move farther away into my side of the couch.

"Stop that," he grits out between harsh breaths.

"Stop what?"

"Annika," he warns, "we agreed you'd stop feeling so damn guilty about things you can't control."

I slump back against the arm of the couch and lift my legs, gently placing them on his lap. "I know. I know. It's just going to take some more getting used to."

Xander sighs, taking one foot in his large hands and massaging the underside. I groan, leaning back to get comfortable.

"Why didn't you tell me, Nika?"

"What about?" I moan when his thumb presses into the heel of my foot.

"About the baby."

I still. Trying to keep my breathing even, which has slowly gotten easier as the days go on.

"I was scared," I finally say. Xander lets go of my foot and I sit up, folding one leg up on the couch while I turn to face him. "Jack and I were already having problems and I was afraid that if I told him or anyone about the pregnancy, that it would make things worse. He wasn't exactly in his right mind."

Xander grunts, folding his arms cross his chest. "You could've told me what was happening. Maybe I could've... been here sooner." His Adam's apple bobs with each harsh swallow but his eyes are trained on the far wall.

I shuffle closer to him slowly so as not to jostle my side too much and rest my head on his shoulder.

"You're here now," I whisper.

"What are you going to do now? I'm not letting you go back to that house," he says before I have a chance to answer his question.

"Londyn's already looking into lawyers back in Miami since we were married there and it's likely to go through faster there than it is here."

"Even though you technically live here now?"

I shrug. "Apparently Jack was only here on a temporary visitor's visa. His six months are up next week which means he'll have to leave and go back to the States, unless he's already applied for an extension."

"It's only been six months since he's been back?" Xander lets out a harsh breath like he can't figure out where the time has gone.

"A lot has happened in six months," I agree.

"I put in my resignation at work," Xander says suddenly, shocking me.

"You what?" I ask, moving away from him so I can see his face better.

"I put in my resignation," he says again like it's no big deal that he just left a company he helped build from the ground up. K&K Construction wouldn't be where it is today if it weren't for Xander Carter.

"W-why would you do that?" I squeak.

Now it's Xander's turn to shrug. "Got nothing waiting for me back home. Our parents disowned me long before Jack." He turns to face me, a small tentative smile pulling at the corner of his lips. "Figured I would move here and give the Cape Town way of life a try."

"You're serious?"

His face falls and I immediately throw myself at him, forgetting about the knife wound in his side and my broken rib.

"Ow, fuck, shit!" he exclaims and I scramble back in time to see Xander turn a shade of white I've never seen before.

"Are you okay?"

He nods slowly, taking deep breaths through his nose and letting them out through his parted lips. When he no longer looks like he's going to get sick all over Mom's couch, he reaches for me. Gingerly, this time, I fold myself in his arms.

"I'm serious, Nika. There's nothing left for me in the States. I mean, that's if you still consider me part of your family." He says the last part so quietly that if I wasn't curled up in his arms I would've missed it.

"You'll always be my family, X. No matter what happens between Jack and I, I'll always consider you my big brother."

We sit in companionable silence for a little bit and it's only when I hear him take in a shuddering breath do I realize that Xander's crying. I tighten my arms around him a little more, careful to avoid the wound in his side this time.

"You can't get rid of me that easily," I joke and feel some of the tension in my body melt away when Xander chuckles.

Later that night when everyone is settled in for bed, with Xander on the couch and Mom down the hall in her room, I put in a quick FaceTime call to Londyn since it's a little before six there and she should be home from work by now.

"How are you doing?" Londyn says as soon as the call connects, and her face fills the screen.

"Better today." Which is the truth. It was way easier to move around today without feeling like I had to take a breathing break. I was even able to help Mom with dinner this evening.

"Good. I'm glad. How are things over there?"

"Things are... I don't know. I still haven't decided how to go about this whole divorce thing with Jack. Do I give him a heads-up and tell him it's coming, or do I just blindside him?"

The camera jostles and moves as Londyn walks down the hallway of her apartment and into what I'm assuming is the kitchen when I hear the sound of a coffee maker grinding the beans.

"Do you feel like you owe it to him to warn him after everything?"

"God, I don't know Londyn. I feel like I owe it to our history, but I don't really want to see him again."

She's quiet for a few beats and I can see her worrying her lip. Trying to figure out the best way to say what she's thinking without upsetting me.

"Just say it, L."

"Okay, but you can't get mad at me."

"I won't. Just say whatever it is you're thinking."

Her shoulders deflate a little as she looks into the camera nervously. "I don't think you owe him anything anymore, Annika. I think you've already given him enough years of your life. Hell, until recently you were still ready to walk into hell to defend him. I feel like it would be so easy for him to blame his PTSD for what he did to you, if you do go see him, just so that he can get you back. But he could've gotten help, for PTSD, for the nightmares... for the drinking, but he chose not to."

"Are you done?" I ask my best friend when she pauses to take a breath.

"Not quite. He doesn't deserve you, Annika. Not anymore."

"I feel like I should've done more for him, L. Like, maybe I should've forced him to look into support groups here or begged him to quit drinking. Maybe I should've told him about the baby."

Londyn's brows pull together and her eyes narrow at me through the camera. The lighting is already dark so her bright eyes don't stand out as much but with them narrowing at me like they are now, they appear almost black.

"You had an impossible decision. To choose between your love for your husband and your love for your unborn child. You did what any other mother would and chose your child. You made the right choice, Annika. You can't possibly know if Jack would've changed for the better when he found out or for the worse."

"It wasn't enough," I say, wiping at the tears beginning to fall. "I didn't do enough."

"Oh, honey. I wish I was there to give you a big hug. I'll just have to give you extra big ones when I see you at Christmas."

"What do you mean?"

"My boss is sending me to London to help set up the office there," she grins.

"London? London, England?!"

She laughs. "That's the one."

"Shit, L! You'll be able to fly out whenever you want."

"Well, not quite that often. It might be less expensive than flying from the States but it's still an eight-hour flight."

I wave her off. My tears forgotten. "But you'll be so close." I pause, the rest of her statement sinking in. "Wait, did you say Christmas?"

"I did." Her grin is back. "I had to beg, plead, and promise my first-born child but I was able to get a week off at Christmas. So, I'll be flying over on the twentieth and leaving the day after Christmas."

That's like three months away. I can't hold back a fresh wave of tears anymore. Just knowing that I'll have my two best friends close again is making me overly emotional.

"Woah, you okay?"

I nod and try to smile through the tears, but it only aids in make me look even more a mess.

"I'm okay. I'm just really happy that you and Xander will be close again."

Her phone pings from somewhere behind her MacBook and Londyn disappears out of camera view for a couple of seconds before re-appearing in her seat with Kingston.

"I have to take this call from work, Annika, but I'll give you a shout tomorrow."

"Okay. Sounds good. Love you."

"Kingston and I love you too," she says and then the video chat cuts off.

Chapter 26

"YOU SURE YOU'RE GOING to be okay going over there by yourself?" My mom asks, standing between me and the front door of her house.

"I'm sure. Dad is at a meeting with a client right now but then he's going to drive by the house to make sure everything's okay and fetch me," I say, giving her a reassuring smile.

She huffs, crossing her arms over her chest. "I still don't like this at all."

"Me neither," Xander chimes in, shuffling down the hall from the bathroom.

"I'm not a fan of this either, but I need to at least go and get my clothes. And you're not in any shape to start driving again," I say turning to Xander and indicating his still bandaged side.

He grumbles something about taking the damn stitches out himself sooner as he shuffles back to the couch and plonks himself down. As much as he's trying to tune Mom and I out, I know he's still listening to every word we say. Some days I wonder if he shouldn't have enlisted instead of Jack. Or at least become a police officer. He has all the protective instincts.

"I'll be back." I pull my mom in for a brief hug and kiss her cheek before grabbing the keys off the hook by the door and making my way out to the Opal in the driveway.

I shouldn't be driving either, but my ribs feel a lot better as long as I don't overreach for something or do anything to jostle my side too much. Plus, my dad switched cars with me again today so I can have the power steering and if it gets to be too much, I'll leave my car at the house and jump in with Dad. He said he doesn't mind taking Dave to go fetch the car later on if need be.

It takes me just over an hour to get to the house on the R310 freeway and when I pull into the driveway, the bukkie Jack was borrowing from dad is parked in front. I really hope he's not attempting to keep the damn thing. That's not something we need to add on the pile of shit we're dealing with right now.

"Jack?" I call out as soon as I unlock the door and push it open.

All the windows and curtains are closed, and the place smells musky. Like it hasn't been aired out in a couple of days.

"Jack? Where are you?"

I head down the hallway and check all three bedrooms and the bathroom. I return to the master bedroom on my way back down the hallway and grab a few weeks' worth of clothes, shoving them into an empty suitcase that's hiding at the back of the huge armoire.

That's one thing I'd miss about this house. My parents had it built when they first bought the house twenty-seven years ago. All it needed was to be sanded down and a new coat of polish when I bought it back from the in-between owners. It's huge and takes up half the back wall of the bedroom. I love it and hope I can find a carpenter who'll be able to create something similar to it when I find a new house.

Just the thought of finding a carpenter has my mind racing back to images of Nate. A sharp pain pings across my heart, forcing me to stop for a minute and take several deep breaths before I grab the handle of the suitcase and pull it behind me down the hall.

On a whim, I decide to check the kitchen and the carport. And I really wish I hadn't.

A scream echoes through the neighbourhood and I'm not entirely sure that it isn't me screaming. Hanging by a rope from one of the wooden beams is Jack.

The next several days pass by in a blur. This time, though, I don't have to make the call to my in-laws alone. Xander is here and so are my parents. When Deb starts spilling bullshit about how I drove her son to this, how if I was just a better wife to him then he wouldn't have turned to suicide, Xander pries the phone from my tight grip and walks away to talk to his parents in private.

It's no surprise that Deb and Ron never approved of our young marriage, but one would think that after nine years, they would've gotten over it. Apparently not. I guess they thought that I was the reason why their perfect son decided to enlist in the Navy and become a SEAL rather than become a pro-football player or doctor, or whatever the hell they had planned for him. I guess I was the reason why he came back different after being held prisoner in the Middle East for two years. It's all my fucking fault. Well, they can go fuck themselves.

When Xander comes back into the living room of my mom's house and says that his parents have not-so-politely requested that his body be sent back to Miami to be buried there, I readily agree. If they want their precious can-do-no-wrong son back then they can have him. I'm officially washing my hands of the Carter family. Except for Xander. I'm keeping him. Xander doesn't seem to have a problem with that either. Over the last few weeks, he seems to have really found his place within my family and within Cape Town. He seems happier here like maybe this is where he was always supposed to be.

We don't have a funeral for Jack in Cape Town. Instead, with help from my dad, I organize for Jack's body to be sent back to Miami and his parents. Xander and I already said our goodbyes to him during that first funeral when we thought he had died while on a mission. To us, that's when the Jack we knew had truly died. He may have continued to live physically for the next few years after that, but he was in no way the same person who left for that mission.

I thought I'd have a hard time releasing his body to his parents, but it was actually a relief. At first I felt guilty for feeling relieved. Relieved that I could put my past to rest. A past that was filled with memories of Jack. Relieved that I won't have to wake up every morning wondering if this is the day that Jack snaps and won't be able to stop before he kills me. Relieved that I won't have to endure that kind of pain again. But with Xander's and my parents' help, I'm quickly coming to the realization that it's okay for me to feel whatever I'm feeling. It's okay to feel relieved. It's okay to feel guilty, within reason, and it's okay to grieve and mourn even if the person didn't deserve it towards the end.

For the first time in a very long time, I feel free.

Chapter 27

"SOMETHING SMELLS GOOD," I say, walking into the kitchen of my mom's house.

"Good timing. Can you set the table for us, please?"

"Sure thing." I drop a kiss on my mom's cheek and then go about collecting placemats and cutlery from their drawers, followed by the plates, and go about setting the dining room table for us. "Where's Xander?" I ask when I'm done and go to fetch a few glasses.

"Your dad's taking him for a check-up and then I think they were going to get dinner with Dave."

I move out of her way when she pushes past with a steaming hot glass dish filled with homemade mac and cheese. This isn't like that boxed crap. Mom makes the white sauce from scratch and adds bacon bits to it. Then she mixes it with penne noodles and grates more cheese on top of the mixture before putting it in the oven to bake. It's so good. Sometimes she'll add thinly sliced tomatoes to the top before putting it in the oven. *Just like granny used to*, she would say when I was younger.

My mouth waters at the sight of the dish sitting in the middle of the table. After she goes to fetch the salad and takes a seat beside me, I remember that I was wanting to see how she was doing with the divorce.

"I'm okay. Really," she says, leaning across the table to fill her plate with a little bit of salad and the mac and cheese. "I think I always knew that something had happened between your dad and Dave in college, but I didn't want to acknowledge it, so I buried the suspicions deep and pretended like everything was just dandy."

"Mom," I say, filling my own plate. "You really don't have to talk about this if it makes you uncomfortable."

Her fork clangs against the plate when she lays it down. "I don't have anything against your father being gay, Annika. I told him as much when I asked for a divorce. What I do… did," she corrects, "what I did have a problem with was that he lied to me about it for years." She puts her hand up to stop me when I try to interject. "I know it was a different world back then, but he could've still confided in me. And then when I saw how he and Dave acted together that night, I knew that your father had never truly gotten over his feelings for Dave."

I try not fidget and wonder how she can feel so comfortable talking to me about all of this. Other parents would want to hide as much from their kids as they can. Not mine, though. They never tried to shelter me or hide the truth from me after I turned sixteen.

"I'm just… I'm happy that he's happy."

"And what about you, Mom?" I stab a piece of lettuce with my fork and move it around my plate. The hunger I felt earlier, dissipating.

She shrugs, taking a bite of the noodles. "I think there's somebody out there for me, but I'm in no hurry. I have all I need right here," she says, placing a hand over mine and giving it a squeeze.

"So, you're okay with everything? With Dad and Dave being a couple?"

Her lips curl into a slow smile as she takes her hand back and picks up her fork again. "I am."

Chapter 28

Twenty-nine years old

"ANNIKA?" THE DEEP VOICE says from behind me, sending my heart into a staccato rhythm. I haven't heard that voice in a year.

"Nate?" I ask after turning around and meeting the whisky-coloured eyes I fell in love with so many years ago.

After everything that happened with Jack, I often found myself wondering what happened to Nate over the years. If he was still teaching grade one at P.N.P.S. and still coaching the boys' field hockey team. I missed him. A lot. I missed us.

"Howzit?" he asks, wrapping an arm around my shoulders and pulling me into a side hug in the middle of the baking aisle.

God, he still smells the same. Like coconut rum and ocean breeze.

"Good. Good." I nod my head and avoid looking him directly in the eye.

Something about this random run-in is unnerving me and I can't put my finger on why. This man knew the most intimate places on my body, he knew the sounds I made when I... yeah. And I can't work up the courage to look him in the eye. Not only that but I feel ashamed of the way I left things. Nate was right. I should've left Jack back when he and Xander pleaded with me to. Before Xander got hurt and before I miscarried.

"Talk to me. How've you been?" He reaches out to grab my arm and move us out of the way of a lady with a buggy filled with groceries. He releases me right away when he sees me flinch at the contact. I glance up at him then, ready with an apology but words die on my tongue when his eyes turn a darker shade, the gold practically disappearing.

I clear my throat and glance down the aisle. "Things have been… okay." If okay meant only in the last six months after Jack's death. "Jack, um. He, uh… died last year," I stammer out, not sure why I feel the need to disclose that information.

I honestly don't know why half the shit leaves my mouth.

Nate rubs a hand across the back of his neck, a pained expression briefly crossing his face before it's gone. "Ja, I heard about that from your dad."

Of course, he had. Dad and Nate developed a kind of friendship back when Nate began rebuilding the closets and other pieces of furniture for my house. I hadn't been aware they had kept in touch after we broke things off, though.

Nate grips my chin between his thumb and forefinger, forcing me to look him in the eyes again. "I'm sorry, Nika. Your dad said you were the one who found him."

"Are you, really?" I ask, pinning him with a glare. Nate never was a fan of Jack.

"I am. I may not have liked the man or what he put you through, but I know how you felt about him."

I swallow hard and nod, but Nate doesn't let go of my chin. His brows pull together in a frown as he searches my eyes for what… I don't know.

"You know I'm always here for you, yeah? Things may not have worked out between us," he pauses to clear his throat. "But I'm here."

Tears I didn't know I was holding back suddenly begin rolling down my cheeks and before I know it I've thrown myself into Nate's arms, sobbing against his chest. He tries to soothe me by rubbing circles against my back but there's no stopping the dam now that's its broken.

God, my heart hurts so much. I thought I was doing well dealing with my parents' divorce, losing Nate, Dad and Uncle Dave starting to see each other, healing from the abuse, losing a baby, and then Jack's death. But if me sobbing into Nate's chest while he holds me in the middle of the grocery store is anything to go by, I'm not handling it as well as I thought. Not by a long shot.

"C'mon," Nate says, picking up the shopping basket I dropped to the ground beside us. "Let's go get a drink for old time's sake."

"Nate?" I ask around a hiccup. "Take me to Dunes."

A slow smile pulls at the corners of his lips as he stares down at me. "Dunes it is," he says, pressing a soft kiss to the top of my head.

Suggesting Dunes was my first mistake. I thought if we were in our bubble, where only the two of us exist then nothing from the outside world could touch us. I should've known it was a fairy tale. I don't know why I expected Nate to be single all this time. It isn't like I was so why should I have expected him to wait for me. But hearing him say that he was engaged to be married to another woman cut deep.

Was this how he felt when I told him I had to stop seeing him because I owed it to Jack, or when I refused to leave Jack after the abuse started.

God, I hope not.

I don't say anything. I just sit back and begin gulping down gin and tonics like they're water. Our poor server can't seem to bring them out fast enough for me, but I need something if I'm going to sit here and listen to him go on and on about his fiancée and their wedding this Christmas. He wants a small wedding on the beach somewhere, and she wants the whole nine yards. Big church, big dress, big guest list, and big party.

Through all of this, the one thing that keeps popping up in my head is, *that's supposed to be me.* I'm the one Nate's supposed to marry, but I'm not and I can't. So, I sit and gulp down another gin and tonic and paste a smile on my face, trying to be happy for him because he does look happy. And that's all I want for him.

"You were married Annika. I didn't think there could ever be anything between us," he says while I nod absently, my eyes locked on the calm, clear water of the beach in front of us.

I try not to flinch from feeling like a sword's been driven through my heart when Nate says he's glad to have me back in his life as a friend. I was just friend zoned and it's my own fucking fault. I had my chance with him, and I fucked it up.

Chapter 29

Two months later

"JISLAAIK!" NATE EXCLAIMS JUMPING away from the side of the boat.

I grin, leaning slightly over the side and barely make out the outline of a shark swimming away from the boat. *Oh, this is going to be fun.* I managed to score a couple of tickets for this shark expedition and invited Nate to join me.

"You sure you want to do this?" he asks, looking out at the vast ocean surrounding us.

"Definitely!"

"They're huge!" Chantel, Nate's fiancée, says beside him.

Oh yeah, Nate ended up buying her a ticket when she found out he was coming with me. So now I'm stuck on a boat with my ex-boyfriend and his current fiancée.

Oh joy!

Cage diving with sharks, especially Great Whites, has been on the top of my bucket list for as long as I can remember but I've always just put it off... until now. I mean, how many people can say they got to go cage diving with one of the regular divers and cameramen from *Discovery Channel's Shark Week*. Never, that's how much. But I have the opportunity to do that today, and there's nothing on this earth that'll be able to stop me from living out this bucket list item. Plus, I feel like it'll go a long way in making me start to feel like myself again, and to prove to Nate that I can be his friend and hang out with his fiancée.

After Jack put me in the hospital the last time, I began to realize that I'd been slowly losing focus on who I was and what brought joy into my life. I was aging but I wasn't really living. Jack's suicide made me realize just how short life really was, and I was just wasting it. Sure, I wasn't wasting days away in bed, but I wasn't living. I felt like I was on auto-pilot. Doing things by routine because it was so ingrained in me that I didn't have to spare a thought as to what it was I was doing. But I wasn't living. I wasn't enjoying life. Even my laughs had become fake.

No one really knows when they're going to die. But if I'm to go tomorrow, I'd probably be one of those ghosts who comes back because they have some sort of unfinished business. It's a stupid metaphor but an effective one. There's still so much I want to do before that time comes. Cage diving with sharks in False Bay is just one of those things.

I watch as Nate gingerly leans a little way over the edge, just enough to see the water below. I feel like I've come a long way in the last few months where dealing with all the hurt is concerned, and I owe a lot of that to him.

That day at Dunes with Nate, before he dropped the bomb about his fiancée, it felt good to have someone else to talk to other than my parents, Londyn, and Xander. I talked, I cried, I yelled… not at him… talked and cried some more that day. By the end of it, I was spent, and Nate was cradling me in his arms. People must have thought I was crazy, but I didn't care, and Nate didn't seem to mind either.

After I was done, he still encouraged me to talk to a counsellor. Jack may have gotten abusive towards the end, but his suicide still scarred me and left a hole in my heart. I understood why Nate may not have wanted to be the one I talked to about that, and when I brought it up he made it clear it was absolutely in no way about that. He thought I needed someone who was skilled in helping people grieve and heal from a loved one's suicide, and he was not that person. He said he hadn't ever experienced something like and that all he could do was be there when I needed an ear or a shoulder to cry on. He feared I would need that extra support a counsellor could provide. Then he dumped the news that he was engaged.

He was right though. While just having him here to talk to or even just be around when I want company but don't want to talk is amazing in itself, having a counsellor is helping tremendously.

I began seeing her twice a week for the first two months after which we decided to drop it down to once a week. However, if I need to see her more than once in a particular week, she makes time for me. I'm grateful for that. There's a lot I had to adjust to in a short amount of time and it may still take me awhile to work through it all.

Dr. Fester helped me work through my anger issues towards my dad and even invited him to participate in a session, which he gladly accepted. We both spent the entire session in tears, and I don't know about him, but I left there feeling utterly wrecked, but with a new understanding of what my dad had been going through.

Our relationship still isn't what it had once been before I learned the truth, but it's getting there. I've even started going over to have dinner with him and Uncle Dave once a week. I really have to stop calling him Uncle Dave. It just seems wrong now, but that's all I've ever known him as. Dave seems to understand and hasn't blown up at me when I've let it slip a time or two during those dinners.

"Ready?" Chris, the owner of Apex Shark Expeditions asks, zipping up his wetsuit while moving towards the back of the boat where Chantel, Nate, and I have taken up residence.

I nod enthusiastically while Nate groans, curses, and shakes his head before taking a deep breath and standing up to pull up his own wetsuit from where it was sitting around his hips. Chantel stays seated on the bench, flapping her flip-flop against her foot and texting. I didn't even know you could get cell signal this far out from the shore. She doesn't seem really into this and I wonder why she agreed to come along. She also doesn't seem like the type Nate would be into, but what do I know. I realize I sound bitter, but he kind of just dumped her coming on this trip on me this morning so I haven't had time to come to terms with her being here yet. I sigh and paste a smile on my face as I move closer to Nate.

I laugh and decide to take pity on him. "You really don't have to do this, babe." I blanch at the term of endearment that managed to sneak its way past my tongue, but Nate doesn't seem to notice my slip up, and neither does Chantel.

"Ja-nee, I told you I would do this with you."

Water sprays up the side of the boat and we all look over just in time to see a fin descend back below the surface. Nate visibly swallows but continues to zip up his suit before sitting down to pull on a swim fin. Chris goes on to tell us that since there's only three of us diving today we'll get extra time in the cage which kicks my level of excitement up another notch. The cage they have attached to the boat is big enough to fit five people and usually they have a lot more divers which limits each person's time in the cage to about twenty minutes. I don't know why not many people signed up to go diving today but hell, I'm not complaining. My shark loving heart is on cloud nine right now and the more time I can get in that cage the better.

For our first dive, Chris jumps in with us. Once the three of us are in, another guy lowers the lid of the cage, closing us in. The cold is an instant jolt to my system but after a few seconds I begin to relax and start to enjoy being back in the water. All I can see for miles on either side of the cage, is empty ocean. I chance a quick glance down, knowing a Great White's propensity for attacking from the bottom but don't see anything, which in itself should kick my nervousness into hyperdrive but it doesn't. Then I look over at Nate who's practically plastered himself to the side of the cage that backs into the boat and I can't help the grin that threatens to spread my lips. It's not the first time I've realized that this man would literally do anything for me, and if going cage diving with one of the world's biggest predators isn't proof of that, then I don't know what is.

As if I thought it into being, I see movement from my peripheral and turn back to the front of the cage in time to see a thirty-foot Great White swim past us, its dorsal fin slightly breaking the surface.

Fuck, that's a big mammal.

If someone were to tell me that I would be in a cage, in False Bay with the guy from *Shark Week* while having an up-close view at a Great White shark, I would've laughed in their face and told them they were crazy. Other people's dreams come true. Other people get to cross items off their bucket list, but not me. Yet here I am at twenty-nine living a dream I've had since I was a little girl sitting in the back seat of my mom's blue Reno and spotted what looked like a shark in the ocean below while we drove along one of the mountain passes.

This is living.

Nate manages to peel himself away from the back of the cage long enough to take a picture of me with his Go-

Pro, when the same shark makes another pass by the cage. I continue staring at him even after he lowers the camera. Why is it that I'm more afraid of the man in front of me and what he can do to my heart than the shark swimming behind me?

Something curls around my heart and squeezes; I push up to the surface and let out the breath I'd been holding. I'm panting and the pressure around my heart continues to increase. I need to get out of the water. I need to get back on solid ground both figuratively and literally. I push on the lid of the cage, grateful when it lifts easily and then haul myself up and back into the boat, taking in gulps of fresh air.

Fuck, I know I had lamented about death coming unexpectedly but this was not how I wanted to go. If this was God's idea of a sick joke, He and I were going to have words.

"You okay?" Nate asks, coming to sit beside me on one of the two benches. Chantel still has her nose buried in her phone and doesn't seem to notice.

"Yeah, I'm fine," I reply, wrapping my arms around myself. "My hands were starting to go numb," I say by way of explanation when Nate continues looking at me in that way of his that says he doesn't completely believe me. I cup both hands and bring them to my mouth to blow on them and rub them together to emphasize that I really was telling the truth.

Nate takes my hands in his equally cold ones and lifts them to his lips, but then it's like he remembers where we are and he drops my hands instantly, swallowing hard as he glances over at his fiancée who still hasn't looked up. I have a feeling she hasn't missed anything that's happened on the boat today though. It's more like she's choosing to play the distant and unattached fiancée.

He gives me a weak smile, then moves to sit beside Chantel, careful not to get her wet with his suit.

Chapter 30

"**ARE YOU SURE YOU** want to do this?" Nate asks with a box of my stuff under his arm.

I take one last look around the house that holds so many memories of my childhood, of meeting Nate, of Jack... I wipe away the lone tear that manages to sneak its way down my cheek and nod, bending down to pick up the last box.

"I am. It's time to move on," I say, turning to lead the way out of the front door and to the waiting bukkie piled high with my belongings.

I was hesitant to move at first because Nate had done so much work around this house when we first met. He reassured me that my mental health was worth more than a few pieces of wood. He can always rebuild certain pieces for me, but he can't rebuild me and if the memory of finding Jack's body hanging in the carport is going to hinder me from moving on then... well, then it is better to let some other family build their happy memories here unplagued by the tragedy. Plus, I'd be closer to my parents in Simon's Town since Dad ended up finding an apartment in an area close to my mom's place.

Nate packs the last of the boxes in the cab of the bukkie while I take one more look at the front of the house, committing it all to memory one last time.

"Ready?" He pulls me into his side and places a kiss on the top of my head.

"Yeah, I think I am," I say leaning into him.

"Good, 'cause I'm starving," he says patting his belly.

I laugh, "When are you never starving?"

Nate pauses on his way to the driver's side. "Good point. How about a braai and beers by the pool?"

"Now you're speaking my language," I grin, pulling myself up and into the passenger seat. "Are you ever going to get a step ladder for this thing?"

Nate laughs then shrugs turning up the music instead of answering me. I huff, crossing my arms over my chest and look out the window, watching the cream painted houses pass by in a blur.

It feels so surreal moving out of this neighbourhood for a second time, out of the same house for a second time. But it also feels like a new beginning. One I'm looking forward to exploring. As the houses begin to turn into freeway, I lean my head against the window and close my eyes. My body giving in to the tiredness of packing and moving over the last few days.

What feels like minutes later, I feel the bukkie lurch to a stop and when I crack my eyes open, the double garage and huge white columns of the new house greet me.

"I'll help you get the rest of the stuff inside then I'll go get some meat for the braai," Nate says, turning off the engine and pushing open his door.

I sigh, my head rolling side to side against the headrest. I'm already so drained from the long morning and afternoon of moving, I'm considering leaving all the shit in the bukkie and letting Nate borrow my car to go get us dinner, but I know the sooner we get all this inside, the sooner I can set up my bedroom and relax for the night.

I never really worried about getting a new house set up the first night of being in it. Except for my bedroom. I couldn't go to sleep that first night without my bed being set up and made as well as my clothes in their respective drawers or in the closet. The kitchen, living room, dining room, and bathroom could all wait until the next day or the day after that as long as I have the basics.

Nate gins as I drop a lighter box just inside the front door and sigh heavily. "Let me guess, you want to set up the bedroom and leave everything else for tomorrow?"

"Maybe."

Nate takes in the bright entranceway, high ceilings, and the reclaimed wooden stairs that spiral up to the second floor from the right, just beyond the living room. The staircase and the view of the ocean from the upstairs bedroom are a couple of the reasons why I chose this house above the other two that were for sale on the same street. Apart from the fact that it doesn't resemble the previous house in the least. Where that house was tile and dark walls -- except for the kitchen -- this one is all gleaming wooden floors and bright colours. And I'm not going to lie, the pool in the backyard was a major selling point. The kitchen counter is all white marble too which makes the space look brighter. And the view of the ocean from the master bedroom is one I could get used to waking up to every morning.

We manage to get the bedframe, box spring, and mattress out of the bukkie and upstairs to the master bedroom. Correction, Nate and Xander do most of the heavy lifting, once he finally showed up. I'm just here to make sure the ends don't drag on the new flooring and to help direct them up the stairs.

"Hey, Nate," I call towards the living room where Nate's walking through to get more stuff out of the vehicle.

Xander had to run out after helping with the bed and the couch, something about an emergency at the construction site he's been working at this week.

"What's up?" he says, poking his head around the kitchen where I have a box open on the counter and am pulling out plates and cutlery for us.

"Can you get me a potato salad?" In all honesty, I should probably just make it from scratch but I'm tired and the potatoes take forever to boil and then cool enough to mix with the mayonnaise and green onions.

"Sure thing. With or without egg?"

I scrunch up my nose and Nate laughs, rasping his knuckle against the door frame before turning and walking back through the house and out the door.

Wait, he's not getting the one with egg in it, is he? I rush after him and catch him just as he climbs into the bukkie.

"The one without egg, right?"

He chuckles again. "I'll be back in a few minutes," he says, reaching to close the door.

"Nate!"

The ass is still laughing as he backs down the driveway and then heads off in the direction of the Spar a few blocks away.

"You know what this place is missing?" Nate asks, leaning back on a beach lounger with a beer in hand and his sunglasses perched on the bridge of his nose.

"What's that?"

"A dog." He grins a mischievous smile when I groan.

"I am not getting a dog."

"And why not?" he whines.

I roll my eyes. "School holidays are almost done, and I'll be heading back to work soon. I won't have time to house train a puppy or take it on walks."

He shrugs like he sees nothing wrong with that. "We could co-parent on the evenings and weekends. I'm sure your parents will happily dog sit during the week."

"Nathan," I groan. "We are not going to co-parent a puppy. Plus, what kind would we even get?"

"I've always wanted a German Shepherd."

"A German Shepherd?"

He nods enthusiastically like a little kid who was just told they get to go to the toy store and pick out their favourite toy. "And we can name him Duke."

"Duke?" I ask, still bewildered that we're even having this conversation.

"Cause he'll be the prince of both houses." Nate's grin grows into a smile revealing his perfectly white teeth and I can't help but stare at him a little too long. His skin has a soft glow to it, like the beginning of a tan. His hair is a little longer on the top than it usually is, but I think I like it better this way. It gives him a sort of boyish charm.

"I'm not getting a dog," I say again.

He doesn't respond to my protest, but then he's suddenly standing by my chair, his beer bottle now sitting on the small table between the two chairs.

"Let's go swimming," he says, extending his hand to help me up.

The speed with which he's changed conversation topics today has given me whiplash. I'm about to ask him what's up with him today when he begins prowling towards me.

"Nate... what are you doing?"

He lunges towards me, gripping me under my arms and lifting me up. I squeal and automatically wrap my legs around his waist.

"Nathaniel!" I screech as he stalks towards the pool. "Don't you dare."

He readjusts his hold under my arms, but I know what he's about to do -- it's exactly what my cousins did to me as a kid – and I scramble to tighten my arms around his neck so he can't throw me in without falling in with me.

"Annika," he laughs. "Don't think I won't jump in with you wrapped around me."

"You wouldn't dare."

His eyes sparkle and I realize the mistake of my words. Nate never backs down from a challenge, and this one is no different.

"Ah, shit." I bury my nose in the curve of his neck and take a breath right as I feel him move towards the deep end of the pool and jump.

As soon as we're submerged under the water, Nate doesn't let me go. A hand sneaks around to grip the back of my neck to hold me to him and then his lips are descending on mine. Nate kisses me like our lives depend on us sharing breath. I tighten my arms around his neck and my legs around his waist, reveling in the feel of him. God, I missed this. I missed his hands on my body, his mouth moving against mine. This feels so good, and so so wrong.

When I push him away, he reluctantly lets me go and I swim up to the surface, hauling myself out of the pool and through the back door in search of a towel.

"Annika!" he calls behind me, but I don't stop. "Annika, please just stop." I hear him enter the house after me. His wet feet are slapping against the tile of the kitchen.

When I reach the linen closet upstairs, I grab a towel and wrap it around myself, feeling securely armed enough to face him now. When I turn to round on him, I'm taken aback by how close he is behind me. It takes me a minute to find my voice after stumbling back a foot or two.

"You're engaged, Nate."

"I know," he says, running a hand through his hair.

"To be married," I stress.

"Fuck, I know, okay. It's just having you in my arms again…" he trails off.

"Look, I know the waters of our relationship were muddied a little when Jack showed up, but I'm really not this girl, Nate. I don't kiss engaged men."

Nate looks down at me and the hurt look in his eyes makes me want to take him in my arms again and hold him close.

"I don't want to lose you, Nika."

I sigh and decide to say fuck it, stepping close to him and wrapping my arms around his waist.

"You won't lose me, but I think we should probably just stay friends."

He lets out a pained sound but eventually encircles me in his arms. "If that's the only way I can have you then I'll take it." He fiddles with my necklace until the map of South Africa lays perfectly flat just below my throat.

"I'm sorry," I say, choking back tears against his chest.

"I am too."

Chapter 31

"I'M BACK, BITCHES!" MY best friend announces as soon as she enters the main terminal.

Rolling my eyes, I go up to welcome her with a hug and take over rolling her big suitcase. You'd think she was here to stay and not just on vacation for two weeks with how heavy this thing is.

"Londyn, you've been here at least once a year since you moved to London." I giggle. "Londyn from London."

Now it's her turn to roll her eyes. "How long have you been holding that in?"

I snort. "A few months."

"You're such a comedian, Nik, Where's X?" she asks looking around the now empty airport.

"He's meeting us back at the house. He was going to braai, but I thought we could all hit the beach then maybe check out one of the pubs in Simon's Town?"

She shrugs, adjusting the strap of her flowy tank top. "Sounds good to me. I got plenty of sleep on the plane so I'm good to go."

"Ugh, I don't know how you do it."

"Do what?"

"Sleep on the plane. I never can. I'm almost worried I'm going to snore and then people will be silently judging me the rest of the flight."

She laughs, grabbing hold of the other end of the suitcase and helping me lift it into the boot of the car. "You're right. They probably would."

"Hey!"

"What? You said it. I'm just agreeing with you. Isn't that what best friends do?"

I huff and start up the engine. "You could've said something like, 'you don't snore, bestie.'"

"Fine," she sighs like being my friend is such an inconvenience. She's convincing too and I would have believed it if I hadn't known her for fifteen years. "You don't snore, bestie."

I grin and bat my eyelashes at her while I wait for the light to change. "Was that so hard?"

"Brutal."

We lock eyes and then we both burst out laughing just as the light changes. Londyn and I drop off her shit at my house in Simon's Town and fetch Xander before picking up wood for a fire later tonight as well as other bonfire essentials.

"I can't remember the policy of fires on the beach but if it turns out it's not allowed then we'll just head back here. Sound good?"

"Aye, aye, Cap," Londyn says from the back seat.

Xander laughs. "What the fuck's gotten into you?"

"What?" She shrugs "I may have started the pre-drinking on the plane. When in Cape Town, right?"

"I feel sorry for your liver," I say, navigating the car down the road to Fishhoek Beach.

I'm surprised when I'm able to find a parking spot relatively easy. The three of us jump out and start grabbing bags and towels from the car. Fishhoek isn't like Clifton Beach where there are guys you can rent umbrellas and beach chairs from. So, we're pretty much on our own with whatever we brought but I'm okay with that. I'm not a huge fan of having someone come up and ask us if we want an umbrella, an icicle, or a drink. I mean, it's nice but sometimes it gets to be too much when you just want to chill out and ignore the rest of the world for a little while.

We've just set up our towels in a spot that's not too far from but not too close to the water when Londyn looks back up to where we parked the car.

"Is that?" Londyn asks, tipping her sunglasses up to get a better look at Nate and the woman he's with as they navigate their way past beach-goers to get to our group.

"Yup," I reply, laying back and tugging the bill of my baseball cap further down.

"Well," Londyn says, resting back on her elbows. "Bitch ain't got nothing on you."

"Londyn!" This is the first time my best friend is getting a look at Nate's fiancée, but I'm not surprised that's her reaction to Chantel. I may have had a slight bitch fest after finding out about her and then again after she joined us on the cage diving expedition.

"What?" She reaches over to the beach bag between our towels and retrieves a bottle of sunscreen from the side pocket. "I'm just saying. He downgraded, like a lot." Londyn sits up, waves at Nate and Chantel and then uncaps the bottle to squirt some of the white lotion on her arms. She burns so easily that she makes sure to always reapply every few hours. "Xander," she calls out when she spots him making his way back from the water. Tiny droplets dripping down his long torso. "Can you help me with my back?"

"Really?"

Londyn shrugs and gives me a look that says she has no idea what I'm talking about. She and Xander used to circle each other in high school before Kyle moved to town. Once Xander saw that Kyle was also interested in Londyn, he backed off. Now that Kyle's no longer in the picture it doesn't seem to have taken her long to go back to trying to get Xander to notice her again.

"Howzit?" Nate says when they finally reach us. "This is Chantel." He gestures to her as he lays a towel the size of a double blanket on the other side of our group.

"Hi Annika," Chantel greets me after giving Xander and Londyn a half salute.

I tip my chin at her but go back to reading my book. I'm not trying to be rude or anything but this whole situation is awkward. I'm still in love with her fiancé and this whole trying to be friends thing Nate and I are attempting is getting harder and harder as each day passes. If I'm completely honest, I kind of resent her, and I'm mad at myself. But I can't fault him for moving on so I'm just going to have to suck it up and be the friend he needs me to be and hope like hell that I'm not invited to the wedding.

"Baby," Chantel whines after a while. "Let's go in the water."

"Xander and I were going to throw the ball around for a bit. I'll meet you over there later," Nate says, turning back to Xander who's tossing an American football up with one hand and catching it with the other. The two guys head down to a clearing close to the water's edge and begin tossing the ball back and forth. Nate's so focused on the rubber ball when Xander throws a perfect spiral to him that he misses the death glare Chantel narrows on him.

Just when I think I can't possibly hate her anymore she peels out of the t-shirt she's wearing to reveal a tiny black string bikini. The twin triangles barely cover her nipples, and the bottoms just cover enough to not be indecent. Suddenly, I feel way too exposed and self-conscious in my modest turquoise tankini. When she's stripped of everything but the swimsuit – if you can call it that – she prances off towards Nate and Xander, walking between them just as Xander tosses the ball to Nate. He's so engrossed by the blonde bimbo; he misses the ball and instead follows after her like a lost puppy. I glance down at my middle that's not as flat as it was a few years ago. Maybe it's time to go back on a diet and increase the time I spend in the gym.

"Whatever you're thinking right now, stop."

"What am I thinking?" I ask my best friend. I can't muster the will to turn my head away from where Nate is swinging Chantel up over his shoulder as he marches them farther out into the ocean. I know I'm just making myself miserable by watching them, but I can't help it. It's like when you drive by a car accident and you know you shouldn't look but you do anyway.

"That if he's with her then how in the hell did he ever find you attractive? That you can't possibly measure up to her? That you need to lose weight?"

I grumble and flip my best friend off as I turn onto my stomach and kick my legs up. I try to ignore the sound of Chantel's giggles that float on the air towards our group but it's nearly impossible. She has that nasally voice that you either find cute or really annoying, and right now it's really annoying.

Sitting back up, I grab the sunscreen from Londyn and reapply to my front. I'm fully prepared to ask Londyn or hell even Xander for help with my back when a shadow looms over me.

"Here, let me help with that," Nate says, prying the blue and white bottle from my hands.

"Um, uh, that's okay. I was just going to ask --" I point to where Londyn and Xander were sitting but there's nobody there. Sonofabitch. When did they get up and leave?

Nate patiently waits for me to turn over and after some cursing – inwardly, of course – I turn back over onto my stomach and fold my arms under my head. I try so hard to keep my body still while his hands work in circles over my back, but by the time he works down to my lower back I'm putty in his hands.

I shiver when he moves my hair away from my hairline and works some of the sunscreen in from my shoulders and up the curve of my neck. I may have moaned, I'm not sure.

His chest grazes my back and his breath is warm against my ear when he whispers, "All set."

I turn my head slightly towards his lips but before anything can happen he's pulling away and jumping to his feet.

Nate

"You what?" Chantel screeches and I visibly flinch.

Damn, did she always sound like this?

"I can't marry you," I repeat for what seems like the twentieth time.

"And why not?" She crosses her arms under her chest or tries to anyway. The boob job she got last year just pushes them up to her chin. Her tanned skin looks leathery in the light of her kitchen, like it's seen a few too many sunrays.

"I'm sorry, Chantel."

I try delivering the news gently but if she's about to start screaming and throwing shit, then I'm out. Hell, I tried breaking it off with her last year, but she pulled some guilt trip bullshit, so I stayed. And if I'm being honest, I don't even remember proposing. All I know is that we had a conversation or two about marriage, I said I wasn't ready to pull that trigger yet and the next thing I know, the woman's bringing bridal magazines over and talking flowers and colours and shit.

I don't know what made me decide that today was the day I put an end to all the bullshit. That's a lie. Seeing Annika yesterday and how absolutely beautiful she looked in that swimsuit, feeling her body beneath my palms again… it flipped something inside of me. Then watching some dick hit on her when we went to a pub afterward. No woman has ever elicited such a strong reaction from me. I'm not a fighter, but I wanted to punch that dick's teeth in when he kept touching her even after she tried pulling away subtly. For as long as I've know her, Annika has always hated confrontation. She avoids it whenever possible. So, I know she wouldn't have said anything last night unless the guy grabbed her. Fuck, if it hadn't been for Xander stepping in, I would've, and it wouldn't have ended as quietly as it had.

I manage to leave Chantel's without a scratch. Barely. I head to Glencairn.

"So, you finally pulled your head outta your ass," Dean says handing me a beer.

"Yes, sir."

"It's about time."

I chuckle, slipping my free hand in the front pocket of my jeans. The sun had set about an hour ago, but the stars are just starting to make their appearance in the sky above us.

"You don't think this friendship is a little odd?" I ask, gesturing between us with the bottle.

"Being friends with my daughter's ex?" Dean picks up a log from the pile beside his chair and expertly places it on the fire. "I considered you a friend before Annika came home." He straightens in his camping chair and studies me for a moment. "But if you break her heart I'll be forced to unpack one of my guns."

It's not an idle threat either. I've seen pictures of Dean's gun collection and it's nothing to laugh at. I have a feeling it isn't Dean that I need to worry about though. Dave is a cop. Those fuckers don't mess around.

"Yes, Sir," I say again over the lip of the beer bottle.

Chapter 32

Annika

I WAKE TO BRIGHT sunlight streaming through a slit in the middle of the dark curtains I purchased last week. It wasn't even eight yet but if the fact that my bedroom's already hot as balls is any indication, today's going to be a scorcher of a day in Cape Town.

Rolling over, I grab for my phone on the nightstand and bypass all the texts, Facebook messages, and emails to check the expected weather forecast for today.

Yup, thirty-fucking-nine degrees Celsius today. It's already hovering just below twenty. I groan, falling back onto the white pillows and covering my eyes with my forearm. I wonder which beach — if any — will potentially be less crowded. Clifton Beach is out… especially 1st and 2nd. Clifton 3rd might be doable but I doubt it. Not in this heat. Camps Bay is out too. Muizenberg, maybe? Probably not, although it is close. That leaves Boulders or Fishhoek and since Boulders Beach has penguins… well, it's a no brainer. There're more options but those are the ones Nate and I have visited often. Speaking of Nate.

Me: I'm dying. Beach... Ocean... water... Boulders?

It was a tad dramatic but whatever. I flip off the light covers and make a mental note to buy an air conditioner or try and convince Nate to install one for me. I don't know why houses in Cape Town don't already come with them pre-installed. It's gets ridiculously hot here. It's like everyone is always so surprised when their house reaches volcanic levels of heat during the summer months.

Nate: Good morning to you too, Sunshine. Happy birthday.

Nate: Boulders it is. Pick you up in 30.

Me: You're the best. I'll be the one already in a bikini standing in the street.

I mean, I wouldn't *just* be in a bikini, but it was almost hot enough to make me contemplate not wearing anything else. I say almost because even I'm not that stupid. The catcalls are bad enough when I'm fully clothed, I shudder imagining what it would be like if I stood out in front of my house wearing nothing but scraps of material covering my breasts and other lady bits. I'm just grateful I live in this part of the city and not where my grandparents live. Seven-foot-high fences surround most of the houses on their street, some with electric barbed wire running across the tops. Cape Town is beautiful, yes, but the crime rate makes you want to think twice before raising a family here. Just the other year, someone set fire to one of the cars of the commuter train. In the same year, someone stole the copper cables off a train.

As I roll out of bed and go in search of Duke. *Yes, I ended up getting the damn dog.* It dawns on me that today is my thirtieth birthday. When the fuck did that happen? I swear I was just turning twenty-one not too long ago. Yawning, I rub the sleep out of my eyes and almost trip over the pup sleeping on the cold tiles of the kitchen floor. Duke yips, scrambling up to all fours and starts pawing at his empty food bowl.

"Yeah, okay," I mumble sleepily and top up his food and water bowls before turning to the coffee maker and switching it on.

With the mug of steamy goodness cupped in my hands, I lean my back against the counter and breathe a sigh of relief after the first taste. As I'm lowering the mug from my lips, I catch a glimpse of pointy ears moving from side to side. I chuckle when I see Duke sitting at my feet with his little tail wagging, his food untouched. He's been picking up his training so fast, better than Hector, the black and white English bulldog and my first pet, ever could. That lump of fat would bowl you over before you had the chance to straighten up from filling up his food.

"Go on," I tell Duke and grin as his little paws slide across the tile in his effort to race to his bowls.

Checking the time, I hurriedly down the rest of the still hot coffee - I'm so going to regret that – and fetch my swimsuit from the washing line in the backyard. Duke follows me out, immediately finding his ball and begins running around while I dash inside and get changed. I can already feel the sun start to burn my skin. It must have jumped another ten degrees between the time I woke up and now. This day's going to be one of those don't-come-out-of-the-water-unless-you-have-to-eat days. I make a note to put on sunscreen and bring it with for Nate as well. Heaven knows that man burns like Tokai Forest in the driest summer.

Twenty minutes later while I'm throwing the ball to Duke and playing tug-of-war to get it back, I hear the stereo system of Nate's car before I hear him pull into the driveway. I swear there's like some unwritten rule or something in CT that says your music and your car's exhaust have to announce your arrival blocks ahead of your actual arrival.

Duke's ears perk up at the sound of Nate's car door and then he's running towards the wooden door that separates the backyard from the driveway. I hear Nate chuckle at Duke's little barks before he pushes open the door.

And then I see him.

My breath whooshes out of me like I've just been punched in the gut when I get a good look at him in low hanging board shorts and flip-flops. His chest already glistening with sweat when he crouches to pet the pup.

"I was thinking we could bring him with us?" I say, surprised when my voice comes out sounding normal and not dry as the desert like it feels.

"Ja, sounds good. We'd have to go to Clifton 1st then. The other beaches are no dogs allowed."

I groan, already beginning to feel claustrophobic just thinking of the amount of people who would be there today, but when I glance down at Duke sitting perfectly in Nate's arms, his tongue hanging out the side and those big puppy dog eyes pleading with me to take him with us, I know I won't be changing my mind. Plus, Clifton 1st is an off-leash beach so at least Duke will be able to expound some energy and maybe we can even get him in the water. It would be his first time in the ocean if we can.

I roll my eyes. "He's perfectly capable of walking to the car."

Nate cradles the pup like a baby, and scratches behind Duke's ears. "Ja, he can but his poor paws will probably burn on the tar."

"Ready to go?" I ask, gathering my beach bag and few snack items for us for later.

I follow Nate out to his car and settle into the passenger seat before reaching out for Duke and settling him on my lap while Nate drives.

"No bukkie today?"

"No. Got a nail in one of the tires and haven't had a chance to repair it yet."

Duke squirms on my lap and I scratch behind his ear to help calm him while trying to keep my mind from wondering to what Nate would look like covered in grease and working on his truck.

As soon as we're parked, Duke scrambles up to stand on all four paws and pants while gazing longingly out the window. I chuckle and make sure his leash is attached before opening my door and letting him jump down. Nate gathers the bags and the snacks from the back seat, and together we cross the street then make our way down the steps to the beach.

We've set up our towels on the sand, fairly close to the where the water comes up the beach. I take a quick glance around, noting all the other dogs. I'm surprised that there aren't very many here today. There are maybe three other dogs and they all seem to be about Duke's size. I crouch down and unclip his leash, watching as he takes off for the water, his tongue hanging out the side of his mouth. Duke comes to a screeching halt just at the water's edge and when the tide comes in, he scampers back, just out of reach of the water and then chases it when it washes out again.

Nate and I watch him do this several times before Nate takes pity on him and goes to scoop the puppy up. With Duke sitting happily in his arms, Nate wades in the water and when it begins rising higher on his chest, Duke tries climbing higher on Nate's shoulder. I laugh as Nate tries to get a better grip on the wiggling puppy so that he doesn't do a nose dive off his shoulder and into the water.

Eventually, Duke settles down and after a while he seems pretty content sitting in Nate's arms while the water laps up against them. I make sure Nate's phone and wallet are carefully hidden out of sight of anyone who may be wandering around the beach looking for something to steal, and then go join Nate and Duke in the water.

"Where's Chantel?" I ask, after we've settled back on our towels and have eaten our fair share of fruits, vegetables, and dip. "I thought she would've been here."

He mumbles something under his breath, popping a strawberry in his mouth immediately after.

"I'm sorry, what?"

He sighs, scraping a hand down his face. "I broke it off," he says, picking up Duke's ball and throwing it towards the water. The pup chases after it, strutting triumphantly back when he catches it.

I choke and sputter on the sip of sparkling water I just took. When I'm sure that I'm not going to die and can breathe again, I glance over at Nate who has a satisfied smirk on his face. My mouth opens and closes like a fish, but no sound comes out.

"Close your mouth, Nika. I don't think you want any of the bugs here to get in," he chuckles, and I instantly snap my mouth shut and glare at him.

"Why?" I finally ask when I've found my voice.

He shrugs. "It wasn't working out."

"When?"

"Few months."

"That's it? That's all you're going to give me. You were ready to promise your life to this woman."

Shut up, Annika. Isn't this what you wanted? You wanted him to leave her. She wasn't good enough for him anyway.

Nate jumps to his feet after wrestling the ball out of Duke's mouth. "I don't know what else to tell you, Nika," he says then walks away down the beach with the German Shepherd close on his heels.

"You okay?" Nate asks, handing me a glass of white wine before he attends to the braai. After a day at the beach we both decided that the perfect way to end this weekend was a braai with my parents, Nate's parents, and Xander. So while Nate wrestled Duke under a hose when we got back to my house, to rinse the sand from his fur, I call my mom and dad, as well as Xander and invite them over. Nate put a call in to his mom and dad once he and Duke were sufficiently soaked. I laugh then hand him a towel and his cell phone and tell him he can call them from out in the backyard because he isn't tracking water into my house.

"More than okay," I say, taking a sip of the sweet wine while watching Duke lounge by the pool.

"Who ordered the Snoek?" My dad calls from the front door.

"Oh, that's me." I scramble out of my chair, placing the wine glass on a nearby table and wrapping my arms around my dad's neck in a hug. "Thank you, Daddy." Snoek was my favourite fish, especially to Braai but it is getting harder and harder to find in Cape Town despite living right by the ocean. Most people hate it because it is so boney and you spend more time picking out the small bones than you do eating the damn thing, but I don't mind. Somehow, though, my dad manages to find me one today.

"Happy birthday, Peanut," he says with a kiss to my temple.

"Howzit, Dave?"

"I'm good, Bokkie. Happy birthday," he says, pulling me into a side hug after I've let go of my dad. "And you?"

"Can't complain. Nate's got the Braai already going out back."

I hear the slam of a car door and then the beep of the alarm being set after Dad and Dave turn to head out to the backyard to join Nate. My mom ambles up the driveway, her hands full of Tupperware that no doubt contain all my favourite desserts and Nate's favourite pastries.

"Here, let me take that," I say, meeting her on the front step and already grabbing the top Tupperware dish before she has a chance to argue.

"Thanks, honey. Happy birthday, baby," Mom says pressing a kiss to my cheek.

"Thank you."

She follows me into the kitchen where we try to move things around in the fridge to make room for the new additions. I crack open the lid of the dish I was carrying and sneak a chocolate éclair before Mom or Nate notice. I swear that man is like a bear coming out of hibernation when it comes to his pastries. I moan as the homemade filling touches my tongue, effectively putting an end to my stealthness. Yes, I just made up a word. Mom giggles from pulling down a bowl to put the pasta salad in.

"You better hide the evidence. You know what happens when he catches you stealing those," she warns with a smile, eyeing the cream on my fingers.

I roll my eyes. "They're as much mine as they are his. Plus, it's my birthday."

She pulls me into a hug while still laughing. "They're for everyone to share."

"Tell that to the man-like kid out there." I hook a thumb over my shoulder at the door leading to the backyard.

Quiet descends on the kitchen as the scent of wood smoke from the braai drifts in from the open windows. I have a feeling mom's gearing up to ask me something and I think I know what she's about to ask before the words leave her mouth. It's the same question she asks every time we've had lunch or dinner together since the divorce was final.

"How's he doing?"

I shrug. "He seems to be doing okay. He and Dave are planning a trip to Durban next month," I reply, giving her a heads-up. I know my dad probably has plans to tell her himself but if I had been in her shoes I'd have wanted a heads-up to the potential conversation.

"I know. He, uh… we met for coffee last week. He mentioned the trip then."

"Oh. Are you okay?"

Mom smiles, causing little lines to appear around her eyes. Eyes that don't look as sad as they did years or even months ago. I breathe a little easier when it doesn't look like I'll have to prevent a war from erupting in my own backyard.

"More than okay," Mom says, echoing my own words to Nate earlier while pulling me into a hug. "Are you happy?" She asks after she's let go and moves back to transferring the salad from the Tupperware and into the glass dish. I smirk at the action. No matter how many times I tell her we can just serve it out of the Tupperware she brought it in, she never listens. It doesn't matter that it'll be the only dish in a glass bowl on the table.

"I really am," I answer after a couple of beats. "Dr. Fester has been great, and Nate has been…" I shake my head. "I couldn't have asked for a better friend during all this."

I feel a slight a pang of regret at saying that, but it's true. Londyn wasn't able to stay very long or come back for Jack's funeral and while she's been just as supportive as Nate I just can't help but think my friendship between the two is completely different. One more intense than the other. Although, it could be that I'm still in love with Nate which makes the difference.

Mom nods, moving to rinse out the Tupperware. "If it looks like a duck, Annika," she says with her back turned to me.

There was never any sense in hiding anything from her. She's a bloodhound when it comes to sensing the truth, but oddly enough never saw Dad's realization coming. I immediately shake off that thought. Sensing things in other's relationships is different than your own. When it comes to our own relationships, we're flying blind because we're too close to the situation.

"We already tried that. It didn't work."

She turns off the tap. Grabbing the dish towel and drying off her hands, she turns to face me again, leaning back against the counter. "It didn't work because of Jack. That man out there has never stopped loving you, Annika, and I don't think you ever stopped loving him either. I know your dad and I splitting up after so many years scared you and then what Jack did…" She trails off looking away before clearing her throat and meeting my eyes again. "Don't let that stop you from chasing after the happy ever after. I've seen the way Jack looked at you and I've seen the way Nate looks at you. And, honey, that's a look a man gives the woman he loves. One he's not going to so easily give up."

"He hasn't made a move or indicated he wants anything more than friendship right now."

"Annika, it's the twenty-first century. You want him? You go after him. So, he hasn't made the first move? Then you make it. You've been lucky enough to get second chances with both loves your of life, don't pass this one up. It may never come around a third time."

She is right. Of course, she is right. Mother's intuition or whatever freaky shit it is. I help her gather the pasta and bean salads and follow as she leads the way into the covered part of the backyard and over to the new table Nate just finished building and glossing last weekend. After I place the glass bowl in the center, I glance up and find Nate already watching me. A smile spread across his face, beer in one hand, and Braai tongs in the other, his focus is purely on me and not the conversation my dad, Dave, and now my mom are having around him.

It may never come around a third time.

Maybe it is finally time that Nate and I have our shot. Maybe it is time to fan the flames that seem to spark whenever we are close. Mom is right, though, I don't think this thing between Nate and I has ever only been friendship. A few minutes later Nate's parents show up with more meat and sides and a Potjiekos, and before I know it, the seven of us are sitting around the newly built table overflowing with food and drinks. The door to the backyard opens again sending Duke darting towards the incoming figure. Xander laughs, bending down to scoop the spoilt puppy up.

"Sorry I'm late," he says, pressing a kiss to the top of my head before greeting everyone else around the table. After the wound in his side healed, Xander ended up finding a house not far from this area. He also got hired on at one of the best construction companies in town as a contractor. Xander still comes over for Sunday dinner at my mom's house and he and I often meet up for coffee in town or lunch if I can I swing it with school.

"Wash your hands before you sit down," my mother reprimands and I can't help the giggle that escapes my throat.

Xander shoots me a dirty look but I just smile back sweetly. The way we act around each other you never would guess that we aren't even related. We're constantly teasing each other and giving each other shit like siblings do, and at the end of the day, I couldn't have asked for a better adoptive brother. Most in-laws fall out of touch after the death of the family member that brought them together. Xander and I, though, we're stuck with each other for life. Like peanut butter and jelly. I inwardly groan at my lame attempt at a metaphor.

They say if you ever find the one love of your life you're lucky, and if you ever find two you were never truly in love with the first. Well, I can say with absolute certainty that I truly did love Jack... once. Maybe it took his death for me to realize that while I loved him, I wasn't exactly in love with him anymore because my heart had been given to someone else. Someone who understands me better than Jack ever could or did.

For once in my life I'm going to take my mother's advice without whining or complaining and go after what I want. And that starts with Nathaniel Walker.

"Who ate one of my éclairs?" Nate's voice booms from the kitchen while the rest of us are sitting around a fire nursing our drinks.

I try to hide my smile behind the rim of my wine glass but when my mom shoots me an I-told-you-so look I can't hold the laugh back anymore. Especially when Nate bounds out of the kitchen, Tupperware dish in hand, one éclair missing as evidence. His eyes scan the group and then narrow into slits when they land on me.

"Uh oh." Carefully, I place my wine glass on the bricked ground beside my chair and rise with my hands held up in surrender. "Nate..."

He growls, and I begin backing away and towards the grassy area. He blindly hands the dish to Xander and I briefly consider telling him what a mistake that is. Xander's just as big a slut for my mother's baking as Nate is. A chorus of laughter sounds around the circle when Nate charges and I squeal, turning tail and running to the far end of the yard. Duke, thinking it's a game, gives chase after Nate and me.

I don't make it far before Nate gets a hold me. He bends his shoulder hitting my middle and then one second my feet are on the grass and the next I'm upside down. My hands grappling for purchase on Nate's back.

"Seriously, it was one éclair."

His palm comes down to slap my ass and I yelp. "It was my éclair."

I roll my eyes as Nate walks us back over to the still laughing group. A blush blooming up my face when I realize that everyone must have seen the slap he landed on my backside.

I can feel the moment he realizes his mistake with handing Xander the dish when his entire body stiffens under me.

I sigh. "At least put me down first if you're planning on murdering him."

No sooner are the words out of my mouth, am I being flipped right side up again. Woah, head rush. Nate steadies me for a beat, with his hands clasped on my arms. When he realizes I'm okay and not going to pass out, he releases me and goes after Xander who's still stuffing the cream filled and chocolate covered pastries into his mouth.

"You just had to bring those," I say glaring at my mother who has a shit eating grin on her face.

"Worth it," she shrugs, clinking beer bottles with Nate's mom.

Somewhere in the back of my brain a thought takes root and I wonder if the two moms foresaw this happening. Me and Nate. After all, it doesn't seem like it's coming across as a surprise to them the way he's treating me this evening.

It's giving me a migraine though. Trying to figure out what Nate and I mean to each other now that we're both single.

248

"More wine?" Nate asks holding the almost empty bottle of Two Oceans out for me.

Both sets of parents and Xander left hours ago, leaving the two of us to clean up whatever dishes were left after the moms had washed up everything else.

"Please," I reply, lifting my glass so he can refill it.

Nate places the empty bottle on the coffee table before taking a seat on the sofa beside me, immediately lifting my feet and placing them on his lap. My eyes roll back when he starts massaging my heels. I had almost forgotten how good this felt.

"That went better than I expected." I manage to say after a few beats of silence.

Nate hums in agreement, his fingers still working their miracles on my tired feet.

"I thought for sure I'd have to run interference between my mom and dad," I add.

Nate remains silent, his gaze laser focused on what he is doing to my feet. I huff in frustration at not being able to take it any longer. I reach over and manage to place my glass on the table beside the empty bottle without spilling any wine (yay me!) before scrambling up and planting a knee on either side of Nate's hips. Effectively caging him in between my body and the couch.

I palm both sides of his face and lean down to kiss him. He freezes the second my lips touch his and when he still hasn't made a move to kiss me back after a few more seconds, I begin to worry that maybe he doesn't want this after all. I start to pull away when his hands that had been fisted at his sides fly to grab my hips and pull me in closer to him. His tongue snakes out and licks along the seam of my lips demanding entry. I give in, feeling my body relax against his as I surrender to whatever has been growing between us.

I feel like the last piece of the puzzle is finally put into place. I won't say that everything makes sense again because life rarely ever makes sense. It's supposed to be messy and unpredictable; it's supposed to have its fair share of ups and downs and random plot twists. I think that's how we know we're really living; when we're down one minute then up the next or vice versa.

What kind of life would it be if every day was the same from the time we wake up till the time we close our eyes at night? Not one I'd want.

My life may have started out as close to perfect as one's life could get, but it wasn't without its fair share of drama and messiness. And I think I like it better this way. Nothing's ever perfect.

When Nate finally draws back letting us up for air, I rest my forehead against his while I tried to catch my breath.

"I love you." The words tumble out before I could stop them, but they seem so right in this moment. "I don't think I've ever stopped loving you, Nathan."

He grips my face between his hands and pulls me in to another kiss. "Ek is lief vir jou ook." I love you too.

I can't stop the stupid ass grin from spreading across my face at hearing him say those words again.

"Can we go to bed now?" I ask, burying my nose in the crook of his neck.

Nate chuckles, wrapping his arms around my waist, and stands. My legs automatically wrap around him.

"On a scale of one to ten, how tired are you right now?"

I laugh. "Babe, if you think that's the reason I want to go to bed then you don't really know me at all."

Nate walks us into the master bedroom, kicking the door closed behind us before dropping me on the bed. I bounce a couple of times before settling in to the middle of the queen-sized bed.

"I was hoping you'd say that," he says. The bed dipping with his weight as he crawls over me. "Happy birthday, love."

He slowly pushes my shirt up, peppering kisses up my belly and between my breasts. As soon as the material slips past my fingers, Nate flings it somewhere behind us before curling his fingers in the waistband of my pants and underwear and sliding them over my hips. "So," he says with a kiss to my left hip bone, "Perfect." A kiss to my right one.

When I'm utterly naked, Nate takes a step back from the bed and strips his clothes off in a flash. I will never forget the sight of Nate standing naked, his hard cock in his hand as he slowly strokes it while his whisky eyes blaze with heat and stare down at me spread out before him. Being completely naked and utterly at his mercy both thrills and terrifies me. My pussy drips with anticipation of what he'll do next, and dare I say… impatience?

The corner of his lips curl in a slow, seductive, crooked smirk, his fist still lazily stroking his length until a bead of pre-cum pearls at the head of his shaft. I moan, waiting to taste it.

My pussy clenches. My clit throbs. God, this man is going to kill me. *Can you die from being turned on?* Right at this moment, it's a real possibility and he hasn't even touched me yet except to strip me naked.

"Nathan."

My body buzzes with the need to feel his hands on me. I arch my back as best I can and slip my hand between my legs. I groan and my hips buck with the first rub of my clit. My body temperature's rising and if Nate doesn't touch me soon I'm going to catch fire and go up in flames.

Then, sweet Jesus, *then* I feel the bed dip and his hands are on me again. His fingers lightly tracing a line in from the tops of my thighs to just before my pubic area before they retreat.

Nate runs his nose along the curve of my jaw, he nips at my earlobe before sucking it into his hot mouth. "You're so beautiful." His lips brush against my ear with every word, his warm breath sending goosebumps all down my body.

"Please," I beg, removing my hand from my slit and sliding it through his hair, pulling his mouth closer.

Nate traces a line down my collarbone with his long fingers. Down between my breasts, over my belly button and lower still until he finds the bundle of nerves between my legs. He rolls my clit between his fingers and my eyes roll back. He pinches it and I see stars explode behind my eyelids.

"Your clit's so swollen," he rasps, his lips still so close to mine. "I bet you'll come as soon as I slide home."

I groan, wrapping my legs around his hips. Nate slips a single finger inside me right down to his second knuckle making my back arch. He withdraws slowly only to slide it back in before completely withdrawing. I'm about to silently beg him but then he slips the finger that was just inside of me between his lips and sucks it clean from my juices. Nate's eyes darken. Gone are the flecks of gold, the irises blending in with the pupil.

I swallow hard.

Nate moves down the bed, positioning himself between my bent legs. "So beautiful," he purrs. "So pink and wet." Then his tongue darts out and licks up from my pussy to my clit, swirling his tongue around the bud before sucking it into his mouth. "I could eat this pussy for hours… days," he says when he finally comes up for air after tongue-fucking me to within an inch of my life.

I'm so close to coming, I grab hold of his hair and force his face back between my legs. Nate chuckles and licks me once more before pulling back.

"And this hole," he continues, circling a finger around my ass. "I can't wait to fuck this hole."

I freeze the moment his finger begins sliding in past the tight ring of muscle, but then his mouth's back on my clit, teasing, and I relax again. His teeth scrape against the bundle of nerves and I can't hold back anymore.

"That's it, baby. Come on my tongue. I want to feel your juices running down my chin."

I arch my back, pushing my head back into the pillow, and do exactly that. I come at the same time Nate pushes his tongue back into my pussy. When he's licked me through my orgasm and my spasms have stopped, he rises to his knees and shuffles forward until his thighs brush against my bent legs. Nate takes his cock in his hand and runs the head of his shaft through my swollen lips, tapping it against my clit and sending another round of spasms through my body. I whimper when he pushes the head of his cock in, only to withdraw.

Nate continues his torturous rhythm, running his cock between my swollen lips, tapping the head on my clit before gliding it back down only to push the head of his cock in before fully withdrawing again.

"You like when I tease you, baby?"

I grunt in frustration.

"My cock looks so good sliding through your pussy lips. I'm going to give you exactly what you want, Nika."

Nate grips the base of his cock in his hand, lining up the head with my entrance. He slides in slowly, despite me being soaked and ready from the first orgasm he gave me.

"God, I'll never get used to this, Nik. Your pussy feels amazing squeezing the hell outta my cock," he rasps, bracing himself on his forearms on either side of my head. His thrusts start off slow, lazy while he licks and nips along my jaw and down my neck.

Then his hips snap faster, driving his cock into me harder. The second orgasm hits me fast and I shudder under him. Nate doesn't stop though. His thrusts get more frantic, more demanding. He interlocks his fingers above my head, caging me within his arms as he ruts into me.

My third orgasm rushes through me and I scream from the intensity. My body pulls tight, my toes curl and I don't relax until the last wave is gone.

The last thing I remember before passing out in a state of bliss are Nate's words as another orgasm crashed over me and then Nate's grunts as he comes.

"Mine."

Epilogue

11 months later

AND THEN THERE WAS you, baby girl," I croon as Kinsley stares up at me with those big green eyes while she sucks on my pinky finger. I can't help but run another finger down one of her soft, plump cheeks and admire the pouty lips that look so much like her father's.

The journey to get here was rough with its fair share of ups and down but as I sit, rocking her in the nursery built from love, I can't help but think that I wouldn't have changed a second of it. After all, if we had not gone through those rough years, she would not be here.

"Ah, there are my beautiful girls," Nate says strolling into the room in jeans that have seen better days, his hair a mess from running his fingers through it all day, and his sweat-soaked shirt clinging to his chest. "Don't worry," he chuckles. "I'm about to hit the shower. Just wanted to come say that I'm home." He leans down to press a soft kiss to her forehead before he repeats the motion to mine.

"How'd it go?"

He shrugs. "Framing should be done in the next couple of weeks."

Nate and a few of the other fathers at the primary school volunteered to rebuild the school gym after it caught fire a few months ago. It shook up the whole area since nobody ever expected it. Cape Town was used to its fair share of wild fires in the summer months, but this was the first time in a long time one had sparked in a city. Of course, it didn't help that the grass was incredibly dry with it being one of the driest summers we've had in a while, and with no rain in the forecast, it made for perfect fire condition. We knew the fires were going to be bad, we just never thought one would spark on the playing field of the school I spent the first part of my school age years at.

"Where's my favourite niece?" I hear Xander call seconds after the click of the front door closing.

"She's your only niece," I say, rolling my eyes when he appears in the doorway behind Nate.

"Yeah, yeah," he waves off the statement, moving farther into the room. "I need cuddles."

I sigh, gently settling her into Xander's waiting arms. "If you wake her up, I'll kill you."

He grins down at Kinsley and for the first time in years, I see genuine happiness in his smile… in his eyes. It's like she repaired the hole Jack left behind.

"Why don't you go relax with your husband? I've got the little angel," Xander says, not looking up from Kinsley's sleeping form cradled in his arms.

Some days, it's still weird seeing him here, in my life. After Jack died the second time, Xander made sure to let me know, in no uncertain terms, that I was not getting rid of him. I was and will always continue to be his family. In fact, he's the one who tried to get me to leave Jack when he started drinking more and started becoming abusive. He even flew out to Cape Town from Florida to try and convince me in person. It opened a divide between him and Jack, one I sometimes still felt guilty about, but it seems Xander never did. Feel guilty about it that is. Then after Jack's suicide, Xander decided to just stay here in Cape Town. When Nate came back into my life, Xander took the role of older, protective brother very seriously and must have grilled Nate with a hundred questions, which Nate took in stride. I guess he understood why Xander felt the need to do that and he didn't blame Xander.

I pause on my way out the door with a hand on the frame and glance back over my shoulder at my adoptive older brother holding his niece protectively in his arms when another pair of strong arms wrap around my waist and pull me back into a hard chest.

"She's going to have a hell of a time dating." I grin, leaning my head back against my husband and feeling the growl in his chest.

"She's never dating." I hear Xander say from the rocking chair. Nate gives an agreeable grunt and I laugh as he takes my hand and leads me to our bedroom.

THE END

Playlist

Heaven - Julia Michaels
That Song That We Used to Make Love To - Carrie
Underwood
No Matter What - Boyzone
I Do (Cherish You) - 98
This I Promise You - *Nsync
One More Day - Diamond Rio
Bless the Broken Road - Travis Atreo
Craving You - Travis Atreo, Colton Haynes
Sorry – Buckcherry
Heartache On The Dance Floor – John Pardi
Gold – Matt Hartke ft. Maggie Peake
What If I Never Get Over You – Lady Antebellum

Acknowledgements

Nicole – My right hand. I don't think this book would've been completed if it weren't for you. I love ya, girl! You're not allowed to leave me.

Caleb – We miss you buddy.

Anita Quick – Thank you for letting me talk out some plot points with you.

Nikki Holt Sexton – Thank you for letting me steal your last name haha and for the help with a plot twist.

Alisha Kines - Thank you for being my sounding board and telling me like it is. Thank you for being there when I needed to talk.

About the Author

A.J. lives in BC, Canada with her husband. When she's not writing or working away on her TBR pile, she's studying psychology at the University of British Columbia or enjoying a glass of wine with her friends.

<u>Connect with A.J.</u>
Reader Group: <u>A.J.'s Naughty Angels</u>
Newsletter: To Sign up click here

Also by the Author

Famiglia Series
Dark Desire
Dark Betrayal
Deadly Intentions
Dark Illusion
Deadly Surrender (Part of the Dominated by Desire
Anthology)

Made in the
USA
Middletown, DE